SMALL TOWN ROMANCE

ANNIE MARCUS

Sam,
Enjoy ♡
Annie Marcus

Dear Reader,

Thank you so much for picking up *Small Town Romance*. I think you're really going to enjoy it!

I wanted to let you know that this free copy had some wonky printing issues. However, it's the same great story you would have read if you'd purchased a properly formatted version.

Thanks for spending time with Olivia and Aiden as they fall in love.

Happy reading!

Annie Marcus

1.
2.
3.
4.
5.
6.
7.
8.
9.
10.
11.

I hope this book brings you joy!

Annie Marcus

Please leave a review!

GoodReads

Amazon

BookBub

38.

39.

40.

41.

42.

43.

44.

45.

46.

47.

48.

49.

50.

51.

This one is for Brett and Roz.

Thank you times a million.

Prologue - Aiden

(Thirteen Years Ago)

MGMT's "Time to Pretend" blasted through the speakers of Aiden Wescott's family's hunting cabin, which was overflowing with Gresham High's recently graduated senior class. Smiling faces and dancing bodies bounced on the lawn. Several of Aiden's buddies were doing cannonballs off the end of the dock, trying to splash the girls sitting on the edge with their feet dangling in the water. The girls shrieked in protest through their giggles.

The sense of communal freedom was palpable.

"Aiden, get your ass out here!" his buddy Jake called from the water.

"Nah, bro, I'm good," he yelled back, grinning.

Out past the pond toward the gravel road, dozens of cars were parked half in the ditch, half on the road. The party would probably get busted. If it did, his dad would be pissed, but Aiden was headed to college in less than a month. Who knew when he'd see these friends and classmates again?

Worth it.

He walked over to the keg perched on the edge of a retaining wall, not far from the impromptu dance floor, and pumped the keg's handle. Cheap beer someone's older brother had scored for them poured from the tap. He tipped the lip of his red cup against the spigot, letting the liquid in slowly at an angle to avoid any heady foam.

Out of the corner of his eye, Aiden saw red hair whipping around and did a double take. Olivia Olsen was dancing with her best friend, Maddy. His smile broadened. Seemingly overnight, Olivia had gone from a quiet girl who had doodled her way through class to a free spirit with few inhibitions.

Cold liquid ran over Aiden's hand.

"Shit," he muttered.

He'd gotten distracted by her legs. He let go of the tap, transferred the cup into his dry hand, and tried to shake the beer off his free one, wiping the rest on his khaki shorts before looking back up at Olivia. She was singing along to the music, beaming. Even in the limited light from the cabin, her hazel eyes looked vibrant and full of something akin to anticipation.

This was the third party in a row where Aiden had spotted Olivia floating around like a hummingbird, laughing and dancing with a drink in her hand. Where had this version of her been hiding for the past twelve years? He'd never seen her party before graduation.

Their class had fewer than two hundred students. Everyone knew everyone's story, even if they weren't friends.

Olivia was in the National Honors Society and mostly hung out with the theater kids. Her friend, Maddy, starred in every production while Olivia walked around with paint on her jeans from her work behind the scenes. If she was called on to speak in class, her cheeks would turn an adorable shade of pink. As soon as she was done, she'd look down at her desk, and her soft, shiny red hair would fall forward, hiding her away.

Aiden took a drink of his beer, recalling the time she'd kissed him behind the puppet stage during Kindergarten Sunday School. He grinned and considered what it would be like to kiss her pretty red lips now.

Olivia still hadn't noticed him watching. As she danced, the pale skin of her long limbs glowed softly in the moonlight. When she raised her arms with the rhythm of the music, her yellow tank top lifted, and he got a glimpse of her lean midriff. To his utter surprise, a little diamond hung over her navel.

Holy shit, Olivia Olsen has a belly button piercing?

Aiden's universe shifted. He would have bet a hundred bucks against Olivia Olsen being the type of girl to pierce her belly button.

He lifted his Twins baseball cap off his head and finger-combed his hair back. Then he flipped the cap around so the bill was facing backward before adjusting it back into place. He was going in.

Chapter 1 – Olivia

(Now)

At 7 p.m. on a Friday, the Locals Only bar in Gresham, Minnesota, was filling up with its regular barflies. Most of the patrons were fifty-something men staring with open-mouthed captivation at the flatscreen televisions pulling double duty as decor. The TV images rotated between colorful sports jerseys and the muted hues of cable news commentators.

Olivia Olsen hadn't realized getting beers at Locals Only was what Ethan Wescott had in mind when he'd asked her on a date. Granted, he'd done it in the middle of the plumbing aisle at Hank's Hardware, but he was the manager at Hank's, and she'd been having issues with her irrigation system. However, for the hundredth time since accepting his invitation, her gut was telling her it was a mistake.

At thirty-one, the maturity gap between Olivia and the twenty-three-year-old man sitting across from her felt vast.

By Gresham standards, it was downright inappropriate, and the thought of some townie telling Ethan's big brother Aiden about their date made Olivia cringe.

Ever since Olivia left Seattle to move back to Gresham six months ago, her best friend, Jessa, had been pushing her to "hop on the rebound train." But it wasn't until Jessa told her she'd spotted Olivia's ex-boyfriend, Sam, on a date in Seattle that Olivia finally caved and agreed to drinks with Ethan.

After accepting, she'd created a mantra of sorts. *It's just a drink. He's cute. How bad can it be?*

It's just a drink. He's cute. How bad can it be?

How bad could it be?

Well, she hadn't anticipated going to Locals Only, and she certainly hadn't expected to have her former high school physics teacher leering at her the whole time from a nearby table. Olivia suspected she needed to get off the Gresham rebound train as soon as possible because there weren't enough boxcars, and it was definitely headed in the wrong direction.

To be fair to Ethan, he was behaving like a perfect gentleman, if a little clueless about where to bring a date. With his classic Wescott good looks–dark brown hair, glacial blue eyes, chiseled jaw, and full lips–he probably didn't need to make much of an effort with other women. His looks and last name made him a big fish in the small pond that was their hometown.

She still had a hard time imagining him taking dates here, regardless of his catch-worthy status. But maybe he enjoyed saying hello to all of his Hank's Hardware customers when they walked through the door. Maybe he thought it was good for business.

"So, is Locals Only really your scene?" Olivia asked after the waitress set a bottle of Budweiser and a pint of Blue Moon on their table.

"No, not so much. My friends and I usually hang out at The Whiskey Warden."

"Oh?"

"Yeah, but I thought we'd be more comfortable here."

"Interesting. Why is that?" She might be older than the women he was used to dating, but there was no way he thought she fit in with this crowd. Right?

"Well, Aiden said he was meeting his buddy Jake at The Whiskey Warden tonight, and I didn't want him giving me a hard time."

Olivia's heart pounded. "Wait. Aiden is in town? Aiden? Your *brother*, Aiden?"

She whipped her gaze toward the door and scanned the bar. The only thing worse than Aiden hearing about this unfortunate date through the town rumor mill would be him witnessing it in person.

Fortunately, Aiden must have stuck to his plan because the coast was clear.

"Well, yeah," Ethan said, as if he were surprised by her reaction. "He just moved back to Saint Paul, so he came up for the weekend."

"Aiden moved back to Minnesota?"

"Yeah, he's starting a Pediatric Fellowship on Monday. I thought I mentioned that."

"Nope. Nope, you didn't."

Olivia grabbed the laminated menu off the table in front of her and fanned herself. She could feel her neck doing that ugly red splotchy thing. It used to happen every time she had to stand in front of a class to give a presentation.

After a few seconds pause, Ethan tilted his head to the side, narrowed his eyes, and grinned. "Wait, did you and Aiden hook up in high school?"

"No! No. Of course not." The idea was beyond ridiculous. "But you know what? I think I'm going to call it a night. I'm tired, and I have to be up at five tomorrow for the farmers market. I should get to bed." She spun on her bar stool and stood.

"Wait. Are you sure? We were just getting started. I mean, we haven't even ordered cheese curds yet," he said with a flirty smile, dimples appearing on his clean-shaven cheeks.

Jesus, he has the baby face of his youth while I'm over here counting crow's feet every morning.

Olivia shook her head and grabbed her purse off the back of her chair.

True to her word, Aiden and Olivia had not hooked up in high school. Despite graduating together, they hadn't even been friends. She had been shy and had taken every art class her high school offered. Eventually, the theater kids took her under their wing after her friend Maddy recruited her to help with the sets for Gresham High's theater productions.

Aiden, meanwhile, had been the captain of the basketball team and their class's prom king. Everyone in their school had followed the day-to-day drama of Aiden's high school romance with Ashley Lund.

Regardless, Olivia hadn't moved back to Gresham to connect with the past. She smiled and shrugged her shoulders apologetically. "I better go. But thanks again for the invite. I'll see you at the hardware store next week. I'm still in a fight with my irrigation system."

Ethan, affable as ever, returned her smile. "Okay, no worries. I think I'll hang out and finish my beer. Drive safe." He saluted her with his bottle and took a deep drink.

"Okay, bye!" Her voice was awkwardly upbeat.

Her body felt tight as she forced her legs to move toward the exit at a normal pace while doing her best to avoid eye contact.

Olivia stepped into the cool, damp evening. As was common in early June, it had rained hard all day. A deep breath brought in the clean smell of wet earth and washed away the lingering stench of stale beer. She let out a sigh, knowing in her gut she'd just dodged a bullet. She needed to be careful if she didn't want to become the talk of the town, especially now that Aiden was living a mere two hours south of Gresham.

She paused under the buzzing yellow light illuminating the bar's entrance and watched a lone car drive down the street. With its tail lights in view, Olivia walked across the empty road to her car.

As her seatbelt clicked into place, her phone buzzed.

Ethan: *Let me know if you change your mind, I think we could have a lot of fun together. (Smiley winky face)*

The text made Olivia want to point her car toward the setting sun and keep driving until she reached Seattle and the relative anonymity it had provided for the past thirteen years.

Chapter 2 - Olivia

As much as Olivia wanted to bury her face in a bowl of ice cream before crawling into bed after her mortifying date with Ethan, she had one more errand.

She made a quick stop at home before heading to her parents' house. After turning her silver Prius right at the large metal sign that read *Olsen Farm*, she drove slowly up the quarter-mile-long driveway to avoid kicking up gravel with her car tires, one of her dad's biggest pet peeves.

Her parents' square, two-story house was surrounded by huge sheds, shops, barns, and other buildings that littered their property, not to mention the various mud-caked tractors, trucks and other farm equipment. Beyond the buildings, her dad had cultivated endless rows of wheat, still short and green this early in the growing season.

Stepping out of her car, Olivia opened the rear driver's side door for her dog, Ms. Darcy, a four-year-old Blue Heeler and Border Collie mix. Ms. Darcy, whom Olivia had nicknamed Missy, hopped off the backseat and landed with a soft thump before sprinting to the house's side entrance.

Olivia followed and knocked before letting herself in. Ms. Darcy wove around Olivia's legs, running straight to Olivia's mom, Gail, who was perched on a bar stool at the beige Formica kitchen counter. Her mom's hand paused, holding a page of the cookbook she was looking through. She glanced up with her kind hazel eyes and smiled at Olivia as she reached down to scratch Ms. Darcy behind the ears.

"Hey, sweetie girl!"

"Hey, Mom, thanks again for taking Missy. You have no idea how helpful this is. The market is going to be way too hot for her tomorrow, and if I left her home alone all day, she'd probably eat a chair or something."

"Oh, no problem. Taking care of two dogs is like having two kids. If you have one, you might as well have another so they can entertain each other."

Ms. Darcy gave Olivia's mom one last lick on the hand before prancing over to Jackie Onassis, her parents' thirteen-year-old chocolate lab, who was showing her age and didn't have a ton of patience for Ms. Darcy's boundless youthful energy.

Ms. Darcy sidled up to Jackie O's bed and did a play-bow, but Jackie looked the other way. In a pout, Ms. Darcy lay down on the carpet next to Jackie and sighed.

Chuckling, Olivia's mom glanced at the clock on the white oven that had been part of the kitchen since Olivia was in middle school. "Aren't you home early? I thought you said you had a date."

"Oh, well, let's just say I severely underestimated our age gap."

"What are you talking about? You graduated high school together."

"Uhm, nope. Ethan is like eight years younger than me, Mom."

"Hold the phone. I thought you were meeting Aiden."

Hold the phone? "Wait, how did you know Aiden was in town?"

"Carolyn told me ages ago he was moving to Saint Paul to do a Medical Fellowship. I think she said it was in Pediatric Emergency Medicine. I guess it's quite prestigious. She's thrilled about it. I'm sure I told you."

Carolyn Westcott and Olivia's mom had become good friends over the last few years through their volunteer work. This fact had not eluded Olivia when she'd agreed to go on a date with Ethan, and yet, she'd made her bed, so to speak.

"No, Mom, you didn't." Olivia didn't bother to hide her irritation. "And thanks to you, I had a near miss with Aiden catching me on a date with Ethan. Do you know how humiliating that would have been?" Olivia groaned.

Olivia's mom clenched her lips between her teeth, but a loud snort trumpeted through her nose. Her laughter burst out of her like someone letting go of an untied balloon, loudly and wildly.

"Oh my god, Mom. This is not funny."

“It's a little funny,” she squeaked. “Why did you go on a date with a high schooler? Isn't that illegal?” More shoulder-shaking laughter rolled through her.

“Great, let me know when you're done,” Olivia grumbled.

Olivia's dad, Bill, walked into the kitchen. “What's so funny?”

“Nothing,” Olivia and her mom said in unison.

Her mom straightened and wiped her round cheeks, which were pink and wet from her laughter. She was fair-skinned with red hair that was now mixed with light golden gray strands. Olivia had inherited her fair Irish complexion from her mom’s side and her height and fast metabolism from her dad’s Scandinavian roots.

Sensing he'd missed the joke, her dad moved on. “So-ah, you selling at the farmers market tomorrow, then?” His elongated O’s made him sound like a parody of the Minnesotan farmer he was.

Olivia had hoped to be in and out before her dad could start up his ongoing campaign to convince her she should drop all of her dreams of becoming Gresham's first small-scale local produce and flower farmer in favor of taking over the family's commercial farm. This dream of his would not only allow him to retire without the “tragedy” of selling off the farm, but he’d also be able to hold his head high in front of his farmer friends.

“Yup. I’ll be selling at the market. Just like last Saturday and the one before that.” Maybe her tone was a little snotty, and it would likely provoke her dad, but she was so tired of having this conversation.

She’d explained a dozen times that her Community Supported Agriculture business was fairly common in Seattle, and she thought it had a lot of potential to take off in Gresham. Her CSA gave her customers a share of her farm, which meant they received a box of freshly harvested seasonal produce each week. In addition to the CSA, Olivia sold excess produce *a la carte* at the Saturday farmers market in order to distribute as much of her small crop as she could.

“Mom says you're still looking for subscribers to that service of yours. Gettin’ kinda late in the season, isn't it? What are you doing with all the extra produce? You can’t possibly be selling it all at the market.”

“I’m donating it to the food bank.”

“Hmmm, that’s not a very profitable business model.”

Here we go again. “Dad, I told you, I’m not all that worried about money right now.”

“Yah, but Olivia, you can't pay the bills with potatoes. If you could, I'd be growing potatoes.” He chuckled softly, and Olivia fought the urge to roll her eyes.

“Fine.” She placed her hands on the counter, deciding to be honest with her dad about her finances–even though it felt like breaking one of the most sacred rules of Midwestern civility. “I didn't want to make this a thing, but here's the deal. I could basically retire at this point if I never leave Gresham. With all of the stock grants I got from working in tech, I achieved the four percent rule as soon as I sold my townhouse.”

“The what now?”

“The four percent rule. It means if you can live off four percent of your total investments each year, you can retire. And with the cost of living so much lower here, it doesn’t take as much to get by.”

The furrow between her dad’s brows deepened, and his jaw went slack. Olivia wasn’t sure if he was stunned because she was sitting on a decent nest egg or that she’d foiled his surefire plan to get her to take over the farm.

After a beat, he sounded perplexed as he said, “Good Lord, Olivia. Man was made to work, not to sit back and make money off other people’s hard work.”

“Well, it’s a good thing I’m a woman then. And I am working! I’ve started a business.”

His face reddened in frustration.

“We don’t need you to start a new business. We need you to take over this one. You think you own the moral high ground here because you’re growing *local produce?* How many families are you feeding with your vegetables and flowers, Olivia? Twenty? We grow enough wheat to feed half this state. Where’s the shame in that?”

"There's no shame in it, Dad. It's just not what I want to do. You know who taught me to love growing food? You did. Every summer when you asked me to help you in our garden and showed me how delicious freshly harvested veggies and fruit taste."

This seemed to settle him a bit. He sat on a stool next to her mom.

"Plus, we've talked about this a million times. Why don't you give the business to Philip? He already knows the farm inside out."

Philip was Olivia's cousin, but growing up, he'd been more like a big brother to her and her sister, Grace, as well as a surrogate son to their parents. He'd been working on the farm since he was twelve, and he knew the ropes better than anyone. He also had a knack for putting up with her dad, which was no easy feat.

"Look, Philip is a good, hard-working man. He's great with day-to-day fieldwork and brilliant at fixing anything."

Olivia raised her eyebrows. She did not see the problem.

"But," her dad continued, "he doesn't have the business experience to run an operation this large. The farm is four times the size it was when you left for college. We've got three employees and millions of dollars' worth of equipment in those buildings out there. I need someone who can keep it all in their head and see the big picture."

"Can't you just hire a bookkeeper?"

"If you worked with me on this, you'd understand why that isn't a solution. It's like what Father Justin said at church last week…"

Olivia's mom stepped in. "Okay, Bill, you've made your point. Let's give it a rest now."

She turned to Olivia, giving her a look that told her to back off from the conversation.

"Yeah, I should get going," Olivia said, taking her mom's cue. "Thanks again for watching Missy. I really appreciate it."

She walked over and gave Ms. Darcy a kiss on the head before hugging her parents.

When she was back in her car, driving toward the Ben and Jerry's Cherry Garcia in her freezer, she thought about her narrow escape from her date with Ethan.

After buying her farmhouse, she'd headed straight to Hank's, where she ran into Ethan. He'd introduced himself as Hank's assistant manager and offered his help. It turned out he knew his stuff. He'd been working there since he was fourteen and could explain the purpose of every tool in the store. Over the next few months, she began relying on Ethan's advice as much as YouTube to answer her DIY questions.

Sure, their conversations had gotten a little flirty, but he was so young, not to mention Aiden's little brother, she assumed it had been nothing more than a little fun for both of them.

Why, god, why had she let Ethan wear her down? And why did Aiden have to move back to Minnesota? Maybe she should throw in the towel and head back to Seattle before things got more awkward.

Then, in a moment or clarity, she rolled down the window to let the fresh air blow some sense back into her. She was a grown-ass woman. She was not going to let Aiden, someone she hadn't seen in thirteen years, have this much power over her.

Chapter 3 - Olivia

The Gresham Farmers Market opened most summer Saturdays at 8 a.m. on the dot, and its first patrons were older, early risers hoping to beat the heat. Though it was a bit unusual for early June, especially after a heavy rain, the forecast predicted a scorcher with highs in the nineties.

Despite the heat, the market would soon be bustling. The whole place smelled like the sugary doughnuts the local Lions Club was frying for their annual summer fundraiser. Olivia's fellow vendors were hawking everything from canned jams to handmade fishing lures. There was only one other vegetable farmer who also sold eggs as well as a berry farmer selling strawberries that week. While those two stands were technically Olivia's competition, without them, it wouldn't have been much of a farmers market.

When Olivia's CSA customers opened their boxes that week, they would find an assortment of late spring vegetables, including lettuce, kale, snap peas, asparagus, radishes, and a bundle of dill. These little veggie babies filled Olivia with pride. She'd always loved watching seeds sprout, grow leaves, and produce food, but unfortunately, her passion didn't translate to her family's five-thousand-acre farm. At that scale, farming meant being stuck in a tractor from sunrise to sundown. Sure, it wasn't the same as sitting in front of a computer all day like she'd done for the previous decade, but for Olivia, it felt too disconnected from the earth.

Furthermore, the crops grown at that scale were invariably commercial products like wheat, corn, and soybeans, which were sold on a global market. Like she'd told her dad, there was absolutely no shame in producing food to feed the masses, but it didn't inspire Olivia to jump out of bed in the morning. What did get her moving was the motivation to increase access to fresh local produce, especially for a rural community like Gresham. If this year was successful, she was hoping to create an income-based subscription model going forward.

Unfortunately, she was more worried about the immediate viability of the CSA than she'd been willing to admit to her dad. At only fifteen subscribers, she was barely breaking even. If she was going to keep her business going next year, she needed to reach thirty subscribers by mid-July, which was only about a month away.

Looking around at the crowd dressed in shorts and T-shirts, she wondered how she might lure a few more families into her CSA. Then, out of the corner of her eye, she spotted Ethan Wescott headed her way. Her nightmare date wouldn't end. How had she forgotten the cardinal rule of small-town living? There was no such thing as anonymity.

She turned, pretending to grab more lettuce for her display, avoiding eye contact. Olivia prayed Ethan would take the hint and keep walking. However, through her peripheral vision, it was obvious he was walking straight toward her. *Damn.* She resigned herself to the forthcoming awkwardness.

"Hey, Olivia." His deep voice was undeniably appealing, but he had to stop. Had he not gotten the message when she'd ignored his three texts the night before? Apparently ghosting didn't work in small towns…or when your moms are friends.

She spun around to put an end to his pursuit, once and for all. "I'm not going on another date with you, Ethan. I told you…"

Olivia froze because she was not looking at twenty-three-year-old Ethan Wescott. She was face-to-face with his older, oh-so-similar-looking brother, Aiden. The resemblance was uncanny.

"I'm sorry, but I think you've mistaken me for my little brother," Aiden said, laughter dancing at the edge of his words. "I'm flattered."

Olivia's mouth dropped open as she took Aiden in. Sure, he definitely looked like Ethan, but he was so much more–for lack of a better word–manly. *Holy hell.* She suddenly had the urge to fan herself like a Southern belle. Where had that come from?

"Aiden! What are you doing here?" It came out more as an accusation than a question.

"I'm in town visiting my family. How long has it been anyway? Like thirteen years since we graduated high school?" he said in a relaxed voice.

Olivia, stop being weird. She recalled her vow to act like a grown-ass woman. She would not revert to the gangly teenager she'd once been. Who cared if the most popular boy in school was talking to her?

"Right! Family. Great! Did you…want to buy some vegetables?"

"Oh, my mom asked me to pick up their CSA box. And obviously, I wanted to see this for myself and say hello. So, ya know, hi."

"Ah yes, that makes sense because you're Aiden Wescott, and your mom is Carolyn Wescott, one of my CSA subscribers who also happens to be Ethan Wescott's mom. Have you ever noticed how small this town is?"

She'd lost control of her mouth. It just kept talking, and every word that came out sounded more inane than the last. Cool and confident? Any hopes of cool and confident had gone ass over teakettle as soon as Aiden showed up.

Olivia splayed her hands. "So, um, yeah, let me grab your mom's veggies."

She turned away to grab the box labeled 'Carolyn Wescott' before she drowned in her own ridiculousness. When Aiden accepted it, his fingers grazed hers, making her fidget.

“Oh, wow. I'm impressed. You're doing all this by yourself?” Of all the awkward vibes leading up to this moment that might have made her blush, it was his compliment that did the job.

“Yeah, thanks. It's, um, growing, I guess. I’ve still got a lot of work to do to get it where it needs to be, but I’m hopeful.”

“Well, Gresham can use all the fresh produce it can get. It’s crazy how many diseases are preventable with better diets, but access to fresh veggies can be challenging in rural communities.” He sounded earnest. She didn’t think she’d ever heard Aiden Wescott sound earnest before.

“Wow, thanks, you make it sound so noble,” she said. “But seriously, I’m really grateful for your parents’ business. Please thank them again for me.”

“Sure, no worries.” He smiled, and his dimples created valleys in his cheeks. *God, those dimples.*

“Oh, and these.” She grabbed a bouquet of light purple daylilies and awkwardly placed them on top of the box in Aiden’s arms. “I try to include flowers whenever I can,” she added, not wanting him to think she’d just given him flowers.

Aiden watched Olivia closely through the whole interaction, but she struggled to meet his captivating blue eyes. She wondered what he saw. What changes or similarities to her eighteen-year-old self did he notice?

Her hair was definitely less orange, thanks to the low lights she spent far too much money on, always hoping for a Julia

Roberts-red, circa her *Pretty Woman* days. Her skin was still fairly freckled, especially given how much time she had been outside that spring. One thing definitely hadn't changed: her 5-foot 9-inch skinny frame. Okay, maybe she'd graduated to a B cup through sheer force of will and ice cream, but that was pushing it.

Olivia was about to turn around again to avoid his gaze, but Aiden spoke. "You know, I have to admit, I was a little surprised to hear you and Ethan were going out last night, but now I have to say, I get it. I mean, at least from Ethan's perspective."

"Oh my god, Aiden. Stop. I'm pretty sure this is the exact scenario that kept me two thousand miles away for the last decade."

"You stayed in Seattle because you were worried about me complimenting you at a farmers market?" His teasing tone surprised her. *Was he flirting?*

"Umm. I'd say it was the fear I'd be desperate enough to go on a date with someone half my age. But for the record, I immediately called it off." *As soon as I heard you were in town,* Olivia admitted silently to herself. "It lasted like, five minutes, tops."

Still talking. She was *still* talking. Why was she telling him this? Her cheeks were getting warm again.

Why does it feel so intense when he looks at me? Beads of sweat formed at her hairline, and she surreptitiously wiped them away with her forearm.

"I know. He told me last night," Aiden admitted. "I promise I won't mention it again. And also, no judgment. Ethan is a catch."

A guffaw burst out of Olivia. Despite his promise to stop teasing her about Ethan, Aiden's eyes were mirthful, and a grin lingered at the corners of his mouth.

Olivia's face turned serious as she remembered what her mom had said about Aiden's dad's stroke. It was exactly the reality check she needed. Aiden had much bigger fish to fry than wasting time talking about her silly date with Ethan.

In a softer tone, she said, "Hey, so, I hope you don't mind me saying, but my mom told me about your dad's stroke. I'm so sorry. How's he doing?"

Aiden's smile faltered. "Not so great, unfortunately. I'm hoping to be around more to take the pressure off my mom and Ethan a bit."

"Ethan mentioned you moved to Saint Paul?"

"Yeah, I just started a job at Saint Paul Children's."

Olivia noted how understated this was—what he'd omitted despite having earned legitimate bragging rights.

"Well, that's great you'll be closer to Gresham…for your family, obviously."

“Obviously.” Although his eyes were laughing, he only smiled as he lingered in front of her stand. “What about you? What brings you back to Gresham? A bit of a change from Seattle, no?”

Olivia tilted her head and scratched her nose as she considered which of her lines about moving back she should give. She could use the “closer to family” line or the “cost of living” line. She could pull out the old, “had always planned to come back, just took a little longer than I thought.” Or she could fall back on, “life is hard to predict sometimes.”

In the end, she settled on something generic while hinting at reality. “I guess the same reasons anyone moves back. Aging parents, opportunity, and all that. And I think I was ready for a change of scenery.”

“Fair enough.” He nodded. “Hey, would you want to grab a beer after you're done here? For old time’s sake?”

“Old time’s sake?” Olivia glanced at him sideways, her voice full of skepticism. “What times are those?”

The last time she remembered talking to Aiden was during a class project in the eleventh grade, most of which he’d spent sleeping face down on his desk. She was pretty sure he had been hungover, but she hadn’t fully understood the mechanics of alcohol yet. It would be another year before Olivia and her best friend Maddy giggled their way through a strawberry wine cooler in her childhood bedroom after her parents had gone to sleep.

And yet, if she was honest with herself, she'd had a little, tiny crush on him in high school. The kind a teenage girl has at a distance, knowing full-well the feeling is completely one sided.

Aiden was looking at her quizzically, as if he were considering his next words carefully. "Are we going to pretend like you didn't kiss me behind the puppet stage in kindergarten?"

Olivia grinned. She shook her head and rolled her eyes. He wasn't wrong. They had been kindergarten sweethearts. But he'd dropped her in first grade for Jessica Thompson.

"Maybe next time?" She hoped her answer sounded friendly but firm. "I've been awake since five-thirty, and it'll probably be dinnertime before I'm home. I'm pretty sure I'd fall asleep in my beer."

"No problem. Another time works for me. Anyway, it was great to see you again, and it seems like you're taking Gresham by storm with these CSA boxes and produce and flowers." He nodded at each item in her stand to emphasize his point.

"Oh, I don't know about that." She smiled, appreciating the encouragement.

As she said it, Pam, another CSA subscriber, hesitantly approached her stand. Olivia waved at her encouragingly to come forward, and Aiden glanced over his shoulder.

"Looks like I'm holding up the line," he said. "I'll let you go, but I hope I'll see you around."

"Sounds good. Take care, Aiden."

Olivia's eyes lingered on the V-shape of his torso as he walked away before she turned toward Pam.

Pam stepped forward with a bounce in her step. As a seventy-one-year-old retiree, Pam worked out at the YMCA every morning and was one of Olivia's first subscribers. While her gray hair suggested her age, she had the energy and healthy aura of a much younger woman. Classic CSA early adopter, Olivia thought to herself. *Where do I find more Pams?*

"Good morning," Olivia said cheerfully, hoping to draw in other folks who might be hesitant to approach. "How is your Saturday treating you, Pam? I see you have your coffee."

"Another day above ground. Can't complain, but I probably will anyway. What are we getting this week?"

Olivia proudly opened a box with a flourish, and Pam peered in. "I remember you said radishes give you heartburn," Olivia said. "So I substituted a few early potatoes in your box."

Pam's face split into a mischievous grin. "I feel so spoiled. I promise not to tell your other CSA folks I got potatoes, and they didn't."

"Well, I appreciate you watching out for me, but in all honesty, anything you can do to spread the word about the

CSA would be helpful. I was hoping for thirty subscribers this year, and I'm only at fifteen. Maybe you could tell all of your YMCA friends about how healthy my produce makes you feel?" Olivia lifted her voice in question, leading the witness.

"Oh yah, I'd be happy to help," Pam responded enthusiastically. "Do you have a business card by chance? I could tack it to the YMCA community board for ya."

"Ah, yes, you're brilliant. That would be great." Olivia handed Pam a stack of cards.

Their banter helped bring Olivia back to herself, but in the lull following Pam's departure, she replayed her interaction with Aiden.

Yes, okay, he looked great. To be honest, he was certifiably dreamy. He'd definitely gotten more handsome since she'd seen him last. Maybe a bit Patrick Dempsey-esque? Or was she thinking that because of the whole doctor thing?

But he was also…different than she remembered. Perhaps this is what she should expect from all of her former classmates who were now full-blown adults, but it felt like more than that. Although he'd teased her, he'd also seemed genuinely curious about what she was up to and had been generous with his praise. Meanwhile, she felt like she'd reverted to her high school days, self-conscious and gawky around the cutest boy in town.

It resurfaced the question she had continually asked herself since moving back home. Was it possible to hold onto her identity and remain unhindered by the town's expectations of who she was supposed to be? Or did Gresham only have enough room for her to be forced back into an outdated mold? Because that brief interaction, with all of her blushing and fumbling for words, suggested the latter, and she didn’t love it.

Chapter 4 - Aiden

Before leaving the market, Aiden turned back to take one last look at Olivia through the bustling crowd. She wore jean shorts, a tie-dyed tank top, and Birkenstocks, but all he saw were her lithe, muscular legs. *Christ, was she always so tall?*

When she'd turned her back to him, he'd wanted to reach out and touch her thick braid of dark red hair, which looped gracefully over her right shoulder. She was beautiful in the most natural, down-to-earth way Aiden could imagine.

Was this the same girl, er, woman, he'd gone to high school with? Sure, she was embarrassed about the whole Ethan thing, but she held her own. And her concern for his dad seemed genuine, which impacted him more than he'd have expected.

Now she stood talking to the older woman who had waited patiently for him to leave. As she spoke, Olivia gestured openly at her produce and flowers. She seemed so confident standing there under a tent banner that loudly proclaimed her vegetables were from the *Olivia Olsen Farm*.

Something Olivia said made the older woman laugh. Any wallflower tendencies she may have had in their youth seemed to have been washed away in the years since high school.

Realizing he was staring with a dorky smile on his face, he turned away and walked to his car. He gently placed the vegetable box and flowers in the backseat before climbing into the driver's seat.

Even though he'd invited her to grab beers, hoping to see her once more before he went back to Saint Paul, it was for the best she'd blown him off. *Did I just ask her to grab a beer when she went on a date with Ethan last night?* Even if Ethan shrugged it off, it felt wrong.

When Ethan first told him he'd asked Olivia out, Aiden was convinced it was a different Olivia Olsen. But then Ethan sent Aiden a link to Olivia's website bio, confirming it was the one person from high school with whom Aiden felt like he had unfinished business. Although the idea of Ethan dating Olivia made him uncomfortable, it was also downright laughable. What had she been thinking? There was no way that was going anywhere.

Yet, the night before, Aiden couldn't stop wondering how their date was going. When Aiden finished having beers with his old high school buddy, Jake, he'd driven by Locals Only to see if he could spot Ethan's truck in the parking lot. When his search came up empty, Aiden swung by his parents' house, where Ethan still lived, and was relieved to find him sitting on the couch in the basement watching TV.

Aiden had tried not to laugh when Ethan told him about their date. "Well, it wasn't great. She ditched me about fifteen minutes into it and has been ignoring my texts since. Anyway, I think Jennifer is going to be in town next week, so it's probably for the best, timing-wise."

Aiden truly appreciated his brother's laid-back personality and rubber skin. Whatever life threw at him, he rebounded without a scratch. Not only did Aiden admire it, but at that moment, he was relieved. He had no claims on Olivia, but the thought of her sitting next to Ethan at their family dinners made something tighten in his chest.

Regardless, even if Ethan gave Aiden his blessing, Olivia was far too sweet to be messing around with. Some things hadn't changed. The way she'd blushed when he'd teased her had boosted his ego, which ultimately made him feel like an ass.

But she'd acted confused when he'd alluded to their history.

Granted, calling it history might be a stretch. He rubbed his thumbs against the steering wheel as he thought back to that one night they'd hung out the summer after graduating high school. It was the first time Aiden had really seen Olivia, with her bright red hair, cute little freckles, and big, charming smile. Sure, they'd grown up in the same small town, but she had always been in his periphery, never in his line of sight. But that night, Aiden saw her for what she was—a hummingbird. She hovered directly in front of him for a moment before flying off to Seattle.

But if she wasn't going to acknowledge it, neither was he. So he'd played it cool and made a joke about their time as kindergarten sweethearts instead. Did she really not remember, or was she messing with him?

Regardless of the past, they didn't have a future.

He was telling the truth when he said he wanted to be around more to help out with his dad's stroke recovery, but the two-hour drive between Gresham and Saint Paul was there for a reason. He had been so relieved to escape Gresham's communal gaze after high school. Furthermore, he loved city life. He depended on having a coffee shop within walking distance of his bed.

Meanwhile, Olivia had put down literal roots in Gresham.

Even though he was closing the door he'd just cracked open, he pondered Olivia's decision to move back to Gresham as he drove home. How could Olivia cope with Walmart being her closest option for browsing books? Or that both Mexican restaurants were owned and run by white people who'd never even been to Mexico? Or that her mom would know everything about her dating life?

Fifteen minutes later, Aiden opened the door to his parents' house. When he set Olivia's produce on the counter, he handed the flowers to his mom and leaned down to give her a kiss on the top of her head. His mom was still slender at sixty-four. Though most of Aiden's siblings took after her in looks, her hair was slightly wavier than his and his siblings'.

Her skin tanned deeply every summer, even though Aiden nagged her to wear sunscreen.

She narrowed her eyes at him, like she was trying to read his mind.

"What?" he asked, his tone flat and suspicious.

"How was your time with Olivia?" she asked, her hopeful voice giving her away.

Well, he supposed it wasn't rocket science. Olivia was sweet, and his mom's friend's daughter, Gresham-born, raised, and returned. What a fortuitous match, she must be thinking.

"Think again, Mom. Not happening," he said aloud.

"What? What's not happening?" she asked coyly.

"Mm-hmm."

"Okay, but you can't deny it. She is darling."

Then, opening the box, she said, "Will you help me put these groceries away?"

He reached over his mom's shoulder and grabbed the lettuce. She was obviously stalling for time.

"Did you know Olivia bought a five-acre farm and started the CSA all by herself? She's Gresham's first CSA farmer, and she's done it all on her own," his mom said.

"Oh really? Good for her." Aiden hoped he sounded uninterested, even though he was hanging on every word, hungry for more answers to his Olivia questions.

"Yup, and you should have seen all the work she's done to help grow the farmers market this year. She even lobbied the City Council to change the market stall fee to an income-based sliding scale model to make it more equitable. In case you haven't noticed, this young woman is very impressive." His mom's voice carried so much pride for everything Olivia had accomplished that it sounded like she was speaking about one of her own children. "Olivia is a needle in a haystack, Aiden. She is very special."

"Well, Mom, maybe Ethan can give it another go since you're obviously hoping Olivia will be your daughter-in-law someday." He wanted to lower her hopes back down to earth.

His mom laughed exasperatedly and shook her head before lightly hitting him in the arm with the back of her hand as if she were scolding a teenager.

"Ouch," Aiden teased, rubbing his arm. "Look, I appreciate the thought, but I'm not interested. Anyway, I gotta go. I told Ethan I'd help with the dock today."

He let his mom give him a kiss on the cheek before he walked toward the basement to find Ethan. They had been tasked with putting the dock in the lake, one of his least favorite chores, preceded only by the worse job of pulling the dock out of the frigid lake in fall before it froze over.

His family's lakefront property was a privilege, so he'd vowed never to voice his complaints. But he was also coming to terms with his dad's illness and that it meant he and Ethan would need to take the reins of caring for their parents' home indefinitely.

Chapter 5 - Olivia

Olivia stepped onto the wrap-around porch of her two-story farmhouse. Unlocking her door, she briefly debated between a shower and dinner, but her growling stomach made the decision for her. She hadn't eaten since the quick salad she'd devoured for lunch.

Too exhausted to cook, she snacked on raw snap peas and strawberries leftover from the market while microwaving a veggie corn dog and a chicken tamale from the frozen Trader Joe's hoard she'd acquired in Minneapolis the week before.

After the farmers market closed, it had taken almost two hours to break down her tent, load everything into the back of her "new" 1994 Ford F-150 truck, and drop off her leftover produce at the food bank. She'd inadvertently purchased the truck as part of her five-acre farm. Still in great shape, it had been among a long list of miscellaneous possessions left behind when the previous owner's adult children had opted to cash out on their inheritance.

Of all the miscellany she'd acquired, the truck had come in especially handy on market days.

As exhausted as she was every Saturday evening, she was grateful the market gave her a sense of purpose. She felt briefly untethered when she'd left Seattle and all of the plans she'd been making there.

In Seattle, she'd been climbing the tech industry ladder straight to Director of Sales for her company's Home and Garden Division. Now she was trying to turn her newly acquired land into a viable, small-scale farming operation. She supposed that technically made her CEO of the Olivia Olsen Farm.

A farm CEO—touting the benefits of local produce while taking a culinary tour of Trader Joe's frozen food offerings. She shoved some more snap peas into her mouth between bites of chicken tamale. As she was about to devour her last bite, a knock sounded on her screen door, followed by a dog whining and thumping its tail against the porch banister.

Her mom let herself in, and Ms. Darcy bounded through the door. "Hi, sweetie, how was the market?"

Ms. Darcy put her head in Olivia's lap, hoping for scratches behind her ears, and her whole body wiggled with excitement. Her "happy to see you" dance always made Olivia smile.

She obliged Ms. Darcy with pets while smiling at her mom. "Hey. It was better this week. I got three new CSA subscribers. Only twelve to go. How did Ms. Darcy do? Did she and Jackie O get along okay?"

"Oh, she was fine. You should have seen her trying to coax Jackie to chase the ball with her. Absolutely hilarious. Poor Missy. Jackie just laid there and pretended to be asleep."

They laughed. "Well, thanks again."

“No worries, lovey. I’m thinking I might borrow her from you some time to hang out with my kiddos.”

“Sure. Anytime.”

When Olivia's dad got busier and busier farming their family’s land, which seemed to expand by five hundred acres every spring, her mom was able to retire early from her dental hygienist job. She'd spent thirty years cleaning people's teeth and had been ready for a change. She used the extra time to volunteer as an opportunity to spend time with her nephew Phillip’s daughter, Fiona, who attended the camp every summer. Olivia had been meaning to join her at the YMCA but kept getting swept up in farm projects.

“Are you still planning to come over for Sunday dinner?” By dinner, her mom was referring to the pot roast lunch she religiously served after church.

Her mom had given up asking her to attend services with them after Olivia returned home from her freshman year of college, ranting about the patriarchal nature of Catholicism. Still, Sunday family dinners had remained a staple of her family’s life.

“Yup. I’ll be there, and I’m bringing a lot of veggie sides, so don’t worry about those. Oh, and grab some lettuce from the fridge. I’m drowning in it.”

Her mom stood. “Okay, will do. I gotta head out. We’re having the Lindens over to play cards tonight.”

“Sounds good, Mom, I'll see you tomorrow.”

"And sweetie…" Her mom paused before walking to the fridge to grab the lettuce, chuckling as she said, "No offense, but you stink. I don't think that hippy deodorant is working."

"Very funny, Mom," Olivia replied good-naturedly. "You try being outside all day in eighty-five percent humidity without smelling a little."

"No, honey, you don't smell a little. You stink." She laughed hard at her own joke before bending down, lettuce in hand, to give Olivia a kiss on the cheek. She let herself out and quietly closed the door behind her, laughing as she left.

"Love you, too, Mom," Olivia called after her, her tone full of mock indignation.

She could still hear her mom giggling through the screen door as she got into her car.

Chapter 6 - Aiden

"You do know you could stay here, right?" Aiden's mom said for the millionth time since he'd graduated high school.

"Yeah, but I'm more comfortable hitting my bong at the cabin."

"Ha ha," she said dryly.

Aiden tried to come up with a new outlandish excuse for sleeping at his family's hunting cabin instead of his parents' home every time he visited. The truth was, he preferred to have his own space. After spending time with his family, he looked forward to the cabin because it gave him the freedom to decompress, and he could come and go whenever he liked.

He didn't know how Ethan did it–living in his parents' basement long after graduating high school. What he did know was Ethan's presence at home took loads of pressure off him and their other siblings, who had long since flown the coop. Far from a deadbeat son, Ethan worked hard to earn his keep, from mowing the lawn to cleaning out the gutters. Since their dad's stroke, many of Ethan's chores had gone from a nice gesture to a family necessity.

"Well, will you at least stay for dinner?" his mom asked.

"Yeah, of course. Should I get Dad?"

"He was asleep when I checked on him last. I think we should probably let him rest. I'll save a plate for him, and he can eat a little later."

Aiden knew his dad was uncomfortable eating in front of others. His stroke had paralyzed his right side, and he'd been having some memory issues, but otherwise, his recovery was going smoothly, if more slowly than they would have preferred.

Sitting down, Aiden and Ethan looked at their plates while their mom said grace.

"Looks amazing, Mom." Ethan grabbed his fork and knife to dig into the salad made from Olivia's CSA. "Thanks for cooking."

"Yeah, thanks, it looks great," Aiden seconded. He grabbed his fork and cut off a piece of the seared salmon seasoned with lemon and Olivia's dill. He rolled the salmon in his mouth, taking a moment to enjoy it before looking toward Ethan curiously. "How are things going at Hank's?"

"Good, yeah, really good. I think I might buy the place in a few years."

"Really?" Aiden was surprised, though he wasn't sure why. Ethan had been at Hank's for almost a decade and would be more than capable of taking over the business.

"Yeah, he's been talking about retiring for a while now, so I finally talked to him about it. If everything goes according to plan, I'll buy Hank out in three years. In the meantime, he wants me to start taking business classes at the community college."

"Ethan, that's great." Pride filled Aiden's chest.

He loved his little brother, but he'd also written off him as the least ambitious of the siblings. Maybe he hadn't given him enough credit all these years. Ethan had somehow found a way to grow up without leaving home. More than that, Ethan was poised to own a very successful business without having a penny of student debt at the ripe old age of twenty-six. Meanwhile, at thirty-one, Aiden was just starting his official pediatrics career and was up to his ears in medical school debt.

"We're so proud of you both." His mom beamed at them.

His parents had never pushed any of them down a particular path. Even when Ethan had lingered at home, it never seemed to bother them. Aiden wondered if having five kids with very different personalities had helped manage their expectations. Or maybe they were just tired.

"Okay, enough, enough. I heard you saw Olivia today." Ethan's face was one big accusatory grin.

"Yeah, Mom asked me to pick up her CSA box. I'm nothing if not a dutiful middle child."

"She's hot, right?" Ethan asked, eyebrows raised.

Aiden's gut clenched. Something about this casual statement went straight under Aiden's skin, but he kept his now-strained smile. “Oh, little brother, I think you missed the boat with that one.”

“Yeah, duh.”

Their mom laughed. “Well, if either one of you manages to marry her, I’ll be very pleased.”

“Jesus, Mom!” Ethan laughed loudly. “And you wonder why Aiden refuses to move back to Gresham.”

As usual, Ethan laughed at his mom’s bluntness. Aiden, meanwhile, felt his toes curl in discomfort.

With guilty relief, Aiden left after dinner to drive the short distance to the cabin. Ethan was well-suited to being the sibling who was still living at home. He had always been a “go-with-the-flow” kid. For every tantrum Ethan’s twin sister Lauren threw, Ethan counterbalanced it with his ability to make everyone laugh. And he did it while somehow bringing Lauren into the joke with him. They were two peas in a pod. Or maybe an edamame and a pea that happened to share a pod.

Regardless, Aiden had never been more grateful for his goofy little brother. Ethan was a rock for his parents, and he imbued a much-needed lightness into their dad during his slow recovery.

Better Ethan than me. Aiden unlocked the cabin’s door, letting out a deep breath as he crossed the threshold.

The little cabin on a secluded pond was exactly where Aiden wanted to be at that moment. He loved how dark it got in the rural countryside. It was the thing he missed most while living in the city.

Grabbing a beer from the fridge, he made his way outside to the end of the dock.

Aiden hadn't stopped thinking about Olivia for more than five minutes since seeing her at the market. As much as he tried to pretend otherwise, he was impressed by everything he'd seen and heard about her.

In high school, Olivia had been quiet and bookish, tending to keep her head down in class. She'd been involved in a bunch of the school plays and had hung out with the "smart" kids—the type who would later become his closest friends in undergrad and beyond.

Wanting to map these two versions of Olivia, he opened his phone and looked her up on LinkedIn. She had stayed in Seattle after graduating from The University of Washington to work at an online retail company. Her profile listed promotions every couple of years, and her most recent position was a senior something or other. She'd left all of that success behind to start a CSA in Gresham? At every turn, this woman created more questions than answers.

Chapter 7 - Olivia

Hours after her mom left, Olivia was still sitting at the table in front of her empty plate. The sun had gone down, and Ms. Darcy lay at her feet, her big brown eyes staring up at Olivia with mournful neglect. She had gone deep into the rabbit hole that was her phone–email replies, social media posts of pics from the market, and random Google searches about issues she was having with her onions.

And…she still smelled awful. Her mom's laugh trilled through her mind.

She needed a bath.

"Let's go, Ms. Darcy."

She stood and headed to the porch, where she had propped up an old neon pink, ten-speed Huffy she'd found in the garage when she'd moved in. She hopped on and gathered speed, peddling the rusty bike down the gentle slope of her oak-tree-lined driveway toward the country road. The crunching gravel under her fat mountain bike tires cut through the buzzing sound of cicadas. Ms. Darcy ran beside her, tail wagging in wild delight.

At the end of the driveway, Olivia turned the bike right toward the pond less than a mile down the road. Over the last couple of weeks, she had found a quick swim before jumping into bed helped erase the day's heat from her body so she could fall into a dreamless sleep.

Growing up on her parents' farm, she had taken the vastness of rural Minnesota for granted, disdaining it by the time she left for college. Now, here she was, relishing the solitude, not to mention the space for Ms. Darcy to roam.

She dropped the bike in the long grass next to the pond. Ms. Darcy knew the drill and began to frolic. Meanwhile, Olivia peeled off her clothes and walked straight into the water without a shiver. Having soaked up the day's sun, the water near the shore was warm and inviting. She splashed it on her face to wash away the dried salt clinging to her cheeks and forehead.

She had always found skinny dipping liberating and had done it as a small act of rebellion in her youth. As an adult, it still gave her a thrill.

Once fully submerged, she flipped onto her back, face pointed up at the quarter-moon and the stars showing up in droves. She moved her body just enough to stay afloat, relaxing as she glided across the pond's mirror surface. Her loose hair tickled her shoulders.

The pond was one of the main reasons she had bought the farmhouse. It was big enough that the water was free of algae and cattail weeds and small enough that it hadn't been overrun with "second homes" owned by wealthy cabin weekenders. Instead, one tiny cabin sat along the shore, which had a healthy buffer of trees before transitioning into farmland.

After driving by the pond for several months, she realized whoever owned the cabin had the kitchen and living room lights on a timer. They turned on from 5 to 10 p.m. every day. Once she'd cracked the code, all bets—and clothes—were off as soon as the temperature hit eighty degrees.

While floating toward the cabin's dock, she recalled her awkward interaction with Aiden at the market. Yes, he'd teased her, but he'd also been kind. She couldn't deny thirty-one looked good on him. Unlike his little brother's soft, youthful beauty, Aiden's features had gotten more defined with age, all of which had been accentuated by day-old stubble and a V-neck T-shirt. It was both a shame and a relief he lived two hours away. If and when she ran into him next, she was going to be cool as a cucumber. She would stay rooted to her adult self. None of those awkward teen vibes.

This resolve gave her some relief, and her mind wandered to Pam. She was curious about where Pam would leave her business cards. Maybe she could create a recruiting deal where Pam would get a free veggie box for every three new subscribers she recruited. Olivia's CSA was growing through word of mouth. It was just slow to take off.

In hopes of catering to the local palate, she had tried to keep her produce fairly mainstream with only one unusual vegetable per week. This week, the customers had gotten very standard fare, but next week, she was going to introduce endives and include a recipe for a delicious grilled version she'd stolen from a friend.

A deep voice cut through her serenity, "Hello?"

She bolted upright, but not finding solid footing below her, she sank. Her limbs flailed about gracelessly, and she accidentally swallowed a mouthful of pond water before popping back above the surface, coughing and sputtering. Ms. Darcy was barking anxiously, and Olivia tried to get control of herself so Ms. Darcy would calm down.

"Is that Olivia Olsen? Are you okay? Do you need me to jump in?" A man stood on the dock, yelling over Ms. Darcy's barks.

The whole thing was causing Olivia's brain to short-circuit, but she registered the voice and silhouette.

Aiden fucking Wescott? You have got to be kidding me.

"No!" she yelled back in a panic. "I'm fine! Do *not* jump in!"

She got her flailing limbs under control and started to tread water, attempting to keep her chest as far below the surface as possible without taking in another mouthful of water.

"Missy, calm down," she yelled, not actually expecting her dog to relax.

After taking a few breaths, she turned to face the situation head-on.

"Aiden. Hello again. I have to ask, are you stalking me?"

Her attempt at comedic relief came out sounding more like the situation demanded, as though she were living out a nightmare involving public indecency.

"Excuse me, miss, but I believe you're the one who swam up to my family's hunting cabin, dare I say, sans clothing?" His voice was full of mirth and contained laughter.

"This is your family's cabin? Well shit, I didn't realize anyone used it." As she said it, Olivia was hit with the vaguest memory of coming to a party here after her senior year of high school when she'd finally let loose.

"Yeah, I usually stay here when I'm in town."

"Got it. Well, sorry to interrupt your peaceful evening."

Olivia was dying to extract herself from the scene. The one in which she was swimming around in her birthday suit and having a conversation with Aiden fucking Westcott.

Okay, I need to get over that last part because we're not in high school anymore.

"Wait," he said, "why are you here?"

"Oh, umm, I bought the farmhouse up the road, and I wanted to cool off before I went to sleep…and…usually nobody's here. I wasn't expecting to get caught, I guess. Ha!" Olivia let out a manic, staccato laugh. "So, I'm gonna swim back over there and get my clothes. It'd be great if you would look the other way. Please."

She dog-paddled toward shore where she'd left her clothes, praying her ass was safely hidden under the water. As she paddled, it occurred to her that Ms. Darcy was no longer losing her mind, so that was one bright spot.

She glanced back toward Aiden and did a double-take. Her dog was standing on the dock next to Aiden, panting and dripping pond water all over his legs. He reached down to pet her head, and…he was laughing.

More laughter thanks to Olivia's sudden onslaught of poor choices.

"Missy, what are you doing? Get over here."

Her words were a mistake because instead of running back along the shoreline, Ms. Darcy took a running leap off the dock to join her in the water. Now they were both dog-paddling away.

Excellent. So freaking great.

"Seriously, Missy?" she chided.

"So, is this not a good time to offer you a beer?" Aiden barely managed to say through his laughter.

"Very funny!" she yelled over her shoulder. "You're worse than Ethan."

"Swim safe," he choked out, apparently needing to have the last word.

Aiden's laugh tapered off as he walked back up the dock and into the cabin.

As soon as she got to shore, she grabbed her clothes and hastily pulled her shirt over her head. But the motion was useless because she was soaking wet, and everything got tangled and bunched.

"Damn it."

She sighed and fought with the fabric, conscious her ass was likely reflecting the moon's glow like a white T-shirt under blacklights. She wrestled into the rest of her clothes and slipped into her flip-flops.

She pushed her bike back onto the road. While peddling home, her mind was stuck on Aiden. He'd gone to the University of Minnesota, studied pre-med, and gotten married to his college freshman sweetheart, according to her mom. At some point during his first year of residency in Boston, they got divorced, and he'd been focused on his medical training since. Add that to what he'd told Olivia at the farmers market, and he was back in Minnesota via Saint Paul.

Maybe she'd take him up on his beer offer next time he was in town, if only to hear the story for herself and regain some of her dignity.

Chapter 8 - Aiden

What kind of joke was the universe playing on him? Olivia had swum up to his dock? Naked? Was he being pranked?

As soon as he had figured out what he was seeing, he tried not to see things.

Sort of.

He didn't see much.

But it definitely made him want to see more.

Fuuuuuck.

The whole thing sent him back in time to the party he'd had at the cabin after graduation. The party where Olivia Olsen had actually shown up. He wondered if she still had that diamond studded belly button piercing.

Shit! You gotta stop. He tried to remember all of the resolutions he'd made this morning and why asking her out was a bad idea. The distance. Moms are friends. Not gonna work. *Don't go there.*

But also, that adorable dog. What had she called her? Missy? He'd been in tears, laughing at the sight of them dog-paddling back to shore together. Absolutely hilarious.

Still, he held strong to his resolution to keep as much distance as he could between them… Which lasted until he went to the YMCA the next morning to meet Ethan for some one-on-one basketball, where he spotted an *Olivia Olsen Farm* business card on the community bulletin board. Olivia's phone number was right there, practically begging him to add it to his contacts.

Maybe he'd text her once, so she had his number…in case of emergency. Easy peasy. No big deal. What's the worst that could happen? But Aiden saw right through his own supposed good intentions. In reality, he wanted to be certain the next time he was in town, he could get in touch with Olivia and see her again.

Aiden: *Hey, it's Aiden. Did you make it home ok?*

Olivia: *How did you get my number?*

Aiden: *I'm standing in front of your business card on the community bulletin at the YMCA.*

Olivia: *Wow, Pam works fast. Maybe I should hire her as a part time marketing consultant.*

Pam? He had no idea who she was talking about.

Aiden: *What?*

Olivia: *Never mind. You go to the Y at 8 a.m. on a Sunday? So ambitious.*

Aiden: *I'm shooting hoops with Ethan. He has to work at 10.*

Olivia: *Of course you are*

Aiden: *What's that supposed to mean?*

Olivia: *Mm-hmm. You wearing your letterman jacket?*

He couldn’t help but give her points for that one. Grinning, he typed out his message.

***Aiden**: For the record, I’m taking offense to that*

***Olivia**: I made it home ok. See you around.*

***Aiden**: Glad to hear it. Take care.*

Oh man, he’d clearly been dismissed. But she was fun, and he wanted to keep texting her.

How long should he wait to make the trip back to Gresham? What was a reasonable amount of time to keep anyone–let's be honest, his mom–from getting suspicious about his intentions?

Chapter 9 - Olivia

Olivia had woken up sore from all of the lifting, loading, and unloading she'd done at the farmers market the day before. After making a mug of pour-over coffee, she crawled back into bed and grabbed a book off the top of her TBR pile. As she read, she savored the peaceful, sunny morning. Ms. Darcy lay next to her, head on a pillow, body under the duvet. *What a ridiculous dog.* Olivia smiled and scratched Ms. Darcy's neck.

Her phone buzzed on the bedside table. Assuming it was her mom reminding her about Sunday lunch, she reached over to unlock the screen.

It wasn't her mom. Aiden wanted to make sure she'd made it home okay.

Aiden Wescott texted me to make sure I'd made it home okay? All of this after catching me skinny dipping last night. Are we flirting? Is this what flirting looks like in Gresham at thirty-one? I am so out of my depth.

Even if he was flirting, which she wasn't totally certain he was, how would that even work? He lived in Saint Paul. Was he looking for a one-night stand sort of thing? She'd never had a one-night stand before. *Can it be considered a one-night stand if you kissed the person in kindergarten?*

She wasn't going to pretend hooking up with Aiden wasn't appealing. He was very nice to look at, and she kind of liked the idea of a short-lived, low-key fling, especially after her last relationship, which had lasted five years too long.

Rather than creating an online dating profile after breaking up with Sam like a normal human, Olivia had fled the state—nay the entire region—to start over. Back to the safety of the Midwest.

Sam had been a classic never-committer. He couldn't commit to Olivia, nor could he *not* commit to Olivia. They'd lived in ambiguity for so long Olivia had feared coexisting in limbo until her biological clock ran out. She had started to worry she'd wake up one day and realize she'd settled for something she didn't want.

Olivia had finally given Sam an ultimatum. Four times.

It took four "marry me or else" conversations before she'd gotten the nerve to tell his self-satisfied ass to move out of her townhome. The one she'd purchased with income from a job he frequently criticized as being *so corporate.*

She'd known deep down he would never cave. Honestly, she would have been in a heap of trouble if he had. Because in her heart of hearts, the idea of a wedding day standing next to Sam, who had always been a tad too "cool" for her with his tattoos, gauged ears, and fixed-gear bike, had filled her with dread.

There was a distinct lack of joy in that daydream, but it was easier to use Sam's inaction as the lever Olivia needed to get the hell out of there than to leave of her own accord. One day, she might need to apologize to him, but it had only been six months since all that went down. She assumed she had until she was eighty or so to come clean.

Not yet, though, because Olivia was still in the "screw that guy" phase of grief. Funny how grief was like that. She could know with one hundred percent certainty she'd made the right decision, and yet, she had to cry the allotted number of tears some god of grief had determined she owed as penance for being too weak to walk away sooner.

The thought made her laugh. It sounded so very Catholic. Penance, guilt, wrongdoing. In all reality, it had probably been random chance and hormones.

Regardless, it was time to stop staring at her ceiling and take a shower. She was planning to make at least *three spring vegetable side dishes you will crave on repeat* that she'd seen in her Bon Appetit magazine that month: mixed greens with lemon tahini dressing, charred and chilled asparagus, and shaved snap pea salad with goat cheese and dates. She would also grab a jar of the strawberry rhubarb compote she'd canned a few weeks before. They would have it for dessert with some of her parents' ever-present vanilla ice cream.

Covering vegetables with tasty sauces like lemon tahini dressing was her surefire approach for getting her dad to try new vegetables like mustard greens and jicama. When her dad asked what the sauces were, Olivia always told him they were ranch dressing.

His response every time? “Mmm, delicious, honey.”

When Olivia parked her car at her parents’ house with Ms. Darcy in tow, her parents’ car was gone, which meant they hadn’t gotten back from Sunday mass at Our Lady of Holy Sorrows yet.

Before going inside, she crossed to her parents' vegetable garden to see what was growing. The garden sat in full view of their living room picture window, right next to the old swing set, which was almost paint-free thanks to Minnesota’s harsh winters.

She reached down to touch a cherry tomato plant before lifting her hand to her nose. The lingering scent epitomized the word *green*. Smiling, she dropped her hand and walked to the door, letting Ms. Darcy run into the house ahead of her.

The smell of her mom’s pot roast and potatoes overtook the fresh tomato smell and wrapped Olivia up like a warm, comforting blanket. Though the warm blanket was also a bit stifling, given it was eighty-five degrees outside.

Cue the never-ending debate about whether a giant beef pot roast was seasonally appropriate between Memorial Day and Labor Day, not to mention morally appropriate given climate change. She could already hear her mom's response, with her singing, "Traditioooon, tradition!" in a false baritone, *a la* Tevye from *Fiddler on the Roof.*

Grinning and shaking her head at the thought, Olivia pulled plates and glasses out of the antique corner hutch in her parents' dining room. The small room's walls were covered in the same floral wallpaper her mom had put up when Olivia was in grade school.

She set their four-person table but left her sister Grace's spot empty. Grace lived in Austin and wouldn't be back to visit until July for the town's over-the-top Independence Day celebrations. Four years younger than Olivia, Grace was absolutely killing it as a recruiter for the University of Texas.

She had texted the family two weeks before to say she was bringing her boyfriend, Abesh, home for the first time, and they were all very excited to meet him. Olivia hoped their dad wouldn't ask Abesh something uncomfortable about his "heritage," but she wouldn't hold her breath.

She'd just sat down and pulled out her phone when her parents walked in the door, plastic grocery bags dangling from their hands.

"Hi," all three said in unison.

Olivia walked over to help unpack the groceries and inspect the contents. Among the cans of tomato sauce and hunks of meat were mayo-drenched potato and macaroni salads.

"Mom, I told you I was bringing sides," Olivia said without managing to hide her annoyance.

"I know, I know, but you know we like to stock up when we're in town."

"Okay, whatever, lady." Olivia gave her mom a kiss on the cheek. "Hey, Dad." She gave him a hug.

They worked alongside each other, falling into old roles established as soon as Olivia was old enough to be trusted with glass jars. As a little one, she'd been assigned to the vegetable drawers, but after her middle school growth spurt, she'd towered over her mom and had been reassigned to manage the highest shelves in the pantry.

Olivia turned to catch her dad gazing at his wife with soft eyes and a smile. Her parents had been high school sweethearts. Thirty-three years later, they still looked at each other in a way that embarrassed Olivia's inner fifteen year old. They'd been apart only once since they were sixteen, when Olivia's mom had spent two years in St. Cloud, Minnesota, getting an associate's degree in dental hygiene.

Meanwhile, Olivia's dad had never lived outside Gresham. As the oldest—and the only boy in his family—he began farming with his dad full-time after high school, eventually inheriting the land on which they now lived. He'd slowly expanded his acreage year after year, buying out other small farmers. Most of the neighbors who'd sold him their land had done it because they were ready to retire, and their kids weren't interested in taking over the family business—a fate her father perpetually feared.

"Hey, sweetheart. How's the truck running?" Her dad always asked her this when there was a pause in a conversation.

Olivia told herself it was his way of saying he loved her. "Good. Thanks. I just changed the oil."

"Smart girl. Did you do it yourself like I taught you?" Olivia could hear hope in his voice.

"No, Dad. I brought it to a mechanic like everyone else."

"Well, that's alright," he said, though it was clear the alright-ness was debatable.

Once they'd completed the dance of setting the table, they sat down. Olivia's parents prayed, and they dug into the feast of thinly sliced beef, baked potatoes, gravy, and the veggies Olivia had supplied. Olivia knew the store-bought salads would be showing up on their dinner table the next day, but she wouldn't hold it against them.

After they'd all enjoyed a few bites, her mom put down her fork and turned to Olivia. "So, you know how I asked if Ms.

Darcy could come and meet the kiddos at my summer camp?"

Ms. Darcy's ears perked up at the sound of her name, but she didn't lift her head from the chair's armrest. She'd been pouting since she'd lost her campaign to get Jackie O to chase her. Ms. Darcy had performed so many adorable (yet fruitless) play bows.

Olivia smiled and said, "Yeah, of course."

"Well, I talked to Maya, and she loved the idea. She said she was already planning to do a healthy kids day program next Thursday, and she thinks Missy's demo could be a great way to get the kids engaged. What do you think?"

"Sure, that sounds great! I just need to be home by noon so I can start prepping for my Friday harvest."

Olivia could have sworn her father grunted his disapproval at the mention of her CSA but chose to ignore him, mostly for her mom's sake. She and her dad had been avoiding the topic since she'd declared her financial independence.

"That shouldn't be a problem." Her mom smiled and clapped her hands in anticipation.

"Okay, great. It'll be so fun to see Fiona," Olivia said with equal enthusiasm.

Her cousin Philip's seven-year-old daughter, Fiona, was one of the YMCA campers with special needs her mom volunteered with each week. Fiona had been diagnosed with Down syndrome at five days old.

It'd been at least a month since Olivia had seen Fiona. She made a mental pledge to do better. Spending more time with Fiona had been one of the things she'd been most looking forward to when she'd moved home, but the farm consumed most of her waking hours and several of her sleeping ones as well.

"Speaking of volunteering, Carolyn told me Aiden hung out with you at the market yesterday."

Wow. There are no secrets in this town. Noted.

"Hung out?" Olivia asked skeptically. "If him picking up her CSA subscription is considered hanging out, then yeah, we had a great *hang*."

"Okay, okay, no need to be so sarcastic. I'm just saying, Carolyn shows me pictures of her kids all the time, and that Aiden is haaaaandsome!" she said. "He's back home now, so why rule him out?"

"Mom, he got a job at Saint Paul Children's. That's not exactly moving home."

An anticipatory smile took over her mom's face. "Oh, so you did catch up then?"

Oofda. The traps had been laid.

"Yes, we talked for maybe five minutes, and he mentioned it."

And then he saw me swimming around naked in a pond...

Her mom smiled at her and raised her eyebrows questioningly. Her dad was decidedly no longer part of the conversation because he pulled out his phone to scroll through what Olivia was sure would be the current prices of his crops.

"And?" her mom asked, sounding hopeful.

"I don't want this to come as too much of a shock, Mom, but he proposed. Yeah, we're getting married next week. I was going to mention it, but I was waiting for the right time."

"Ha ha," her mom said dryly.

"Well, *honestly*, what do you expect happened? We haven't seen each other since high school, and even back then, we didn't talk to each other."

"Yeah, but you've both grown up. You're adults now."

I guess. But it sure didn't feel like it.

She'd felt like she was fifteen again. Flustered and blushing through the entire conversation at the market, not to mention the whole date-with-his-baby-brother thing. Then, what would surely be one of her most cringe-worthy memories until she died, he caught her skinny dipping. So yeah, things were going swimmingly, so to speak. Both memories made her want to crawl under the table.

Instead, she bit the inside of her cheek. "Let it go, Mom. Let it go." She'd keep telling herself the same thing.

"Okay, fine." Her mom raised her hands in surrender before changing the topic to their plans for Grace and Abesh's visit in a few weeks.

Chapter 10 - Aiden

It had been almost a week since Aiden had seen Olivia, but the image of her swimming in the pond was burned into his memory. Strands of red hair floating on the water, the fair skin on her clavicle glowing in the moonlight. His desire to see her again was becoming an itch he was desperate to scratch.

When could he get back to Gresham? The last thing he needed was their moms talking. His new fellowship program was extremely demanding, and he was still relying on his more experienced peers to help him with complex cases. Plus, he was also studying for his medical licensing exam in the fall. With all of that on his plate, he should have been strictly focused on establishing himself as a competent pediatrician.

And yet, Olivia Olsen was a welcome distraction. After three years of intense residency where medicine had been the only thing he'd had the time and energy to focus on, he wanted a life again. As it turned out, he did have more hours to fill. The first few weeks as a fellow in the Saint Paul Children's Emergency Department had been intense emotionally but less so physically. He no longer had to contend with a night shift rotation, and most days, he worked eight to ten hours per day as opposed to the twenty-four-hour shifts he'd become accustomed to during residency.

In truth, he didn't know how to fill all of his downtime. He studied. A lot. And as much as he loved eating out, he didn't love doing it solo. He got most meals to-go and ended up eating them in front of ESPN or The History Channel.

On the rare nights when their schedules lined up and his best friends Isaac and June were able to get a babysitter, they gathered with a few other friends from undergrad for dinner and drinks. Those were easily his favorite evenings. He loved that, regardless of how much time had passed since they'd struggled through pre-med together at the University of Minnesota, he and his friends, especially his best friend Isaac, could pick up right where they left off. However, those nights were much harder to come by now in their early thirties than in their early twenties.

As for Olivia, he kept checking his phone for texts. Every time he looked at his phone hopefully, he asked himself the same thing. *Why would she be texting you, doofus? Get over yourself.*

He'd then spend the next few minutes reminding himself why texting her was a dumb idea before throwing himself back into work or studying for a few more hours before repeating the cycle.

He was grabbing lunch in the hospital cafeteria, arguing once again with his phone about the pros and cons of texting

Olivia, when his new colleague and fellowship advisor, Dr. Joanna Chan, asked if she could join him.

He'd enjoyed getting to know Joanna on a personal level over the past week or so. She was around twenty years Aiden's senior and had two teenagers at home. When she was nine years old, she immigrated to the U.S. with her parents as refugees from Cambodia.

After making his way through medical school and residency with all of the advantages he'd grown up with, not to mention his own father being a doctor, Aiden was truly in awe of non-native English speakers who made it through medical programs successfully.

"So, Aiden, how are things going? You settling in okay?" Joanna sat down on the chair across from him. She spoke louder than usual to be heard over the busy cafeteria, which was filled with a steady hum of voices and the clatter of plastic flatware moving food from plates to mouths.

"Yeah, I'm doing okay. Thanks. How are things going with you? How are your girls?"

"Oh, you know, they're…" She paused. "A lot."

He laughed. "I can imagine."

"How are you managing your patient load?" she asked.

"Good. It's definitely intense, but the senior physicians have all been really supportive."

"That's good to hear. And I'm here if you ever need second or third opinions. I know they teach you this during your residency, and the same is true here at Saint Paul Children's: we are a team, and our goal is to provide excellent care to our patients."

Joanna had been a great advisor so far, showing him around and introducing him to the nurses and other hospital staff without being overly directive. It was easy to see why she was so respected and liked, a balance some doctors weren't able to achieve because they took themselves too seriously.

"I appreciate that," he said. And he did.

He was perpetually impressed by more senior colleagues who managed to retain and increase their medical knowledge on a day-to-day basis. His first year of residency had knocked him on his ass, and he was forever indebted to the doctors who had come before him and passed along their knowledge from one intern to the next.

"It's good to hear you're managing well. How do you like being back in Minnesota? Do you have family nearby?"

"It's great. And yeah, not too far. Most of my immediate family lives a couple of hours north, in Gresham, but I have a few friends from undergrad who live in Minneapolis. Though most of them have gotten married and have kids, so they're harder to pin down these days."

Joanna nodded knowingly. "Yup, I remember that feeling. Though, having kids completely puts you back in time debt, so let me know if you'd like to do any babysitting," she joked. "Seriously though, if you're looking to meet people and make friends, I do have one idea, but please tell me if I'm overstepping."

"Okay," he said, his voice encouraging her to continue.

"Do you remember the niece I told you about?"

Aiden nodded, sensing where Joanna was headed.

"If you're at all interested, I could ask her if she would be comfortable with me giving you her number."

It wasn't like he hadn't been asked out or set up at work before, but the offer didn't sit completely right with him because he had a nagging feeling, like maybe he wasn't single? But he was. He was one hundred percent single and should be dating women in the Twin Cities, so why not?

Hoping he hadn't paused too long, he said, "Yeah, sure. It would be great to meet more people in the area."

"Wonderful." Joanna smiled. "I'll text her and let you know. Anyway, I better get going. Thanks for letting me join you."

"Sure thing."

He picked up his phone and saw two missed calls from his mom. Worried something was wrong with his dad, he immediately called her back.

"Aiden, sweetie."

"Hey, Mom. What's up? Is Dad okay?"

"Yes, sorry, this isn't about Dad."

"Oh good." Aiden let out a breath as his body relaxed. "What's up?"

"Well, I have a tiny favor to ask."

Arriving back at his empty apartment, Aiden changed into workout clothes but made himself sit at his desk to cram in a study session first. He shook his head at himself. He'd agreed to drive two hours one way for an hour volunteering with his mom's campers for their 'Healthy Kids Day' on Thursday. When she'd mentioned Olivia would be there, he tried to play it cool, but he wondered if his mom suspected he was actually going so he could volunteer alongside Olivia.

At the very least, his mom had given him an opening to text her.

Aiden*: Looks like we'll be volunteering together on Thursday.*

He forced himself to refocus on the material and ignore her silence. It was a full hour and a half before Olivia responded. The notification brought him to his feet.

Olivia: *Oh, I guess that makes sense. Healthy Kids Day and all*

Aiden: *I guess so. But who is Mrs. Darcy? My mom said something about you two doing an agility demonstration. Are you secretly a gymnast or something?*

Olivia: *Lol. Ms. Darcy is my dog. I did a bunch of agility training with her when she was little so she'd stop eating my couch.*

Aiden remembered the dog who had dripped water all over his legs while Olivia was trying to swim off. He laughed afresh at the memory.

Aiden: *I thought her name was Missy?*

Olivia: *Yeah, it's short for Ms. Darcy*

Aiden: *Well that sounds pretty badass. You are full of surprises, Ms. Olsen. Looking forward to this demo.*

Olivia: *(winky face, dancing lady emoji)*

A jolt of delight shot through him, and he caught himself bouncing on his toes. He shoved his phone back in his pocket and put on his running shoes. He needed to burn off some adrenaline before he'd be able to fall asleep.

Chapter 11 - Olivia

By the time Thursday morning rolled around, Olivia had spent far too many hours analyzing her text exchange with Aiden. Had their moms planned the Healthy Kids Day event to set them up? That seemed far-fetched. They'd likely just seized the opportunity to get Aiden and Olivia back in the same vicinity. She'd called her mom to scold her, but her mom had claimed innocence. She'd told Carolyn that Olivia would be there, but that was it.

Trying to ignore the quiet buzz of anticipation at seeing Aiden so soon, Olivia told Ms. Darcy to load up into the truck so they could head to town. She had packed some treats and agility toys. Per her mom's request, they were going to do an agility demonstration for Fiona's fellow campers to make Healthy Kids Day more engaging.

Olivia had given herself extra time to stop at Jill's Diner to grab a coffee and one of Jill's famous sourdough cinnamon rolls.

When she pulled into the parking lot, Olivia lowered the windows halfway. The morning had been mercifully cool, and Ms. Darcy would be comfortable waiting in the truck for ten minutes.

A bell chimed above the diner's door when Olivia walked in, a bouquet of sweet peas in hand. She approached the cash register with a huge smile on her face to greet her old boss. Jill had purchased the restaurant from the previous owner twenty years prior and changed the name from Jack's to Jill's. *Only in Gresham*.

"Do these old eyes deceive me, or is that little Miss Olivia Olsen?" Jill smiled broadly, revealing her crooked incisor.

Olivia's visit was overdue, and she'd brought the flowers as a token of apology. Jill had given Olivia her first job, waitressing on the weekends when she was sixteen. In hindsight, Olivia knew Jill had done it as a favor to her mom.

In the years since, Jill's hair had gone from mostly gray to fully white. She kept it short in a no-fuss style. Jill's apple-shaped middle spoke to the hash browns and bacon she nabbed during a busy shift rather than taking the time to sit down for a meal.

Olivia looked into her smiling eyes.

"A little birdy told me you were back, and I've been waitin' for you to walk through them doors."

"Jill!" Olivia's smiled around her words. "It's so wonderful to see you!" She handed Jill the bouquet.

"What is this about?" Jill asked, inspecting the flowers skeptically.

"They're for you. I think mom told you I'm selling flowers and veggies?"

"Oh my gosh, they're so fancy. I better hide them, or people are gonna realize what an old dump this place is."

Olivia laughed and reached out for a hug. "Sorry it took me so long to stop in, but I'm here in search of coffee and a cinnamon roll."

"You need a job?" Jill asked. They both knew she didn't, but Olivia appreciated the offer. It was the closest Jill would ever come to saying she cared about Olivia.

"If I do, I'll know where to come."

"Good girl." Jill paused to inspect Olivia once more. "I just have to say that this town is better off with you back in it, not to mention how happy it makes your folks."

"Awww, thanks, Jill. It's good to be back."

"Your mom told me about your market stand and your vegetable boxes. You know, I'd be a customer myself if I didn't eat every god-forsaken meal in this hellhole."

Olivia laughed. "Of course, no worries at all. Though, now that you mention it, do you mind if I leave a few business cards with you? I've still got a few subscriptions to fill."

"Absolutely, darlin'. Why don't you pin one up on the bulletin board over there as well."

"Awesome, thank you. I will."

"Alright, well, let me go grab your stuff. Don't wanna keep you here all day."

"Thanks again, Jill. It's so good to see you. I'm forever indebted to you, ya know. You kicked off my career."

"Pfft." Immune to flattery, Jill dismissed the compliment with a flap of her pudgy hand and turned toward the kitchen.

She walked with a slight hiccup in her step, which Olivia knew was the result of forty years on her feet running the restaurant.

Jill returned a minute later with the breakfast, and Olivia tried not to cringe at the Styrofoam containers, reminding herself to maintain a "when in Rome" attitude. She'd had to adjust her expectations regarding micro-level solutions to macro-level issues when she moved back. If she hadn't, she would have lost her mind and alienated the whole town trying to fight for progress on every issue Seattle had achieved years ago, like banning Styrofoam.

Olivia paid and left a fifty percent tip before turning toward the exit. She called over her shoulder as she opened the door, "Thanks again!"

"No trouble, sweetheart."

Olivia got in the car, and Ms. Darcy's nose wiggled as she sniffed curiously. Drool dripped from her mouth onto the vinyl seat.

"You're not wrong, Missy. This thing smells amazing, and it's still warm." Olivia reached over and scratched Ms. Darcy behind the ears.

She started the truck and turned up the volume on the radio. The classic rock channel, the only radio station the truck's broken antenna would pick up, was playing "Jack and Diane" by John Mellencamp, which always reminded her of her parents. As she drove across town, she thought back to her years working at Jill's and how she used to eat a giant cinnamon roll every time she worked a shift.

Why was I so skinny in high school? It does not add up.

Tearing off pieces of the roll gleefully, she shoved them into her mouth as she drove. Doing so while driving a manual truck wasn't her smartest choice, but she couldn't help herself. She licked her fingers between each shift of the gears, and she only stalled the engine twice.

Like most drives in Gresham, the distance was beautifully short, taking only five minutes to reach the YMCA.

When Olivia opened the door for Ms. Darcy to hop out, Fiona saw them and squealed with delight. Olivia's niece ran over and buried her round face into Ms. Darcy's neck, mingling her blond pigtails with Ms. Darcy's fur.

"Hi, Ms. Darcy!" Fiona yelled as she pulled back.

Equally excited, Ms. Darcy gave a few quick, delighted barks before aggressively licking any remaining breakfast off Fiona's face. Fiona squirmed and giggled hysterically.

The sight of Fiona and Ms. Darcy together, both contenders for the title of *greatest love of her life*, always warmed Olivia's heart. She pulled out her phone and snapped a photo, capturing Ms. Darcy mid-lick and Fiona mid-giggle-squirm. She took a moment to send the picture to her sister, Grace, who immediately responded with three lines of heart eyes.

With her arms wrapped around Ms. Darcy's neck, Fiona looked up and said, "Hi, Auntie Olivia!"

"Hello, my sweet Fiona." Olivia squatted to her level. "Do you think I might be able to get a hug, too?"

"Okay." Fiona giggled and ran straight into Olivia's arms. Olivia let out a dramatic "oof" and fell backward, pulling Fiona on top of her, amping up the pitch and decibel of Fiona's laughter.

"Auntie Olivia," Fiona chided.

"Sorry, Fiona, you're too strong. I couldn't help it." Olivia gave Fiona a big smooch on the cheek.

"You're silly," Fiona giggled.

"It's true. I am a silly goose."

"Honk," Fiona replied with more peals of laughter.

They'd been working on the routine for years, and Olivia thought they'd nailed it that time.

"Did Nanna tell you we were coming?" Olivia asked.

While not technically Fiona's grandma, Olivia's mom loved that Fiona called her Nanna.

"Yes!" Fiona made her way back to Ms. Darcy's side.

"I've been missing you, little girly."

"I've missed you, too. Can I stay over at your house tonight, and Ms. Darcy can sleep in my bed?"

Was there anything better than a seven-year-old's ability to shamelessly ask for exactly what they wanted? *A lesson for us all.*

"That sounds *so fun*! Buuut, I have to ask your mom."

"My mom will definitely say yes."

Olivia laughed. "Are you sure about that?"

"Yes, I'm pretty sure," Fiona said confidently.

Olivia gave Fiona one more kiss on the forehead before standing back up and holding Fiona's small hand in one of hers while the other gripped Ms. Darcy's leash.

"We'll see. I'll text her, and if not tonight, soon! Your mom might just need a little more notice so she can plan for it, okay?"

"Okay," Fiona said happily.

"Okay," Olivia mimicked before adding, "Ya know, Ms. Darcy is here to meet all of your friends. We're gonna do some cool tricks. Does that sound good?"

"That sounds awesome," Fiona confirmed.

"Awesome possum!"

"Awesome possum!" Fiona mimicked back.

"Can you hang onto Ms. Darcy's leash while I set up the agility course?"

"Yes," Fiona said, in her most serious voice, tightly gripping the leash with both hands, her face the picture of stoicism.

Olivia told Ms. Darcy to lie down and stay. She wouldn't leave Fiona's side. "Good girl, Missy," Olivia said when Ms. Darcy planted her body onto the grass, laying her snout next to Fiona's pink shoes.

As Olivia turned to grab Ms. Darcy's obstacles out of her truck, a black sedan pulled up next to her, and Aiden stepped out.

She froze momentarily before spurring herself back into motion. She waved and smiled at Aiden but used the excuse of grabbing the agility obstacles out of the back of her truck to give herself a moment.

Aiden walked toward her. “Hey, Olivia.” His characteristic mirth danced in his eyes.

“Hey, Aiden.” Gratefully, her hands were full, so she didn’t have to worry about whether she should shake his hand or reach for a hug.

She took Aiden in. He was dressed in what she guessed was his doctor garb–slacks and a button-up shirt.

She looked down at her casual outfit–shorts, a T-shirt, and Birkenstocks. She was suddenly self-conscious about the friendship bracelet she’d worn. Her friend, Jessa, had made it as a joke for her last birthday, but Olivia wore it often because the bright, interwoven colors made her happy.

“It’s nice to see you again. Can I help you carry anything?” Aiden asked, gesturing toward the back of her truck.

“You, too. And sure. Can you grab that circle thing and that little table?”

“Of course.” He reached over the side of the track to grab the obstacle course materials before following Olivia toward the lawn where several kids were waiting.

"So, is agility training a side hustle for you?" Aiden asked, sounding genuinely curious.

Olivia looked at him and laughed. "No. Not at all. I just do it because it makes Missy happy. How about you? Are you required to volunteer a certain number of hours as a doctor?"

"Nope. I just do it because it makes my mom happy."

"Well, that's generous of you. How was the drive?"

Olivia motioned for him to put the stuff down, and she walked around, setting it all up. It gave her an excuse to look somewhere besides his face because his ridiculous dimples and twinkly eyes were out in force, and it made her feel jittery.

"Not bad. I left Saint Paul at six, so I think I beat most of the morning traffic."

"That's good. Are you staying for the weekend? Should I be expecting you at my farmers market stand on Saturday?" She wondered if she sounded flirty.

"Unfortunately not. I have to work this weekend, but I'm having lunch with my mom after this if you want to join us."

"Oh." The invitation caught her off guard. Did he just invite her to lunch with his mom? "Um, sorry, I can't. I have to start harvesting flowers today and get ready for my big veggie harvest tomorrow. The end of the week is kind of crazy for me."

By the time Olivia had finished setting up, she hadn't stopped analyzing the invitation to lunch with his mom. Had he sensed she was flirting and tried to shut it down? Was he trying to establish a clear friend zone? Because she didn't need a friend zone. She was good with staying off the field entirely.

In hopes she came across as equally friendly, she asked, "Do you want to meet my niece, Fiona? Well, technically, she's my cousin's daughter, but we're all pretty close."

"Absolutely, I'd like that." Aiden followed her over to Fiona, and Olivia watched him kneel so they were eye-to-eye in height.

"Hey, Fiona, sweetie, this is Dr. Wescott. He's here to help out today, just like Ms. Darcy and me."

"Hi!" Fiona said. She smiled but did not take her hands off Ms. Darcy's leash.

Ms. Darcy thumped her tail happily against the ground, but she held her stay.

"Hi, Fiona. It's nice to meet you. You can call me Dr. A. Is this your puppy?"

"No." Fiona giggled. "This is Missy, Auntie Olivia's doggy. She's not a puppy!"

"She's not?" he said in mock surprise. "Well, she's a very well-behaved dog. Do you mind if I pet her?"

Fiona leaned down to whisper loudly into Ms. Darcy's ear, "Dr. A. wants to pet you, okay?"

Ms. Darcy licked her cheek. Fiona giggled and wiped her face. "Okay, she's ready."

Aiden reached down and scratched Ms. Darcy on the cheeks, then rubbed her ears. “Hi, Missy.”

Something about Aiden’s ease made Olivia feel strangely happy. She shouldn't be surprised Aiden was good with small creatures. He was a pediatrician. However, she hadn’t anticipated what it would be like to see him in action with *her* small creatures.

All of it reminded Olivia, once again, that it had been thirteen years since high school. Like Olivia, Aiden had grown up.

Both Aiden and Olivia's moms made their way over and gave them their respective hugs before each taking a turn to hug Fiona. “Hi,” they said, big smiles on their faces. They looked expectantly from Olivia to Aiden and back again.

“Hi.” Olivia silently begged her mom to please stop with the obvious grin already.

“Hi, Mom. Mrs. Olsen,” Aiden said.

He reached out and shook her mom’s hand, and Aiden’s mom gave Olivia a hug. She felt like she’d somehow stumbled into someone else’s family reunion.

Fortunately, Maya, the head teacher and the only paid adult, called everyone to attention.

Once everything and everyone were in their place, Maya gave an overview of what to expect.

Olivia looked around. All eight campers were in attendance, and their special needs ranged from being very able-bodied, like Fiona, to being wheelchair-bound. Their cognitive levels varied as well.

One of the kids was a local fifth grader named Cole, who had been diagnosed with Spinal Muscular Atrophy, or SMA, when he was a year and a half old. Olivia's mom had gotten very emotionally connected to Cole over the past few summers, and it had been hard for her to see his muscles weaken each year. When Olivia's mom had first started volunteering with him and the other kids, Cole could walk with braces and crutches, but now he was fully dependent on his chair.

In addition to Fiona, four other children had Down syndrome. The final two campers were on the autism spectrum.

Maya introduced Olivia, Aiden, and the two other healthcare volunteers–a local dentist and a nurse practitioner.

After completing introductions, Olivia and Ms. Darcy took their places. Self-conscious with Aiden watching, Olivia was glad they knew their routine well.

For the kids' sake, she said, "Ms. Darcy, say hi," while giving her the hand signal to bark twice.

Ms. Darcy obeyed, and the kids cheered and said, "Hi!" loudly back.

"Okay," Olivia said as the kids settled down. "Are you ready?"

"Yes!" they called back.

"Okay, here we go."

She unhooked Ms. Darcy's leash and took her through an old routine they'd had to learn for the level three agility class. They easily completed each obstacle, and the kids squealed with delight. They absolutely lost it with giggles when Ms. Darcy wiggled her way through the long tunnel. When Ms. Darcy finished her routine with a "bow" on top of her dancing table, Olivia's heart was bursting with joy and pride for her pup.

Calling her back to her side, Olivia gave Ms. Darcy treats and pets, scratching behind her ears and cheeks. She spoke sweetly into Ms. Darcy's ear so she would know what an incredible dog she was. Everyone cheered, and Olivia caught Aiden's smiling eyes. She gave Ms. Darcy a hug to hide her grin.

Finally, they walked around and said hello to each child so they could pet Ms. Darcy. Olivia let Ms. Darcy kiss their hands, eliciting delighted squeals every time. After each camper had a turn and a cuddle, it was time for Aiden and the nurse practitioner to go to work.

Olivia's mom held Ms. Darcy's leash and gave her belly rubs while Olivia quietly disassembled the course and packed it up in the back of her truck. As she turned back to the event, Mrs. Wescott blocked her path.

"Olivia, that was so great," she said quietly. "The kids absolutely loved it!"

“Oh, thanks, Mrs. Wescott. Ms. Darcy loves showing off,” Olivia whispered back, not wanting to distract the kids.

“Oh, please, call me Carolyn.” She took in Olivia from head to toe before meeting her eyes. “Well, I can see how you've won over two of my sons. Fortunately, Nathan won’t be coming back until Ellen’s wedding in September, or we’d have a real pickle on our hands.”

Olivia was speechless, her mouth opened in surprise, and her cheeks burned with embarrassment. She snuck a glance at Aiden, wondering what he’d told his mom.

What does she know?! Olivia panicked silently. *Please, god, not about the skinny dipping. I'm a good person. I don't deserve that.*

“I…” She couldn’t think of a response.

Faced with Olivia’s open-mouthed panic, Carolyn continued, “Well, either one would be lucky to have you, but let it be known that I'm rooting for Aiden.”

“Thank you?”

What does she know? And what exactly is she rooting for?

“Oh dear, I can see I've embarrassed you.”

Olivia’s blush crept toward her neck.

“I'm sorry,” Carolyn continued. “I sometimes forget that we Wescotts tend to be very blunt. All the same, thank you again. This was just wonderful. Hopefully, I'll see you again soon. I'll let ya get going.”

“Okay, thanks, Mrs. Wescott. See you around.”

"Carolyn," she said quietly but firmly.

Olivia smiled and walked toward her mom, who lifted an eyebrow questioningly.

Olivia shook her head in several small rapid movements, willing her cheeks to cool, and whispered, "Not now, Mom."

Olivia gave her mom and Fiona quick hugs goodbye. Catching Aiden's eye, she gave him a small wave. He tilted his head as if to ask if she was leaving, and she nodded. He smiled and waved back. She got herself and Ms. Darcy situated in the truck. Before driving off, she sent a text to Fiona's mom, Cassie.

Olivia: *Hey, any chance I can have Fiona over to spend the night again sometime soon?*

Cassie: *That would be amazing! Philip and I are SO overdue for a date night. I know you have the market on Saturdays. Would this Sunday work?*

Olivia: *That's perfect! Feel free to bring her by any time after 3. If it's helpful, I can drop her off at camp on Monday morning.*

Cassie: *You're the best! Thank you!!!*

Olivia: *My pleasure! :)*

About to put her truck in gear, she sent one more text to Jessa, her best friend in Seattle.

Olivia: *I think I have boy troubles.*

Jessa: *Already? I thought you said moving back would force you into a life of celibacy*

***Olivia**: I mean, the celibacy situation is intact, but I might have gotten caught skinny dipping by a guy I went to high school with, and there is a small chance his mom knows about it.*

***Jessa**: Woah! Awkward! LOLOLOLOL!*

***Olivia**: I know!! Can we video chat soon? I think I need to talk this one through*

***Jessa**: Yas! Call me tonight after 7 my time. What time will that be there?*

***Olivia**: 9. It will always be plus two hours from where you are. That never changes.*

***Jessa**: Hey lady, it's confusing. That never changes*

Chapter 12 - Aiden

Aiden was no longer on the fence about texting Olivia. He grabbed his phone and began typing out a message.

***Aiden**: You left without even a goodbye? Were you afraid I'd try to rope you into lunch with my mom again?*

Forty-five minutes passed before he finally heard back.

***Olivia**: Lol, your mom seems great. But I really do have a ton of work to do. My farm is sort of blowing up. Or should I say blooming-up? No, I probably shouldn't ever say that again, right?*

He laughed softly. So she still had a bit of a nerdy side to her.

***Aiden**: LOL*

***Aiden**: Well, I was hoping to run some ideas past you before you left, so maybe you can let me buy you a beer next time I'm in town. I have a lot of questions about your genius dog and how we might take that show on the road and make millions. There's gotta be a Shark Tank opportunity here somewhere.*

***Olivia**: (crying-laughing, dog face, & dollar bill emojis)*

After that, he sent her silly gifs and videos of dogs doing cool agility work. Her response times were so unpredictable it reminded him of a study he'd had to review in medical school about gambling addicts and unpredictable dopamine triggers.

Though, to be fair, she was busy with her farm. He assumed she couldn't look at her phone and dig holes at the same time…or whatever it was she was doing on her farm from one day to the next.

Digging holes? Was that a thing she did? Maybe he should Wikipedia small-scale farming so he didn't sound like an idiot the next time he saw her. Damn, he wanted to see her again.

***Aiden**: What do you do all day? Does it involve digging holes? Asking for a friend.*

Three hours later, she finally responded.

***Olivia**: Lol. You're kinda clueless when it comes to farming, huh?*

***Aiden**: 100%. Maybe you could offer classes?*

***Olivia**: Hmm… Might be a good way to generate revenue in the winter? How much would you pay for one?*

***Aiden**: Depends. What's the teacher to student class-size ratio?*

***Olivia**: (smiley face emoji)*

At one point, Olivia sent a picture of herself and her niece Fiona in their pajamas, each with braided pigtails. It was adorable.

He'd been out grabbing beers with friends, so he sent a selfie of himself holding a beer up in salute and smiling what he hoped was his most charming smile.

Their texts kept his days interesting, and he knew Olivia was the reason he hadn't opened a dating app in weeks. She was also the reason he hadn't yet reached out to Joanna's niece, Sarah. He needed to text Sarah soon if he didn't want to look like a total dick. Begrudgingly, he pulled out his phone.

Aiden: *Hey Sarah, how's it going? Your Aunt Joanna gave me your number, and I was wondering if you'd want to grab a drink next Tuesday evening?*

Unlike Olivia's standard texts, Sarah's response was immediate.

Sarah: *Sure, that'd be great! I'm free after 8.*

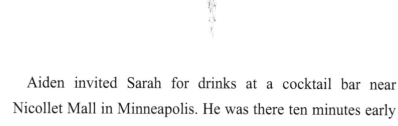

Aiden invited Sarah for drinks at a cocktail bar near Nicollet Mall in Minneapolis. He was there ten minutes early and was trying not to text Olivia. Instead, he opened his Kindle app to keep his mind occupied.

Aiden hoped that no matter what happened, Sarah would report back to her aunt that he'd been a gentleman. He generally tried to avoid mixing his dating life with his work life, but he'd also had many well-meaning colleagues set him up with this cousin or that friend once they found out he was single.

When Sarah walked up to his table twenty minutes later, Aiden startled. Her wide, red-lipsticked smile accentuated her high cheekbones, and her black hair was loosely curled. The deep V-neck of her dress put her ample chest on display, but he made himself focus on her face. She wore high heels that brought the top of her head to just below his chin.

"Hi." She smiled hesitantly, "Are you Aiden?"

"Yes. Sarah?" Aiden stood and shook her hand. "Nice to meet you."

"Nice to meet you, too." Sarah's smile relaxed.

Aiden gestured to her chair. "Please, have a seat."

He didn't mind blind dates. His adventurous side appreciated the slight mystery they created. Although some were better than others, they were rarely uninteresting.

"So, Sarah, did you grow up in the Cities?" Aiden asked, opening the conversation.

She had. As it turned out, they'd also attended the University of Minnesota at the same time for a couple of years. His last two and her first. She'd studied marketing and now worked for a small tech company in Minneapolis.

She asked him about his time in Boston and growing up in Gresham. How did he like working at the Children's Hospital? What were his favorite sports teams?

Sarah was lovely and smart. She even made him laugh a time or two. When they said their goodbyes, he gave her a polite hug, and they went their separate ways. He could see himself going on a second date with her, for sure, and yet...he wasn't sure whether there would be a second date.

Despite his efforts not to, he'd spent the entire time comparing Sarah to Olivia. Maybe it was the circumstances of their shared history or that he'd caught Olivia skinny dipping in what he thought of as his family's pond, but he was being pulled in a direction, and it wasn't Sarah's.

It wasn't just Olivia's beauty winning Aiden over. She worked so hard to grow her business while making time to bring her weirdly talented dog to the summer camp where their moms volunteered. She was obviously a good human, and *good human* was a top requirement for Aiden these days, not to mention how truly down-to-earth she seemed.

To be fair, Sarah seemed great, too, but he was pretty sure his heart had already chosen another. He texted Olivia as soon as he got into his car.

Aiden: *Are you going to be around this weekend for the Independence Day celebrations?*

Chapter 13 - Olivia

Parked in the cell phone waiting lot of the Minneapolis-Saint Paul International Airport, Olivia smiled down at her phone when she saw Aiden's text. She excitedly unlocked the message. Already feeling Grace's influence, she leaned into her silly side.

Olivia: *Yes! My sister is coming home and bringing her new man friend! I'm so excited! Can you tell?!!! I'm at the airport right now*

Aiden: *Haha, great. Well maybe I'll see you this weekend?*

Olivia: *Sure, that'd be fun*

Olivia had debated telling Aiden she was coming to the Twin Cities, but after weighing the pros and cons with Jessa, she decided against it. She didn't want to seem desperate. Despite all of their texting, she wasn't sure where Aiden's head was. And now this? A text that said he hoped he'd see her in Gresham, but he hadn't specifically asked her to meet up at a specific time and a specific place?

It left her even more uncertain. They'd been communicating for multiple weeks, yet he left the whole thing up in the air. *What is that about?* Maybe she was exceptionally bad at boys after being off the market for so long.

The next text was from Grace.

Grace: *The chickens are in the henhouse. I repeat, the chickens are in the henhouse.*

Olivia laughed to herself as she put her car into drive and made her way to Arrivals.

She had insisted that her parents let her drive solo to the Cities to pick up her sister and her new boyfriend, Abesh. Olivia wanted to make a good first impression on behalf of their family.

As she pulled forward slowly along the Arrivals driveway, Grace waved her arms frantically, like she was stranded on a desert island. Even after making eye contact, Grace continued to dance around like an idiot, which made Olivia laugh out loud.

Standing calmly next to Grace was a handsome, well-dressed man holding two suitcase handles–Abesh. His black hair, dark brown eyes, and olive skin were a beautiful pairing with Grace's blond hair, blue eyes, and pale complexion. Abesh watched Grace's silly antics with the happy satisfaction of a man in love.

Dang, girl. Well done. Olivia pulled over and got out of the car to say hello.

"Sister!" Grace yelled, wrapping her arms around Olivia and swinging her from side to side.

Olivia laughed and hugged her tightly in return. "Wow, so you act like a dork in front of your boyfriend, too?" she teased.

Grace laughed and tickled Olivia's side, Olivia's weak spot. She eek'ed and pushed her sister away.

"Some respect for your elders, please," Olivia mock scolded. "You haven't even introduced me!"

They turned to Abesh, who waited with a good-natured smile. He reached out his hand and said, "Abesh Hossain, nice to meet you."

"Olivia." They shook hands warmly. "Thank you for putting up with Grace for an entire four-hour plane ride. I've been there, and it's not easy."

Grace laughed. "You're a turd."

Olivia's face hurt from smiling. "I'm so glad you're here," she said without sarcasm. "I've missed you, and we've all been so excited to meet the famous Abesh."

Grace gave her another hug, this time without wiggles.

They loaded up the car and climbed in. Grace settled in the passenger seat, and Abesh took the back.

"So, we have news," Grace said as they buckled up.

"Oh yeah?"

"Yeah. We're moving in together!"

"Yay! Congratulations! Very exciting," Olivia said in a sing-song voice.

"Do you think Mom and Dad will freak?"

"Nah, I think I paved a smooth path for you on that front with Sam."

“Okay, good. How are you doing with all that, by the way?”

“Honestly?” said Olivia, considering. “Good, I think. The first few months were hard, but it’s gotten easier since I started working on my farm. Now, I honestly don't think about him all that much. We haven't texted since…” Olivia paused, thinking. “March?”

“That's good. I'm glad you're doing well.”

“Thanks, yeah, me too.”

The conversation evolved, and Olivia made sure to include Abesh, asking him questions about his teaching and research at UT Austin. He struck Olivia as calm, kind, and confident, which seemed to be a good balance for Grace's bouncy energy.

I wouldn't be surprised if he ends up being the one for her. Olivia’s thought was accompanied by a feeling of contentment.

By the time they rolled into their parents’ driveway, it was a little after 10 p.m. Their parents were watching the news, and dinner leftovers were warm in the oven.

After Grace introduced Abesh, their mom gave him a hug, and their dad reached out his right hand and gave him a serious “man shaking another man's hand” look. Olivia glanced away, feeling embarrassed for her dad.

When they sat down to eat, Grace told the story of how she and Abesh met when Grace recruited him for the Economics

Department at the University of Texas. Abesh chimed into Grace's story with important details and teased her for coming on strong. They were very charming together.

When their dad pointed out Abesh didn't have an accent, Abesh took it in stride, for better or worse. He told them his parents had immigrated from Bangladesh when he was a baby. His dad had gotten a visa to work at the University of Ohio as an academic researcher in agronomy to study crop production. Eventually, they all become citizens through his father's green card.

At that, their dad couldn't help himself. "That's such a wonderful testament to hard work."

Oh god, where is this going? An ominous pit formed in Olivia's stomach.

"This is why it's so important we fight illegal immigration because it's not fair to people like your parents who have had to work so hard for it."

"*Dad*!" Grace and Olivia protested in unison.

"Bill, no politics, please," their mom said.

Olivia quietly seethed and mentally told him she was never taking over his stupid farm because he was a terrible person. *So there*, she thought with a final childish flourish.

Meanwhile, Abesh deftly steered the conversation into safer territory, asking their dad about the farm. After listening patiently to their father's ramble about his expected yields, Abesh told a story about his paternal grandfather, a tea farmer in Bangladesh, and how growing up on a tea farm led his father into agricultural research.

"Your dad sounds like a great guy. I'd love to meet him," their dad said matter-of-factly.

"Sadly, he passed away a few years ago," Abesh responded.

"Oh, I'm so sorry to hear that." Their mom's voice was filled with sincere sadness for Abesh.

"Well, he must have been very proud of you," Dad added.

"Thank you, both. That's very kind." Abesh sounded genuinely touched.

For a moment, Olivia reflected for the millionth time on the split personalities of so many old white Midwestern men. She couldn't count the number of times her dad had pulled someone's car out of a ditch with his tractor when they had slid off an icy road or fixed a neighbor's roof for free when they were down on their luck.

One minute, they'll figuratively spit on someone who lives outside their narrowly defined boundaries of decency, and the next, they'll show up in grand ways to help someone, no questions asked.

It added evidence to Olivia's ongoing hypothesis that humans were rarely black and white.

Despite the awkward moment, the rest of the dinner went smoothly, and Abesh seemed mostly relaxed with their family, for which Olivia was grateful. She couldn't help but wonder what it would be like to introduce Aiden to her parents like this. She hated considering it because she didn't want to crave her dad's approval, yet she wondered how Aiden would measure up to his high expectations. Though, given Aiden's lack of visible tattoos alone, he was sure to impress her father more than Sam had ever managed. The two had mixed like oil and water.

Regardless of her dad's opinions, she hoped she would see Aiden at the festival the next day. Again, she wondered why Aiden hadn't tried to make a more formal plan to meet up.

Chapter 14 - Olivia

Each year when Independence Day rolled around, Gresham briefly redirected all of its energy to the four-day weekend celebration. After spending the morning with her family and trying to subtly search for Aiden in every crowd they passed, Olivia and Grace had gone their separate ways with a plan to meet up at the street dance after Olivia finished taking care of Ms. Darcy.

Making her way through the growing crowd of people ready for dinner, drinks and dancing, Olivia searched for Grace while also hoping to spot Aiden.

"Hey, sister," Grace called from the picnic table she and Abesh had claimed.

"Hi, Olivia." Abesh gave her a friendly smile.

Olivia's eyes locked with Grace's, and a broad smile rearranged her features. She approached, stepping over the long bench attached to the green picnic table.

"Hey, you two. How was the rest of your afternoon?"

"Good, we taught Abesh how to play Nut," Grace said. Nut was a classic, fast-paced card game their family played, especially during snowstorms. It had a tendency to turn their mom, otherwise relatively calm and composed, into a cutthroat competitor, willing to slap someone's hand away from her card piles if they encroached.

“Oooh, how’d that go? Did Mom get mean?” Olivia asked conspiratorially.

“Abesh only cried twice, so it wasn’t too bad,” Grace teased.

“Her fingernails are sharp,” Abesh said, laughing along with them good-naturedly.

“Hey,” Grace said abruptly, “let’s get food and beer before the lines get too long. Abesh, you stay here and guard our table. I’ll get food, and Olivia, you go buy us some beer.”

Olivia lifted her hand in a salute and stood. “Aye, aye, captain.”

The beer trailer’s line was long but not unbearable. She played on her phone while she waited, wondering why she hadn’t yet seen Aiden and trying not to feel disappointed. She repeatedly reminded herself they hadn’t made *actual* plans to meet up. They had kept it casual. Then she would wonder once again why he had kept it open-ended. Maybe he was less interested than she thought. Had she been reading the energy between them all wrong? She really hoped she’d see him to get a better sense of things.

But what if we don’t, a whiny voice in Olivia’s head asked.

She mentally smacked herself in the butt, telling herself to get it together. Nothing was going on between them. She had misjudged his texts entirely because if he’d wanted to see her, he would have made it happen.

Maybe he's just not that into you. She hoped that telling herself this would ground her, but instead, it made her feel sad and a little pathetic.

She collected three red cups filled with locally brewed IPAs, balanced them in a triangle between her two hands, and turned to walk back to Grace and Abesh.

Someone to her left called her name. "Olivia! I thought that was you."

She turned to see Aiden, hand raised in a greeting. She couldn't stop her mouth from breaking out into a happy smile. He was standing near a woman who looked a lot like him and a stocky man who had his arm casually draped across the woman's shoulders.

"Ah, hello!" Olivia said. She wove through the crowd, trying not to spill beer on anyone. "I didn't know if I'd see you."

She hoped it sounded more nonchalant than she felt, given how tingly her toes felt.

"I made it up for the weekend, but I have to work on the Fourth."

The couple smiled politely at Olivia.

Aiden quickly added, "This is my sister, Ellen, by the way, and her fiancé, Tommy."

They gave friendly Midwestern waves in place of a handshake.

"This is an old friend, Olivia Olsen," Aiden explained.

Olivia nodded her head over the beers. "Nice to meet you."

"You all went to high school together?" Ellen asked.

"Yup," Aiden and Olivia replied in unison.

After an awkward beat, Olivia excused herself. "Well, it was nice to meet you both. I should get back." She nodded toward the picnic table where Grace and Abesh were waiting with burgers and fries. "We were just about to eat."

"Oh right, er," Aiden said. His eyes darted to Grace and Abesh and then back to Olivia. "Um, can I buy a drink later? After you've had some time to catch up with your sister?"

Olivia heartbeat picked up, but she tried to keep her smile and voice casual. "Sure, that would be great. I'll catch you a little later."

She nodded once more to Ellen and Tommy. "It was nice meeting you."

She wove through the festive crowds, who were ready for beer, food, and music. Grace helped her as she set down the beers.

"Was that Aiden Wescott?" Grace asked, sounding surprised. "What did *he* want?"

"Oh, um, he was just saying hi," Olivia said as casually as she could.

"Why?"

"What do you mean, 'why'?"

Grace looked at Olivia incredulously. "Wasn't he an ass in high school? I thought you hated him."

"What? No." Olivia paused to consider. "Did I?"

"You *definitely* complained about him."

Olivia shrugged. "Well, I guess we grew up."

"Interesting." Grace grinned.

"What do you mean *interesting*?" Olivia retorted. Apparently she needed a lot of clarification.

"You *like* him." Grace's grin broadened to a knowing smile.

"Do not!" Olivia said, sounding like a defensive teenager.

Grace's raised eyebrows told Olivia that Grace wasn't convinced.

"Whatever," Olivia said in a huff.

Grace's grin expanded to all-out howling laughter.

"I hate you." Olivia laughed. She threw a French fry in Grace's beer for emphasis.

"Hey! Party foul!" Grace yelled. She fished the soggy fry out of her beer and dropped it back onto Olivia's plate.

"Okay, okay. Tell me about the best fries in Austin," Olivia said, trying to change the subject.

As they ate, Grace and Abesh told Olivia about their life in Austin and the friends they hung out with. She enjoyed seeing how obviously smitten they were, finishing each other's sentences, and finding excuses to touch. It was all pretty adorable, even for someone who had recently ended a six-year relationship.

“The next time you visit,” Grace said, “there's this chips and queso place…”

Chapter 15 - Aiden

Two hours and two beers later, Aiden walked toward Olivia. She'd looked his way from time to time throughout the evening, and he was glad to know she was keeping tabs on him.

"Hi again," Olivia said as he approached.

He smiled. "Hey."

After Olivia introduced everyone and they made polite conversation for a couple of minutes, Aiden turned to Olivia and asked, "Will you dance with me, Olivia?"

Aiden had been waiting for a song he hoped Olivia would appreciate. As an outdoorsy woman from the Pacific Northwest, he pegged her for a folksy-music lover, so when he heard the opening notes of "Look at Miss Ohio" by Gillian Welch, he took his chance. The song was full of twang and sap, and it had been one of his sister Lauren's favorites for years.

"Oh, I don't know," Olivia said, looking down at her hands, which were cupping her nearly empty beer.

Grace squinted at Olivia, studying her for a beat before saying, "Good idea."

She clapped her hands once and stood. She reached back to grab Abesh's hand, pulling him upright. They walked toward the other slow-dancing couples, leaving Olivia to fend for herself.

"Looks like you're stuck with me," Aiden teased, throwing a silent thank you to Grace as she walked away.

Olivia took his outstretched hand. He pulled her close and guided her around the makeshift dance floor.

They were quiet through the whole song, swaying from side to side, nothing fancy. Even so, he felt like the man in the game Operation he had played as a kid–every time their thighs touched or her hand moved on his shoulder, his body buzzed.

And, god, she smelled like a potent mix of floral lavender and earthy leather. *Is this what all farmers smell like?* He smiled at the thought.

When the song ended, he stepped back, but he wasn't ready to let go of her hand, and she didn't pull away.

"Well, Olivia," he said as he ran his thumb along the calluses on her palm, "I've now seen you naked and danced with you. Since we're doing this backwards, may I please buy you a beer?"

She grinned, and that familiar blush crept onto her cheeks. Smile lines creased the corners of her eyes, which looked more green than hazel under the street lamps.

"Sure." She ducked her head and tucked a loose red lock behind her ear.

She led him through the crowd, meandering around the edge of the dance floor and back to the picnic tables. Grace and Abesh were nowhere to be seen. Why was he not surprised? He was going to have to thank Grace properly at some point.

Chapter 16 - Olivia

Olivia checked her phone while Aiden grabbed beers. In the brief time she'd been on the dance floor, trying not to swoon while tucked up against Aiden's solid chest, she'd gotten three texts.

Grace: *Have fun! (winky kissy face emoji)*

Realizing they'd abandoned her, Olivia replied with a poop emoji.

Mom: *Did you make it to the dance? Carolyn told me Aiden will be there (winky face emoji).*

Wow. I'm apparently very bad at hiding anything from my family. Also, that would have been helpful to know like, four hours ago, Mom*!*

Olivia: *See you tomorrow at Sunday Dinner.*

Lastly, and least expected, she had a text from Sam.

Sam: *hey, I found some of your pictures and books when I was going through some of my boxes. Do you want me to mail them to you? Not sure if you're planning to come back to Seattle for a visit anytime soon*

She set down her phone and took a deep breath before shaking out her hands, pushing away his unwanted presence. Feeling calmer, she picked up her phone and texted him her new address.

When Aiden returned with beers, Olivia asked, "So what's your story, Dr. Wescott?"

His eyes widened a fraction, and she could tell her use of his professional title had thrown him. It seemed rare for him to be caught off-guard. She smiled, pleased.

"Me?"

"Yeah, what are you up to in Saint Paul? Who do you like to spend time with?" she asked awkwardly.

Gees Olivia, just ask him if he's got a girlfriend, you dork, she silently scolded herself.

He glanced at the teenagers who had taken over the dance floor and were filming themselves before answering.

"Are you trying to ask me if I'm single?" One corner of his mouth turned up slightly.

"Perhaps." She glanced down sheepishly before meeting his eyes. "I'm not all that interested in becoming friends with a man who is in a relationship."

"Would I be asking you to dance and have drinks if I were?"

"You tell me."

"Single." After a pause, he added, "Divorced."

Olivia nodded but didn't say anything, wondering if Aiden would share more of his story.

"No kids, no pets," he added. "If I'm honest, I finally feel like I'm coming up for air after moving back. What about you?"

"Single, no lawyers involved, though. Just old-fashioned heartbreak."

Aiden saluted his beer. "Cheers to that."

They tapped the rim of their cups and drank.

"You know," he said, "people are talking about you."

"*What?* Why?"

"You're new and interesting, and you've got Seattle liberal written all over you."

That made Olivia laugh out loud. "Who are you talking to exactly?"

Aiden paused, making Olivia wait while he took another drink. "John Anderson said something about you 'being alright despite probably voting to legalize pot.'"

"Oh! John!" Olivia said excitedly, pleased to hear she was on John's good side. "He plowed my garden!"

"Excuse me?" Aiden raised his eyebrows, grinning.

Olivia burst out laughing, "No, no, for the…because…" she gave up. "Look, all I'm trying to say is that he plowed my garden. Let's leave it at that."

"That's where we're going to leave it?"

"Yup," Olivia said with a wink in her voice.

"You might be a bit too forward for this town, Olivia. No wonder folks are talking."

The street band started playing an old Garth Brooks cover Olivia and her dad had sung whenever it came on the radio when she was a kid.

"Well, for the record, I proudly voted to legalize weed because the tax revenue is fantastic for schools. But I can also sing every word to this song. There are some things you will always know, no matter how much you pay your therapist." Olivia paused before adding, "Was that TMI? I realize people here probably prefer to drown their sorrows."

"Cheers to that." Aiden raised his beer once again.

"At the very least, beer goggles feel like the only viable option for procreation, given the lack of a vibrant online dating scene," she added, hoping for a laugh. She was happy to see her efforts pay off.

They looked around at the crowd. A few solo men in their late forties lingered near the sides of the dance floor. Most people were paired off and many had several towheaded kids running around.

"It looks like I'm currently your only viable option for procreation in this town, beer goggles or not," Aiden said.

They laughed, and he bopped his foot against hers.

"Excuse me, are you playing footsie with me? That is very forward of you, even if I'm now just finding out how desperate I am."

"Maybe." He grinned. "I'm just glad I get to see you. I wanted to text you, but I knew you were excited about your sister visiting, and I didn't want to intrude."

The weight of her earlier worries washed away.

"I'm glad, too, but next time, feel free to text."

"Noted. In that case, is there any chance I could steal you away for an hour or two tomorrow morning to have brunch with me? I'll make you Eggs Benedict. I bet you haven't had proper Eggs Benedict in a very long time."

Was that an innuendo? Because he wasn't wrong on both fronts. A flutter of excitement tickled her stomach.

"Okay, sure, that sounds fun. But speaking of tomorrow morning, I should take off soon. I have to be up early to get Ms. Darcy some exercise and finish a few chores."

"Oh sure, no worries. Actually, is there any chance I could catch a ride?" Aiden asked hopefully.

Olivia looked at him dubiously. "Did you walk here?" It would have taken him two hours.

"No, my Mom gave me a ride. I knew I'd be drinking, and I figured I'd find a ride home eventually. Worst case, it'd be a long walk home."

"Okay, sure, but I should warn you, I'm driving the truck tonight, and I may kill the engine. I'm still mastering the manual transmission."

"Ah, let me know if you ever need any lessons."

"Ugh, no. That's too cliché." Olivia stood. God forbid she had to rely on a man to teach her how to drive a car.

He laughed and stood to follow her.

"Who taught you how to drive?"

"My dad," she admitted begrudgingly. "Who is a man."

His eyebrows raised briefly.

"Yeah, yeah." Olivia feigned annoyance.

They reached her truck, which was parked in front of the post office, two blocks from the dance. She opened her door, climbed in, and leaned over to lift the lock on his side.

Aiden climbed in beside her and ran his hands along the red and tan leather seats and dashboard.

"It came with the house," Olivia admitted.

"It's well-cared for. What are you working on tomorrow?"

"You know, just general farm maintenance. I have to fix my irrigation hose again and deadhead some flowers since I didn't go to market today. It turns out my sad excuse of a farm is a lot to manage," she added humbly.

"The one John Anderson plowed?"

She burst out laughing. "That's the one."

A comfortable silence settled in for a few miles as they drove through swarms of bugs. She wasn't looking forward to cleaning the windshield, but she made herself focus on the road. She carefully watched for the glowing eyes of deer, which were prone to running in front of, and getting hit by, complacent drivers.

A few minutes later, Olivia pulled up to Aiden's family's cabin, feeling proud for getting there without stalling the engine once.

Aiden turned to look at her. "Should I be expecting you at the end of my dock tonight? I can set out a beer if you give me some notice."

"As a matter of fact, I'm glad you brought that up. You know, you've ruined my swim schedule. I used to have this pond all to myself, but instead, I've been having to take cold showers."

"Me too." Aiden winked and stepped out of the truck.

She shook her head, feeling both idiotic and pleased for having so easily walked into that trap. "See you tomorrow, Aiden."

"See you soon, Olivia."

She pushed in the clutch and put the gear in reverse, but she let the clutch out too quickly, and the engine died. The truck lurched to a halt.

Well, at least we got that out of the way.

She restarted the ignition and managed to successfully turn the truck around and head home. In the rearview mirror, Aiden was standing at his door, smiling into her taillights. He waved and turned into the cabin.

Chapter 17 - Aiden

Aiden looked at his phone. It was late, but he was two hours ahead of his little sister Lauren, who lived in Portland, so he shot off a text.

Aiden: *Hey Laur, I have a friend who just moved back from Seattle coming over tomorrow morning for brunch. What music should I play?*

Laur: *What kind of friend?*

Aiden: *A women*

Laur: *Who?*

Aiden: *Doesn't matter, you don't know her*

Laur: *Tell me anyway*

Aiden: *Why, so you can tell mom?*

Laur: *As if! So I can tell Ethan.*

Aiden: *Well, her name is Olivia.*

Laur: *Seriously?! Tell me this isn't the same Olivia that Ethan went on a date with. What's wrong with you? What happened to bro code?*

Aiden: *Hey. I was the one who went to high school with her, and besides, Ethan said the date only lasted five minutes.*

Laur: *Fiiiiiine. But I need more details. Set the scene so I can get the vibe right.*

Aiden: *Brunch, at the cabin, eggs benedict, sitting on the dock, tomorrow morning*

Laur: *You're cooking eggs bene on that shitty little stove, huh?*

Aiden didn't respond, waiting for her to come through for him.

Laur: *Alright, play the album, "Hello Love" by the Be Good Tanyas, BUT don't push play until you see her pull up. The first song will be critical for setting the vibe! Trust.*

Aiden smiled and shook his head. "Trust." He always did when it came to Lauren's music choices. She'd introduced him to all his favorite bands as soon as she was old enough to peruse YouTube music videos. As soon as he'd left home for college, she sent him weekly emails with music links, and her tastes ranged broadly from classic rock to folk to hip hop.

Aiden: *Always. Thanks little one.*

Laur: *And don't eat inside the cabin. It's creepy as fuck in there with all those eyes looking at you.*

He laughed and looked around the room filled with Minnesota hunting trophies–taxidermied ducks, pheasant, and deer heads covered most wall surfaces. Shaking his head, he opened his phone to preview Lauren's recommendation. He had to admit the music was pretty perfect. He fell asleep to the vocalist's sultry vibrato, looking forward to the alone time he would have with Olivia in a few hours.

Chapter 18 - Olivia

The next morning, Olivia wrapped up her chores and was out of the shower by 10. She didn't spend a ton of time getting ready since she'd told Aiden she'd be there by 10:30. She slipped into shorts and a tank top before adding a touch of mascara to her eyelashes. After scrunching some product into her hair, she headed out the door, letting her hair air dry during the short walk to the cabin. The evaporation felt good on the sunny walk alongside the empty gravel road.

The cabin's interior door was open, so she knocked lightly on the screen door's frame. Aiden opened the door, hair also damp. He sported a well-worn University of Minnesota T-shirt and khaki shorts.

Aiden pulled her in for a hug. "I'm so glad you're here."

She looked around the tiny cabin. Fish, birds, and antlers were mounted on every wall of the tiny interior. A bathroom, a kitchen, and a single bedroom all led off the small sitting area, which had a cozy-looking wood stove surrounded by old, tattered couches that looked like they'd once belonged to Aiden's grandparents. Soft melodic music played from a speaker sitting on top of a bookshelf, and she was pleasantly surprised to recognize the smoky singer's voice.

Looking at Aiden, she said, "Are you kidding me? I would never pass up free Eggs Benedict."

“I should tell you, I don’t actually know how to make them. I just wanted to hang out with you.”

Olivia opened her mouth, flabbergasted.

“*Kidding*.” He grinned. “They’ll be ready in a few minutes. There’s a mimosa waiting for you on the dock. I’ll bring you a plate when it's finished.”

Olivia put her hands on her hips. “Aiden, it is not okay to joke about anything involving Hollandaise sauce.”

His grin told her how pleased he was with himself.

“So, you still think you’re, like, really funny, huh? You didn’t grow out of that phase?” Olivia teased.

“Why would I have stopped being funny? Think of all of the fodder I have gleaned since we were kids. Humor only gets better with age…like wine.”

“Okay, okay, go make the eggs.”

He continued to grin as he headed for the closet-sized kitchen. Olivia glanced in behind him. *He must be an Eggs Benny pro if he’s going to pull them off on a single-burner stove*. She hoped Aiden lived up to his own hype.

Olivia slid open the screen door and headed for the dock, which made a pleasant thump-thump sound as she walked to the end. True to his word, Aiden had placed a mimosa on one of the dock’s wooden slats.

She sat down, dipped her feet in the water, and took in the beauty of the pond, enjoying the gentle morning sunshine on her face and chest. A loon paddled through the calm water, followed closely by her two babies. The pond was still and quiet, excluding the various songbirds singing in the trees along the water's edge.

Between the peaceful ambiance and the champagne in her mimosa, she vaguely wondered if this was what it felt like to be wooed.

After a few minutes, the screen door whirred open and clicked closed. Aiden walked the length of the dock to join her, a plate in each hand. His stride was unhurried. As soon as he handed her a plate, Olivia's mouth watered. He had constructed the Benedict using the classic eggs and Canadian bacon ingredients.

"Oh, I forgot." She reached into her bag. "I brought you something."

She pulled out a jar of strawberry rhubarb compote, made Gresham style, which basically meant you added twice as much sugar as was called for in a normal recipe.

He took it and read the label. "Seriously?" He looked at Olivia with something close to glee. "I love this stuff. My mom used to make it but hasn't gotten around to it lately."

Olivia wondered if it had something to do with his dad's stroke but didn't ask.

"I'm glad you're glad, but let's not waste any more time getting to the important business at hand."

They took their first bites, and Olivia moaned with pleasure.

“Why is this so good?” she asked, incredulous. “This is 'stand in line for an hour' delicious.”

“MSG.”

“Seriously?” she said, surprised but also not.

“Nah, I took a brunch cooking class with Rebecca a long time ago.”

“Rebecca…your ex?”

“Oh right, yes." He scratched his cheek and looked out at the water.

“Well, the class was well worth the money,” Olivia said.

“Thanks. I'm happy you like it,” he said, meeting her eyes again, a smile on his face.

“Oh, guess what? I saw a loon and her babies while you were cooking. They were so cute.” She gestured across the pond. “I think they tucked back behind that tree over there.”

“How many loonlets did she have?”

“Excuse me, loonlets?”

“You heard me.”

“That sounds made up.”

“Did you fail to notice all of the taxidermy in that cabin?”

“Oh, I saw. But isn’t this your parents’ cabin?”

“It is, but that doesn’t mean I was excused from the freezing cold, ass-crack-of-dawn hunting excursions with my dad and Nathan as a kid. *And* given very quiet lectures on the various bird species we saw.”

"Is that why your parents moved to Minnesota? Because your dad's a hunter?"

"That was a factor, I'm sure, but I think the biggest thing was the cost of living. They knew they wanted a big family and for my mom to stay at home with us. The East Coast would have made it a lot harder. And honestly, I think my mom felt safer making that choice for herself here. Less judged, you know?"

"That's interesting. And they did, right? Have a big family, I mean? There are four of you?"

"Five."

"Woah, that is big. Wait, give me the lineup in full from start to finish."

"Ellen, Nathan, me, Lauren, Ethan." He held up a finger for each name until his fist was completely unclasped.

"So, let me get this straight. Your parents, Carolyn and Brendon, had five kids and named them Ellen, Lauren, Aiden, Nathan, and Ethan?"

"Yep, that is correct," he said with a 'what can you do' shrug, making it clear he had resigned himself to the matching second-syllables years ago.

"Okay, but how often does your mom call you by your name and not one of your siblings?"

"I'd say…" He paused as if considering. "A solid twenty percent of the time."

"So a one-in-five chance then?"

He cracked a grin. “Yup.”

“I can’t imagine being around that many other humans all of the time.”

He shrugged again. “You know, it was nice always having someone to hang out with, and now, as an adult, I call on my siblings for different advice. Like, I’ll ask Nathan about anything related to money. Ethan is the best storyteller, so I’ll call him when I need a laugh. Ellen is the best for navigating family politics. And Lauren, well, she’s the hardest nut to crack, but we see eye to eye culturally. She has great music and book recommendations, and she understands my perspective on life given how long she’s lived in Portland.”

“Portland is a great town. Amazing food and excellent Tarot card readings.”

He laughed. “Is that how you decided it was time to move back here?”

“That, and a coin toss.”

“Well, I’m glad you’re here,” he said.

She sensed no trace of irony in his voice as his blue eyes bore into hers. She worried his gaze held meaning she wasn’t ready to uncover. She broke eye contact and took another bite, trying not to drip sauce down her chin.

“Thanks… And thanks again for brunch.”

“You’re very welcome.”

After a beat, he asked, “So what really brought you back? My mom told me you had a pretty good thing going in

Seattle. Sidebar, did you know our moms are, like, best buds now?"

Olivia laughed. "Yes, I've heard. I'm going to have to be more filtered around my mom."

He grinned, looking at her through his long, dark lashes, and Olivia's stomach did a flip.

"It's kind of a long story," Olivia said.

"Well, my parents are at church for at least another hour, so I've got time."

After taking a breath to collect her thoughts, she told him about Sam and their breakup, but she omitted the more embarrassing parts of the story, like her four failed ultimatums.

"I guess I felt like I needed to shake it up, and I'd been missing my family. And then, the day after I broke up with Sam, my team at work got reorg'ed for the sixth time in a year. It was the straw that broke the camel's back, I guess."

"Yeesh, sounds brutal," he said, and Olivia appreciated the validation. "Well, for what it's worth, I think it's pretty badass the way you're striking out on your own. Also, have I mentioned I'm a big fan of strawberry rhubarb compote? This is all working out very well for me."

He grinned, crinkling the edges of his eyes and revealing his dimples through his stubble.

She laughed. "Well, that's a relief."

"Isn't it?" he asked.

Olivia shook her head, grinning. "What about you?"

"What about me?"

"What brought you back?"

"Hmmm…" he said thoughtfully. "Well, there's my dad, obviously."

She nodded, acknowledging his father's stroke, but didn't say anything, hoping for and expecting more.

"And you've probably heard through the rumor mill by now, but Rebecca, my ex, cheated on me, and I was totally blindsided. I knew we weren't in a good place—medical residency is pretty brutal on relationships. I took it for granted that she would never cheat. It—" He paused as if searching for the right word, "—destabilized me. I ended up throwing myself into my residency program, working nonstop, not making time for any relationships, romantic or otherwise. Then, my dad had his stroke, and it was a wake-up call. I finished up my residency, found a great pediatrics fellowship program in Saint Paul, and made my way back to Minnesota."

She felt for him. He'd been put through the wringer. She could also relate to the desire to return to Minnesota's familiar embrace.

"And now?" she asked.

"And now…I'll be focused on my fellowship program for the next three years, and then I'll probably spend the next thirty years paying off my med school loans. And I guess I'd like to give marriage another chance and have kids and all that at some point. What about you? Do you want all that?" he asked, meeting her gaze.

"I think so." Olivia gazed at the water. "But I'm not sure how one accomplishes that in Gresham. I mean, obviously this place is lousy with kids, but I don't know how to even date here. I've been afraid to set up a Tinder profile for fear I'll get matched with a second cousin, or your brother, or something."

He laughed loudly at that.

"God forbid you end up on *another* date with Ethan."

"You have no idea."

They continued chatting, and it occurred to Olivia she enjoyed spending time with Aiden. Yes, okay, he was handsome, he had his life together, and all of those easy boxes to check. But more than that, he seemed like he'd lived enough life to be grateful for what he had without being bitter about what he'd lost. His sense of humor was a refreshing mix of self-deprecation, feigned arrogance, and a healthy dose of teasing. She couldn't remember the last time anyone outside her immediate family or Jessa had made her smile and laugh so much.

After they finished eating, they went inside for coffee. She leaned against the counter while he took his time grinding the coffee beans and boiling water so he could use the Chemex brewing method. His Portland sister, Lauren, had given him the Chemex as a Christmas gift, and he kept it at the cabin since there wasn't room on the counter for a coffee maker. It felt like he had brought some of Seattle's coffee culture into the cabin with them, and it was very comforting.

As they sipped their hot coffees, they sat on opposite ends of the cabin's single sofa, facing each other, and let their feet fiddle in the middle. The casual contact felt right, but she couldn't help but consider for the millionth time where this budding connection was headed.

She wanted to know what he wanted from her, but she was also afraid to ask…because if Aiden were to ask her, she wouldn't have a good answer. She hadn't dated anyone since Sam, other than a short-lived fling with an old crush soon after their breakup. She wasn't sure what she was looking for, much less what she was ready for.

When it was time for her to go, Olivia wondered if he'd kiss her, but he didn't. Instead, he pulled her in for a warm hug and held her. He rubbed her back, and he nuzzled her hair. She felt him inhale the scent of the lavender oil she'd dabbed below her right ear. Despite the technically innocent nature of the hug, it sent shivers down her spine and made her feel a bit wobbly. And she was guilty, too, letting her hands explore the firm contours of his shoulders and back. He had a pleasant, subtle scent, like clean cedar and clove.

They extracted themselves from each other's arms, dopey grins on their faces.

He smiled at her sheepishly. “I'd love to see you again.”

“Me too.”

She squeezed his hand once before turning to walk home, holding on until the distance forced their fingers apart.

Chapter 19 - Aiden

Aiden had a fantastic time with Olivia, and he had been such an idiot saying goodbye to her. *What was wrong with him?* A quick kiss on the cheek would have been totally appropriate. Instead, he'd groped her like a pervert. But she *had* leaned into his desire to explore each other's bodies with hands—if not mouths.

Should I have walked her home?

He was in deep, and he knew it. Sure, technically, there hadn't been a kiss between them, but their chemistry was intensifying. Best not to light any matches in their vicinity.

On the drive back to his apartment in Saint Paul, he thought carefully about how to compose a message to Sarah to let her know he wouldn't be seeing her again. Once that was settled, he spent the next hour and fifty-five minutes thinking about Olivia, her beautiful red hair, her sharp mind, and her disposition—a healthy balance between optimism and skepticism. He had a feeling she saw him for who he was, and if he was going to take a chance with her, he'd have to bring his A-game.

He needed help clearing his head. As soon as he pulled into his apartment building's parking garage, he opened his phone and clicked on the contact for Isaac, his best friend from undergrad.

Aiden: *Yo, any chance you can grab a beer tonight?*

Isaac: *You're welcome to come over. Kids should be asleep by 8.*

Aiden: *Will June be pissed if I come at 7:30 and rile them up a little?*

Isaac: *Don't you fucking dare, man. I will lock the doors.*

Aiden: *I have a key*

Aiden took his silence for what it was, a cold threat of violence, and chuckled. He was definitely going to have to pay his dues someday when Isaac returned all the shit Aiden had given him since he'd had kids.

Aiden: *Ok fine, how about I bring a pizza over at 5:30 and wind the kids up then?*

Then Isaac's wife June joined in the text chain.

June: *If you're coming, bring at least 1 medium cheese pizza, but it can't have any cheese besides mozzarella or Bella won't eat it.*

Aiden: *Roger that. See you in a few hours*

By the time Isaac and June's kids were in bed, and they were free to hang out with Aiden as adults, it was closer to 8:30. They looked shell-shocked and like they had been through a wind tunnel. Aiden handed them each a Coors Light, and they dropped down next to him on the big wrap-around couch in their cozy living room.

Aiden had tried to move some of the toys scattered across their floor into piles but had given up in the end, having no idea what the current rules were for whose toys went where or whose toys were whose for that matter. So he'd done the dishes and taken out the trash instead.

"You two okay?" he asked as they took long drinks of their beers.

"Yeah." Isaac's tone was unconvincing. "George is way too clever for his own good. Every night, we think we're on track to get him to bed on time, and then he Jedi Mind Tricks us, and we've somehow wasted twenty minutes brushing his teeth. Hey, word of advice, have a kid, but just the one."

Aiden laughed. His friend was full of shit and adored his children equally.

"No, that's good advice," June confirmed. "Take it while you still can."

He loved these two. Whether happy or miserable, they were always miraculously on the same page. They'd known each other throughout college but hadn't dated until after June broke up with her high school boyfriend during junior year. Isaac had eventually gotten up the nerve to ask her out, and the rest was history. Aiden knew he romanticized their friendship-turned-relationship, but they seemed to have found the secret sauce, and he admired it, especially after going through his divorce.

"So, what's up, man?" Isaac asked. "Is this a two-for-one convo, or are you in need of some one-on-one advice? In which case, I'll leave you and June to it."

Aiden smiled. "No, June, please feel free to stay or not. It's just…I met someone, or I guess I ran into an old…classmate? And I think I might be into her." He shook his head once. "Fuck it, I'm really into her."

"Hey! Mazel tov!" Isaac said joyfully, clearly missing that Aiden hadn't yet spoken the "but…" part of his monologue.

June eyed him closely. "What's the problem, Aiden?"

Isaac looked at his wife curiously.

"She's in Gresham."

"Interesting. And she told you she's opposed to leaving?" June continued.

"And you're one hundred percent opposed to moving there?" Isaac added, catching on.

To June, Aiden said, "Not in so many words, but I have good reason to believe she isn't interested in leaving. She moved back a few months ago after living in Seattle since we graduated high school."

To Isaac, he said, "I'm at least ninety percent opposed to moving to Gresham, and I'm locked into my fellowship program for the next three years."

"Hmmmm," Isaac hummed.

"That's tricky," June added, "but…you never know. I wouldn't close the door on it. You haven't actually asked her if she'd move to Saint Paul, right? And until you're comfortable having that conversation, it's what, three hours to Gresham from here?"

“Two,” Aiden replied.

“Oh dude, two? That’s nothing,” Isaac said. “June and I did long distance for a year before she joined me in San Diego. We only saw each other, like what? Once every two or three months?” He turned to his wife for confirmation.

She nodded. “Yeah, but we talked almost every day, and we knew the end was in sight.”

“I know, I know,” Aiden said. “Maybe I’m being a coward because it feels like this is a heavy one. Like I can’t dabble. If I’m going to do this, I have to go for it. Gresham is so small, and our moms are friends. And…Olivia’s great. I don’t want to mess with her. I think she went through a tough break-up.”

They eyed him questioningly, as if to say, “And you haven't?”

“Here’s the thing, Aiden,” June said. “We know your divorce put you through the wringer. What Rebecca did was inexcusable, but if this Olivia is as cool as you say she is, I say give it a shot. I'm serious. These opportunities don’t come around every day.”

“Yeah, I guess I’m worried I’m about to repeat history. Does a long-distance relationship while I’m doing my fellowship stand a chance? Especially one that would be brand new? As much as Rebecca screwed me over, I mean, I was never home. And when I was home, I was a total zombie. Olivia deserves better than that.”

"I think it's different, man," Isaac said. "I mean, look, you're here with us. You brought pizza, washed our dishes, and took out the trash—don't think I didn't see that. You'll make it work if it is meant to work. I hope you'll forgive me for saying this, but Rebecca wasn't the right girl for you."

Aiden's eyebrows raised, and he pulled his head back, surprised.

"No, no, hear me out. Do you really think if you hadn't had all the pressure from her and her family to get married before med school, your relationship wouldn't have just ended when she realized the road to becoming a doctor's wife was much less glamorous than she imagined? She didn't have the gumption to see it through, ya know? And can you imagine if, after residency, you told her you were going to do a fellowship? Ha! She would have divorced you then and there if it hadn't already happened."

Aiden knew Isaac was right, even if it stung to hear. "So what do I do now?"

June spoke first. "I think you know what you need and want to do. But based on what you just told us, if you're going to do it, do it right."

"In other words, if you feel like you'd drop everything and drive two hours to see her if she asked you to come, don't fuck it up," Isaac added.

And with that, he leaned over and kissed his wife on the cheek.

“Okay, fine.” Aiden held up his hands in surrender. “You’re right. You’re both right.”

“Of course we are,” June said. “We’re old and wise and shit.”

When Aiden got a text from Olivia’s cousin Philip the next week inviting him to Olivia’s birthday party, he knew he was going. Isaac’s words played in his mind. It didn’t matter what his schedule looked like. He was going to make it work.

Chapter 20 - Olivia

Olivia was one subscriber short of reaching her CSA goal, thanks in part to word of mouth. Five of Mrs. Wescott's friends had signed up, along with two other women who volunteered with Olivia's mom. Pam had recruited the last four from her group of YMCA friends. Olivia was thrilled and insanely busy.

She spent the next few weeks harvesting veggies and flowers from sunrise to sunset. She barely had time to use the bathroom and eat, much less cook the food she grew. She had thankfully restocked her Trader Joe's freezer hoard when she and her mom drove to the Cities to drop Grace and Abesh off at the airport.

She wondered if she and Aiden were at a point in their *friendship* when she could ask him to pick up supplies from TJ's for her when her stash ran out. She'd think on it, but was leaning toward yes out of desperation, if nothing else.

Her cheeks were sore from smiling at the texts Aiden had been sending her. In addition to their banter, she occasionally sent him pictures of inappropriately shaped vegetables, and he sent her photos of latte art.

I guess we each have our kinks. She laughed.

Olivia had barely registered that it was her birthday week when she got a text from Fiona's mom, Cassie, inviting her to come over Saturday night after the farmers market to celebrate.

Olivia replied with a "That's so sweet, you don't have to do that," text, only to receive an emphatic, "If you don't come, I'll think it's because you don't like me," text in return.

Well played, Cassie, well played. Olivia smiled and confirmed she'd be there.

For a moment, she considered inviting Aiden, but she wasn't sure she was ready for a double date with her cousin and his wife–if you could call it a date.

Would I *call it a date?*

In the end, she decided to go stag and put it out of her mind as she scrambled to plan and execute her subscription boxes. Mid-summer produce was hitting fast and hard. She had an abundance of cucumbers, summer squash, and cherry tomatoes, not to mention carrots, potatoes, and beets. She'd even been able to include onions and fennel that week. And most excitingly, her earliest dahlias were starting to bloom. She made sure to include a couple in each bouquet.

She could no longer remember falling asleep each night. She was so tired she was out as soon as her head hit the pillow.

By the time her birthday rolled around, she was absolutely exhausted from a hot, busy day at the market, but she didn't have any other choice than to get in the shower and get ready to celebrate.

If I'm only as old as I feel, I must be turning ninety tomorrow.

Halfheartedly, she forced herself through the routine and gave herself points for putting on a sundress instead of shorts and a T-shirt. At the last minute, she threw on some red lipstick because she needed to pull it together. *This birthday thing only happens once a year.*

With the last ten minutes before she absolutely had to leave, she whipped together a crudités platter. As she locked her house, her phone vibrated.

Mom: *I'll bring Ms. Darcy to the party tonight, but I'm also happy to keep her if you decide to crash at Philip's.*

Olivia: *Great, thanks!*

Why would I crash at Philip's? Also, she didn't know her parents were coming, but she was happy to hear it. She hadn't had time to think past her next tomato and hadn't seen much of them beyond their Sunday dinners.

Olivia was thinking she might need to hire someone to help her during her next CSA season if she was even *considering* adding one more customer. *Only two and a half more months*. It had become a mantra of sorts whenever she felt like lying down in the dirt and taking a nap.

Driving up to Fiona's house, a couple of extra cars were parked in their yard. For the first time since Cassie had texted her, she considered the possibility the party might be more of a *party* party.

When she stepped out of her car, she could smell grilled barbecue chicken and hear kids laughing.

She walked into the house through the side door leading straight to the kitchen, which was busy-family-clean, free of dirt but full of clutter.

Cassie was at the counter making lemonade using frozen concentrate.

Olivia set the platter down next to Cassie. “Okay, I’ve got every type of crunchy veggie you could imagine. Is it summertime yet?”

“Olivia! Happy birthday!” Cassie dropped the wooden spoon she was holding and wrapped Olivia in a tight embrace. “You didn't have to bring anything.”

“Please. This farm is taking over my life, and I’ve got veggies coming out of my ears.”

“Oh, well, it’s sweet of you to show up with food at your own birthday party,” she said.

Just then, Philip walked through the patio door from the adjoining dining room.

“Hey there, birthday girl,” he said with a wink. “You ready to have some fun tonight? I'm pouring G and T's.” Without missing a beat, he handed Olivia a glass of gin and tonic with lime. “Hope you like Tanqueray.”

“Who doesn’t?” Olivia said warmly, lifting the glass to her lips and savoring the first sip.

The piney juniper flavor filled her mouth, followed by the refreshing taste of lime to balance it.

“Yummm…” she hummed.

“So, for tonight, we invited a few friends over. You know, the usual. Your parents, my sister and her family, Don Schwartz’s family. Jill is planning to swing by after she closes the restaurant. And a few others. Oh, and uh…” Cassie hesitated briefly, “I hope you don’t mind, but Philip texted Aiden Wescott as well.”

Olivia suddenly felt a little lightheaded. *Maybe the gin and tonic is stronger than I thought.*

“Great!” she said with forced bravado.

She had forgotten how impossible it was to maintain secrets in Gresham, but since she didn’t know what they knew, she left it there. Now she was torn between fear Aiden wouldn’t show and wariness about putting their budding attraction on display for all of her closest family and friends.

“Cheers.” She lifted her glass to divert the conversation. “And thank you so much for throwing me a birthday party. I had no idea this was going to be a real party.”

“No, no, thank you for giving us an excuse to have folks over. I mean, we have to make our own fun around here, don’t we?” Cassie said. “So here’s the plan. Philip's gonna man the grill, we’ll eat, we’ve got some yard games, bean bags, and that crazy golf ball game, and later, we'll get the fire goin'. We'll break out the S'mores for the kiddos, and you can sit back and relax, okay?"

As an afterthought, Cassie added, "Also, we've got a whole lot more gin and tonic fixings because Philip insisted we buy twenty limes, so drink up."

Olivia chuckled and set her drink on the counter. She reached out to give Cassie another hug. "Truly, this is the most social I've been in ages. Thank you."

Cassie returned her hug before waving her off, and Olivia followed Philip into the spacious backyard. Led Zeppelin's "Black Dog" played on the portable speaker, and she allowed herself to relax and be present. She was genuinely looking forward to the night ahead, though a little nervous about all things Aiden.

She looked around the backyard. Fiona was playing in the swimming pool with her cousins. They called out a quick hello to Olivia and immediately got back to their ring-diving game.

Several picnic tables had been covered with plastic tablecloths held down by potted flowers. The firepit was already filled with a tripod of wood, cardboard poking out through the cracks, ready to be lit, and a dozen miscellaneous chairs circled the pit.

Olivia walked toward the grill to join Philip. While tall like Olivia and her dad, Philip was more barrel-shaped and took up a lot more space in general. Given the number of meals they'd shared in her parents' dining room growing up, she was relaxed by his side. As he flipped burgers and rotated brats, they chatted about Philip's mom and the other endless topics they could jump into the middle of without needing to provide context. They finally circled around to the inevitable—the farm.

"Have you thought more about taking over the farm at some point?" he spoke cautiously, scratching his cheek and looking away as though he was already privy to the conflict.

"Philip, I don't know what my dad has said, but the farm is rightfully yours. We both know that."

He looked over her shoulder as if considering his words before meeting her eyes and cautiously continuing, "You know I appreciate that, even if I don't fully agree. But I have a proposition for you. The truth is, I love the farm, and I'd love to keep it going. But I don't want the responsibility of the business side. I need help with that, and I'd like to partner with you on it."

Olivia began to turn away from him, but with a hand on her arm, he stopped her from leaving.

"Wait a minute, Olivia. Hear me out." With increased determination, he said, "If you can take the office work, I can manage everything else. I'll hire more help, and you'll never have to drive a tractor or deal with harvest. All I need from you is your business brain and organizational skills to help me plan our crops, make sure we get to market at the right time, and all that computer stuff you're a pro at."

Olivia's gut told her Philip was presenting a reasonable picture for the two of them to coexist with the farm and both get what they needed and wanted out of it. She'd always had a knack for data analysis and project management, which is what Philip was asking from her. It certainly appealed to her business brain, and she vaguely considered what changes she would make if she were in charge.

Philip paused a beat, nudging a brat with his tongs. "You could still do your CSA and flower stand, and you could afford to hire help for *your* operation as well."

Another pause.

"It'd mean a lot to me and Cassie if you'd consider it."

She recognized that what he wasn't saying was how Olivia's decision would impact Fiona. They both knew Olivia wanted to give Fiona the world, and she appreciated Philip for not putting pressure on that tender spot in her heart.

Olivia took a deep breath and gazed at Fiona, who was giggling happily in the pool.

"I'll think about it, I promise. But I need some time."

"Thank you for considering it. I have a good feeling about it, but I'll leave it there. Take your time. Anyhow, Cassie would kill me if she knew I'd brought it up since this is your birthday party. So cheers to the day you were born, cousin!

The world is better with you in it, and we're glad you're home."

Olivia raised her glass to his but was surprised to find her G&T empty. *Oops, I'm going to have to slow down.* She excused herself to get a glass of water.

Several hours passed, and about twenty people showed up to celebrate and socialize. When a new car pulled into the driveway, Olivia held her breath until she saw it wasn't Aiden. She tried to hide her disappointment every time.

After dinner, the music and voices got louder. Olivia was on her fourth drink, twice her usual cut-off point.

I should switch to water.

But she was having too much fun to be her own buzzkill.

Fiona and Olivia danced like maniacs along with several other kids and their moms. After one last must-dance song, she took a break and plopped next to her mom and Ms. Darcy. Olivia's dad had come and gone. He'd headed home early so he'd be asleep by his usual nine o'clock bedtime. Olivia was again wondering whether Aiden would show. It was getting late, and she was beginning to lose hope.

Her mom must have read the disappointment on her face because she asked, "Are you having a good birthday, sweetie?"

"I am. Thanks, Mom. I didn't realize this was going to be an actual party, but now I realize I was in need of some fun. I think I've been taking the CSA too seriously. There's just so much to do all the time."

"Well, if I recall, the CSA was a bonus, right? And it was supposed to bring you joy? Don't lose sight of that, even if it means you don't harvest everything on time. Or maybe you could hire someone. Regardless, you definitely inherited your dad's talent for farming."

It might have been the alcohol, but Olivia's eyes teared up with gratitude.

"Thanks, Mom. You're right, that's a good reminder."

Olivia reached over and gave her a hug. Naturally, Ms. Darcy felt left out and jumped up, propping her front paws on Olivia's thighs.

She laughed and gave her dog a hug.

"Love you too, Missy."

"I think I'm gonna head home. I'll take Missy. You stay and have fun."

"Thanks, Mom. Have I told you lately how great you are?"

"The information is always welcome, love." Her mom gave Olivia one last kiss on top of her head.

"You're the best!" Olivia said.

"So are you, sweet pea. We'll see you tomorrow."

As her mom headed out with Ms. Darcy, Olivia caught sight of Aiden standing at the edge of the yard. He was wearing a light blue short-sleeve Riviera shirt. The top two buttons had been left open, exposing the hollow dip at the base of his neck. He walked toward her with his hands tucked into the pockets of his navy chinos, his ankles peeking out above his tan boat shoes.

He came! Little bubbles of *yay* bounced around her chest.

The alcohol dulled any composure she normally would have tried for, and she waved excitedly. Her grin took over her face, and he smiled broadly and waved back.

Her mom and Aiden crossed paths, and he stopped and reached down to scratch Ms. Darcy's cheeks before standing to chat. The music was too loud, but whatever he said made her mom laugh, and she reached out to touch Aiden's forearm in response. He lowered his head to listen more closely to what she was saying, nodded, looked toward Olivia, and smiled.

Olivia squinted and wrinkled her nose at him. *What on earth are those two talking about?*

He smiled, turned back to her mom, nodded again, and said something brief. Her mom reached up to give Aiden a hug. Why was she giving him a hug?

That's weird. Olivia's dulled brain couldn't be bothered to worry about all that when it was her birthday. She was feeling good, and Aiden was there.

As Aiden walked over to join her near the bonfire, Olivia stood, feeling giddy with anticipation.

"Happy birthday, Olivia. Sorry I'm late." He leaned down and kissed her cheek.

She touched her fingertips to the lingering sensation and smiled. "No worries, thanks for coming."

"Did I miss anything?" he asked.

"Just the Chicken Dance, but I think they'll be queuing up the Electric Slide soon, so don't worry about it."

He laughed, took her glass out of her hand, and sipped.

"Olivia Olsen, gin and tonics look good on you."

Her head fell back as she laughed.

Still smiling, she asked, "How was the drive?"

"Not bad. I got on the road a little late. Had to stay an extra hour at the hospital to finish up some paperwork."

"So, you're not a Monday through Friday doctor?"

"No, my schedule varies since I work in emergency medicine, and unfortunately, I have to work occasional weekends and holidays, but it goes with the territory. Anyway, enough about work. We're here to celebrate you and your day of birth. How old are you again? I forget when we graduated high school."

"You'll just have to wonder," she said, batting her eyes coquettishly.

Then, remembering her Midwest manners, she asked, "Have you eaten? I'm sure there is still food in the kitchen, and we can heat some leftovers for you."

"I'm all set, but I could use a drink…unless you want me to finish yours." He flashed a teasing grin.

She cocked her head and raised an accusatory eyebrow. "Excuse me, sir, but are you implying I've had too much to drink?"

"No, it seems to me you've had just the right amount." He held out his hand. "Would you care to accompany me to the bar?"

"I suppose, but only because you're cute," Olivia said as she took his hand, liquid courage coursing through her.

"Huh, and here I thought you liked me for my personality."

She eyed him up and down before resting her eyes on his. "Nah," she teased.

Without thinking, Olivia leaned forward on her tiptoes and kissed Aiden on the lips.

To her surprise, the folks around them whooped and cheered. Olivia immediately buried her face against Aiden's shirt to escape their attention, giggling into his chest. She'd barely had time to register his soft lips before the crowd reminded her that she was in a semi-public setting. However, despite the alcohol and embarrassment, she was delighted to have just kissed Aiden Wescott. She was looking forward to another, less public, opportunity. Maybe she'd have to drag him behind the garage for a do-over.

Instead of seeking alone time, they spent the next few hours moving in and out of conversations with the other guests. They remained glued to each other's sides, and they continually found excuses to bump hips and graze arms.

By eleven, Olivia hadn't had a drink in a few hours and was getting sleepy. She tilted her head to the side so it rested against Aiden's shoulder.

He looked down and put his arm around her. "You're kind of adorable, you know that?"

She smiled, basking in his sweetness.

"I'm also a bit drunk and very tired. Do you think you could be a gentleman and drive me home? Assuming you're good to drive because *I'm* certainly not."

"I think I should be well below the legal limit from my one beer, Scout's honor."

They said goodbye to the folks who had gathered around the fire and were recounting stories they'd all heard a million times but retold for an excuse to laugh.

As Olivia and Aiden walked toward the parked cars, many folks called out, "Happy Birthday!" Several people added teasing shouts of "Have fun!" and "Make good choices!"

She and Aiden laughed as they got into his car. They held hands like teenagers on the drive.

"Did you have fun tonight?" Aiden asked. "I hope you don't mind that I came."

"I had a great time, and I'm so glad you came." She gave his hand a reassuring squeeze. "Sorry I didn't invite you myself. I thought it was only going to be Fiona, her parents, and me."

"Fiona is really important to you, isn't she? "

"She is. Being close to her has been a huge perk of moving back here."

"I get that."

"Do you have any patients with Down syndrome?"

"I have in the past during my residency years, and of course I see all types of kids in the emergency department where I work now. But neurodiverse kids typically see multiple specialists, depending on whether they have any associated complications."

"Yeah, I remember Fiona had to do a lot of occupational and speech therapy when she was a toddler. I felt so sorry for Philip and Cassie, having to drive to the Cities practically weekly. Cassie waited to go back to work until Fiona was five and had started kindergarten."

He nodded knowingly, "Not an easy road, but most roads worth traveling aren't."

"Ahhhh, sage wisdom, Mr. Wescott," Olivia declared in grave voice, and he laughed good-naturedly.

"The years have taught me a *few* things."

"Oh yeah? What else?"

"Well, thanks to some humbling experiences, I'd hope I'm twenty-five percent less of a dumbass than when we were in high school. And I'm also better at recognizing and prioritizing quality humans." Aiden squeezed her hand this time, and her cheeks warmed with pleasure.

"Well, for whatever it's worth, I like this version of you, but I don't feel like I knew high school Aiden well enough to compare you to him."

"It's probably for the best. My ego needed to be put in its place, and it definitely has been. Repeatedly."

He drove up Olivia's driveway, parked, and turned off the car, enveloping them in silence. "I have something for you. Excuse me," he said with a shy smile as he reached across Olivia to the glove box.

He popped it open and pulled out a bag of whole-bean coffee. Olivia recognized the logo but didn't immediately place it.

"You seemed to like this the other day at the cabin, so I wanted to get you a bag. I'm hoping to get you addicted so you'll have to come to Saint Paul and hang out with me."

"That's super sweet. Thanks, Aiden." Olivia turned and reached for a hug. He caught her face with the softest part of his palm and gently kissed her lips.

Pulling back, he looked into Olivia's eyes questioningly. She nodded and leaned forward. Their lips met again, slow, exploratory, patient. Mirroring Olivia, Aiden's lips were supple against hers.

The languid sensuality of the kiss was delicious. She parted her mouth, and he licked her bottom lip before nipping it. Their tongues met, and a shiver ran from the nape of Olivia's neck down her spine.

Aiden slowly moved his hand from her cheek to the back of her neck before weaving his fingers into her hair. He massaged every surface, and it was heaven. His lips followed the path of his hand to the side of her neck, and she let out a quiet moan of pleasure. She cupped her hand against his forearm before sliding it along his arm to his bicep, where his muscle flexed against her palm. She continued her search, threading her fingers through his hair and tugging softly. It was Aiden's turn to murmur his pleasure into her ear.

Olivia pulled back, and he paused.

"Do you want to come in?" she asked.

Because it was her birthday, and he was hot, and he made her feel desired in a way she couldn't remember feeling in far too long.

He hesitated before saying, "Will you please believe me when I say I'm dying to come in, but I think it would be better to wait?"

"Is it because I've been drinking? Because I can promise you I am fully capable of consent."

"Well, I appreciate knowing that," he said with a chuckle, "but I have to drive back home tonight. I have to be at work at six tomorrow, and I'm afraid if I go inside with you, I won't be able to leave."

"Yeah, no, of course." She tried to hide her disappointment, but she suspected the high pitch in her voice gave her away.

“Damn,” he said under his breath. Then, more clearly, he said, “I promise, I'll make it up to you.”

“Oh no, I'm grateful you made the drive, especially knowing it was only for a few hours. You don't owe me anything.”

“Well, let me make it up to myself, then, because I'm feeling disappointed as hell right now. Why did I have to grow up and become all responsible?” He cocked his head and gave her a flirty smile, forcing her to meet his eyes. A grin crept over her mouth. “You have a lovely smile, Olivia. I'm glad I got to see it one more time tonight.”

The sappiness, which would normally make Olivia cringe, had her swooning. *Oh boy, I'm either drunker than I thought, or I've got it bad for Aiden. Fingers crossed, it's the G&Ts.* Her tender heart had been through a lot after breaking up with Sam. She wasn’t sure she was ready to open it for Aiden.

Olivia brushed the hair from her eyes. “Well, in that case, thanks for the coffee, and thanks again for coming tonight. It was a wonderful surprise.”

“My pleasure.”

“Drive safe. And text me when you get home so I know you made it okay.”

“I will.” He leaned over, and she met him halfway for one last kiss.

Before Olivia lost her head and started getting handsy again, she pulled back and opened the door.

“I'll be back soon,” he said firmly.

“Hope so.”

Olivia waved from the porch as he drove off before trudging up the stairs to her bedroom. Absolutely exhausted, she collapsed onto her bed.

Happy birthday to me.

She woke twice in the night, thinking of Aiden with a smile before drifting back to sleep.

Olivia wondered if she’d been smiling in her sleep when she woke the next morning. Her cheeks couldn’t relax, thanks to all of the happy memories from the night before.

But she also had a headache.

In search of a hangover cure, she headed to Jill’s for fried potatoes and eggs. As she made her way toward the entrance, she returned waves to several people she recognized from the farmers market.

The door announced her arrival with a jingle. A group of older men drinking coffee at a nearby table all turned to watch her as she walked in. Olivia knew them well as part of her father's circle of farmer friends, including Don Schwartz, who had been at the party the night before, but she wasn't sure why they were silently staring at her.

Jill, seeing the whole thing, broke the silence. "These here gentlemen have been clucking like a flock of old hens for the past thirty minutes about you, and now they're speechless. Figures."

Her jab provoked several grunts.

Don Schwartz piped up. "So, who was that guy you were so cozy with last night?"

"Olivia, I thought you said you'd sworn off men," Mike Swanson chimed in. "But not all men, I see." He winked and grinned with a nod.

"If you're looking for a man," Pete Jacobson said, "I've got a real nice second cousin in Minnetonka who owns a landscaping business. Let me set you up with him."

"Alright, alright. Don't you all have fields to plow?" Olivia teased back.

"Oh no, honey, not with all the automation they've got going these days," Jill said. "Now all these old duffers have to do is sit around, drink my coffee, and gossip. God curse the man who invented GPS-guided combines."

"Yah, yah," the farmers grumbled in unison. "We're looking out for our girl here."

Olivia groaned.

Jill rolled her eyes in sympathy. "The *woman* lived in a city of four million people. I think she can fend for herself." To Olivia, she said, "They're not exactly feminists, but their hearts are good. What can I do for ya darlin'?"

"Mind if I grab a table in the corner over there? I'm in need of some grease and sugar."

"Sure thing, sweetheart. You know that's all we've got here. Grab a menu and head on over. I'll be there in a minute with some coffee."

As Olivia sat down to breakfast, still catching looks from her dad's farmer friends, she pulled out her phone to text Jessa about the night before. She needed help processing everything because she was as scared as she was excited about the possibility of things moving forward with Aiden. She really didn't want to get hurt again, but the pull to move close to him was impossible to ignore. Because last night, he'd left her wanting so much more. In the light of day, minus the four gin and tonics, she was glad it hadn't gone further than PG13, but it also left her on pins and needles, wondering if and when he'd accept her invitation to come in.

Not only was everything with Aiden spinning her in circles, but it also seemed things with the family farm were coming to a head. Philip had presented a reasonable argument for them to manage the farm together. But, if she accepted the nagging feeling that agreeing to his proposal was the right thing to do, what was the point of getting more wrapped up in Aiden?

Chapter 21 - Olivia

Olivia had been staking dahlias for hours to keep them from collapsing under their own weight, which would break their stems and cause them to become generally useless.

Who thought planting three hundred dahlias was a good idea? It couldn't have been me. That would have been highly irrational, Olivia thought for the hundredth time that day.

But the anticipation of seeing the dahlia field in full bloom, representing every color under the rainbow, kept her going. She expected the flowers to transition from one-off blooms to an innumerable variety of breathtaking beauties in about two weeks. At that point, she was going to have a new problem on her hands—figuring out what the heck she was going to do with more than a thousand dahlia blooms each week, not to mention how she was going to harvest them.

Olivia paused to drink some water and check her phone. She had a ten-minute-old text from Aiden and felt the buzzy excitement now accompanying each text he sent—the sensation was beginning to feel familiar. They had been exchanging messages consistently since her birthday.

Aiden: *I know this is really short notice, but I was able to get someone to cover my shift tonight so I can drive up for my dad's birthday. Any chance I could convince you to come as my date?*

Aiden: *It's not the date I had in mind, but I promise I'll make that up to you soon.*

Olivia waited to respond while she sifted through the onslaught of emotions that accompanied Aiden's text. On the one hand, the idea of seeing Aiden and that he'd unambiguously asked her on a date made her giddy, but on the other? Dinner with his family? The image made her squirm because she felt like going to his parents' home would be crossing lines that couldn't be uncrossed.

Aiden: *Ok, I know this is a lot to ask, but I'll only be in town for the night, and I'd love to see you. It will just be us, my parents, Ellen and Tommy, and Ethan at my parents' house. Very casual.*

Bouncing dots appeared, so she waited for his follow-up text.

Aiden: *The Ethan thing isn't still weird for you, is it? It shouldn't be. I think he's dating someone, and he might even bring her.*

This last piece of information did help, though it wasn't a major concern for Olivia. Despite her discomfort at the thought of crashing a Wescott family affair, she was beyond eager to see Aiden. She'd had far too much quiet time to herself in the field, and her mind kept wandering back to their kiss. Well, in reality, it was like a tennis match in her mind, flipping back and forth between both kisses over and over again. That morning, when she'd glanced in the mirror, she had a dopey smile on her face. She couldn't deny the infatuation tickling her sternum.

Ugh, why did I think a quiet farming life was a good idea again? Now I have all the time in the world to obsess over Aiden. I need a more social job ASAP—something demanding and distracting. Maybe it was time to call Jill about that waitressing job.

She was still holding her phone when it vibrated once more.

Aiden: *Please? I'm not above begging. I promise it'll be fun.*

She exhaled and typed.

Olivia: *LOL. Sure, sounds great! What should I bring?*

Aiden: *Nothing, just yourself! I'm leaving the Cities now. I should be there by 6 to pick you up, but I'll text you my ETA when I get closer.*

Olivia: *(thumbs-up emoji)*

Crap, thumbs-down emoji! Lines were about to be crossed. Her mom was definitely going to hear about this. Should Olivia just text her mom right now–control the narrative and all that? Or did it even matter? If the farmers were talking, half the town probably knew she'd left her birthday party with Aiden.

She had two hours before he arrived, and at that moment, she was covered in sweat and dirt. She needed to figure out what she was going to bring because, duh, she couldn't go over to a…man-friend's…parents' house empty-handed in Gresham.

She dropped the dahlia staking supplies in the dirt. No time to clean up after herself. She grabbed some snips and frantically whipped together a market-style bouquet, stuck it in water on her porch, and ran up the stairs to shower and get ready. Seeing her running, Ms. Darcy barked and chased after her. It made her laugh, and she paused to cuddle and play with her pup for a few minutes. Afterward, she assuaged her guilt for abandoning Ms. Darcy with a rawhide and dashed into the bathroom.

Two hours later, nearly to the minute, Aiden's car pulled up the driveway. She checked her reflection in the mirror once more. She'd had to blow dry her hair, which had given it a little extra volume and a bit of wave. Turning her head from side to side, she liked the way the light brought out various shades of bronze and copper.

Look out, Julia Roberts. I'm coming for you.

She'd settled on a navy blue wrap dress and strappy brown sandals. For good measure, she'd put on her favorite necklace, a small rose gold locket her grandmother had given her, and slipped on her favorite bracelet, which matched the locket.

She greeted Aiden from her porch. He got out of his car and reached his arms above his head as if he were stiff from the long drive. As his arms stretched high overhead, his shirt rode up above the line of his waistband, revealing a few inches of his lean torso. *Damn, he looked good.* He dropped his arms back down to his sides and winked. His light blue button-down, navy jeans, and brown loafers fit his body perfectly.

"Hi." Half of his mouth crooked up in a flirty grin she was beginning to think of as Aiden's signature smile.

"Hi." She leaned her hip against the porch railing, grinning back, before looking down at her toes, which really needed a re-polish. She curled her toes into her sandals, hoping he wouldn't notice.

"You look beautiful." He came closer and leaned down to kiss her cheek.

She leaned into his kiss and inhaled his cedar and clove scent. "Thanks, so do you."

"Thank you for coming tonight. I thought about getting you flowers, but I wasn't sure what the etiquette is for buying flowers for a flower farmer, so I got you this instead." He lifted his hand to reveal a small box of chocolate truffles.

Olivia read the label, 'Earl Grey Sea Salt,' and smiled. "I must say, you have excellent taste."

The corners of his eyes crinkled as he smiled a big "pleased to have pleased you" smile.

"Let me pop these inside, grab my bag, and then we can head out."

"Sure."

In addition to a bouquet of hand-tied sweet peas, snapdragons, and strawflowers, Olivia grabbed a jar of her increasingly handy compote, remembering what Aiden had said about his mom having made it in the past.

On the way to Aiden's parents, they made small talk about his drive from the Cities, the weather, and what she was planning for her CSA boxes that week. Olivia asked him about work, and he told her about a few of his more complex cases.

Aiden turned off the highway onto a paved road, heading toward Lake Susan. Olivia had been to Lake Susan at least once to go boating with friends in high school, but she'd never been inside one of its lake houses. While lakeshore property was fairly prevalent in Creek County, where Gresham was nestled, Lake Susan, in particular, attracted a lot of Gresham's wealthier residents, including several doctors like the senior Dr. Wescott.

Driving around the edge of the lake, she took in the view of one large, manicured house after another, most sporting American flags along with a second affinity flag representing everything from The Minnesota Vikings to the U.S. Navy to Sweden.

Old feelings of inferiority that used to surface when surrounded by obvious wealth tried to sneak up, but Olivia shoved them back down. In her youth, growing up on a farm, she'd felt more average than special. Despite her best teenage efforts, she envied some of her wealthier classmates and all of their shiny new toys and expensive family vacations to Mexico or Hawaii each winter. As an adult, Olivia knew better, but she had to actively quiet her inner fifteen-year-old.

Aiden pulled the car into a short driveway and parked next to a black Tesla Model S. They stepped out, and he guided her toward a path along the side of his massive childhood home.

As they rounded the corner, the lake came into view.

Wow.

The distance from the house to the lake was at least fifty yards, which explained the short distance between the garage and the road. The Wescotts had optimized their nearly water-level lot for privacy and lake access. She'd been on enough pontoon rides with her father to know this kind of property, which didn't require stairs to access the water, was significantly more valuable.

In the water, an expansive dock housed a speed boat, a pontoon, and two jet skis. In the opposite direction, the house was a wall of glass, doubtless to ensure every room had an optimal view of the lake. Olivia took a deep breath to slow her heart rate.

"Oh, there's Ethan," Aiden said, pointing toward the patio.

Chapter 22 - Aiden

Sensing Olivia's nervousness, Aiden reached out and threaded his fingers through hers. She met his eyes and smiled, and he was once again grateful she'd agreed to come. He loved being near her, and he was proud to "bring her home" to meet his family. Sure, she'd met most of them before, but Aiden couldn't help feeling a sense of possessiveness since she was now meeting them as his date.

On the patio connected to the house, Ethan was at the grill. His eyes glanced to their connected hands, but his grin remained as affable as ever, if not a smidge self-satisfied—as if he'd predicted Olivia and Aiden's connection all along.

Ethan jauntily saluted with his tongs. "Hey brother. Olivia."

"Hey Ethan," they said as they made their way over to join him near the grill.

"What's for dinner, little man?" Aiden asked.

"We've got barbeque chicken and brats tonight. And some veggies from your CSA, Olivia," he added with a wink.

"Oh, nice." Olivia's smile seemed a touch wary, and Aiden wondered if she was still feeling uncomfortable about the Ethan date.

If any awkwardness lingered, Aiden hoped tonight would smooth that over because if things went his way, this wouldn't be Olivia's last dinner with his family.

He changed the subject to give her some breathing room. "How's Dad doing?"

"Not too bad. I think he's napping. His physical therapy went well yesterday, but it wore him out a bit."

"Well, that's normal. Glad to hear he's doing alright. How are you?"

"Oh, you know, same ol'," Ethan replied. "I'm heading up to the Boundary Waters with Kyle on Thursday to do some fishing, so that'll be a good time."

"Sounds fun."

The camping and nature part of visiting the Boundary Waters did sound cool, but they both knew Aiden wasn't a fisherman. Aiden had always brought along his Gameboy when their dad took them fishing.

Aiden's mom opened the patio door and stepped out to join them. Her smile was enthusiastically bright. "Olivia! I'm so glad you came."

She walked directly to Olivia and wrapped her up in a big hug. Aiden loved seeing the smile and slight tinge of pink on Olivia's face.

"Thank you so much for having me," Olivia said. She stood at least half a head taller than his mom.

Pulling away from Olivia, Aiden's mom turned to give him a hug and kiss on the cheek.

Focusing her attention on Olivia once again, his mom said, "I hope this is okay. Aiden said you eat meat."

"Oh yeah, no worries, I'm easy…going," Olivia said awkwardly.

Ethan coughed on a laugh, and Aiden glared at him.

"Well, that's great. I also made a salad from your CSA," his mom added excitedly. "We have been so pleased with your produce. It is ten times better than what you can buy in the stores, and I think it's a much better value. You have clearly inherited your dad's skill for growing things."

"Thank you, that's really kind," Olivia said. "Oh, and these are for you," she added, handing over the bouquet she'd held protectively on the drive over. "Thanks again for having me. I love spending time by the water."

"Oh yes, us too, obviously." His mom took a moment to spin the bouquet in her hands and smell each bloom. "These flowers are *so* delightful. Did you grow all of these yourself?"

"I did." Olivia smiled.

"Would you mind arranging them for me, Olivia? I know you'll do a much better job than I would. Aiden, will you get Olivia a vase and some shears from the pantry?"

"Of course," Aiden and Olivia replied in tandem, taking his mother's directions in stride.

The three of them headed into his parents' house while Ethan kept his place at the grill.

His parents' kitchen was modern. They'd recently remodeled it with a white tile backsplash behind the sink, along with natural wooden butcher block countertops, which made it feel more like a fancy restaurant than a Midwest kitchen. He watched as Olivia took it all in and wondered what she was thinking. Mostly, he just wanted her to feel relaxed around his family.

After excusing himself for a moment, he returned from the pantry with a medium-sized crystal vase and scissors, hoping it was what she needed, but feeling very far out of his depth. He added some water to the vase and placed both items on the island counter in front of Olivia.

Olivia set her phone on the counter and carefully unwrapped the bouquet. Her fingers were long and adept. He remembered once telling her she had pretty hands at a party after graduating high school. She'd laughed at him like he was nuts, but they were still lovely, if a little callused. He still wondered how she'd forgotten that night or if she was just pretending not to remember.

Arranging the bouquet on the counter, she carefully selected and snipped each stem and added them to the vase, one by one. It was mesmerizing to watch, and he jumped slightly when her phone buzzed. Without thinking, he glanced down at her phone, which flashed a text from Sam, Olivia's ex.

His gut clenched with dread. Olivia quickly reached for her phone and turned it over, but before he had a chance to ask why Sam was texting her, his mom called from across the room, asking him to help set the table.

His head snapped up. He cleared his throat and shook off his discomfort before asking, "Sure, Mom. What do you need?"

"Grab the plates and glasses, will you? Ellen and Tommy should be here soon. Oh, and we're going to sit outside tonight. If that's alright with you, Olivia."

Olivia looked up, her cheeks a dark pink. "Oh, of course, anything is fine with me."

Setting the table gave him a chance to take a few deep breaths. He talked himself off the ledge and told himself to be cool. It wasn't unusual for exes to text. They were probably still untangling a million details after so many years together, but he definitely wanted to reach into the phone and flick this Sam guy on the forehead. That idiot had missed his opportunity with Olivia, and Aiden wasn't about to leave an opening for him to get a second chance.

He walked back to Olivia as she was putting the finishing touches on her bouquet and placed his hand on the small of her back. The curvature of her lower spine warmed his palm.

"You should put them on the table."

He snuck a kiss below Olivia's ear, and she leaned into his lips. Her response was reassuring, and he let the last threads of jealousy float from his body.

Olivia placed the flowers on the table just as Ellen and Tommy made their way into the backyard.

"Helloooo," his big sister, Ellen, called.

She walked onto the patio and set two fruit pies on the table. Like Aiden and Ethan, Ellen shared their mother's dark hair and blue eyes, but unlike her brothers, Ellen also took after their mom in height.

She locked eyes on Olivia's bouquet. "Woah, those flowers are incredible. Mom, where did you get these?"

"You remember Olivia from the dance? She grows and sells them at her farmers market stand on Saturdays," Aiden said, his voice thrumming with pride.

He was pleased to see Olivia's shy smile.

"That's so cool," Ellen said enthusiastically. "Hey! You should do the flowers for our wedding in September. Do you grow dahlias?"

Olivia laughed. "Yeah. I've gone a little crazy with them this year. I have so much more space here that I sort of got carried away."

"Yay! Okay, let's grab coffee sometime soon and hash out the details. Assuming you'll let me hire you?"

“Oh, sure,” Olivia said. She sounded hesitant. “But I've never done a wedding before. Are you sure you don’t want to hire a professional?”

Aiden understood her reasons, but he didn’t like that Olivia downplayed her talent. He lightly bumped his hip against hers, hoping it would encourage Olivia to own her skills.

“Honestly, don't even worry about it. I'm three months pregnant, so this wedding isn't exactly going to be by the book.” Ellen laughed.

“Oh wow! That’s so exciting!” Olivia glanced at Ellen’s midsection.

Ellen pointed to her stomach. “I'm not showing yet, but I guarantee I will be by our wedding.”

Aiden was happy for his sister and her fiancé, Tommy. They’d been together for years. It was just a matter of time until they got married and had kids–or kids first and then marriage. Whatever worked for them. Although his parents would have preferred the more traditional order of things, they were so excited to be grandparents that it didn’t take them long to get over it.

“Well, congratulations two ways!” Olivia said, making Aiden smile.

Ellen laughed.

By then, dinner was mostly ready. At the grill, Tommy helped Ethan check the chicken.

Aiden's mom popped her head out and asked, "Aiden, can you please help your dad to the table?"

"Sure."

He gave Olivia's shoulder a squeeze before walking into the house toward the back of the main floor to his mom and dad's bedroom. He knocked gently on the door before opening it.

The room was dark, with lines of light seeping in from below the curtains.

"Hey, Dad," he whispered tentatively. "You awake?"

"Ai, uh, Ai-den," his dad said through garbled speech.

Given the memory issues he'd been having since his stroke, Aiden's shoulders relaxed when his dad recognized him. He'd also lost a lot of motor control on his right side, which messed with his pronunciation.

"Happy birthday, Dad."

"Thanks," his father said, but it came out sounding more like "fains."

Aiden reached over to slowly turn the dimmer switch to add some light to the room.

His dad was propped up with several pillows. He lifted his left hand in further greeting, and Aiden walked over to him. When he reached down to give his dad a hug, his dad patted Aiden's cheek with his good hand.

"Want some help getting dressed?" Aiden asked.

His dad grunted his consent.

Aiden grabbed the clothes he found draped over a chair near the bed—dress pants and a Polo shirt. First, he helped his dad pull a Polo shirt over the white T-shirt he'd been sleeping in. After that, Aiden helped him out of his pajama pants and into his clean slacks.

Aiden had done this routine a few times now, and it broke his heart every time. His dad had been such a strong man. Aiden had always felt so safe with him, like nothing could ever possibly hurt their family because his dad was there. The role reversal made him fight back tears and swallow hard.

"So, has Mom been taking good care of you?"

A grunt of assent.

"And Ethan hasn't accidentally dumped you out of your wheelchair yet?"

A deeper, more exasperated grunt this time, along with a few quiet chuckles.

"Hey, Dad, I brought a friend tonight. Hope that's alright. Her name is Olivia Olsen. She's from Gresham. We went to high school together."

At this, his dad raised his left eyebrow questioningly.

"Yeah, I like her a lot."

The left side of his dad's mouth lifted with a smile, and he nodded approvingly.

"Let's get you into your chair."

He lifted his dad onto his feet and pivoted him, gently placing him in his wheelchair. After putting his dad's feet in the stirrups, Aiden unlocked the wheels and pushed his dad's wheelchair through the living room, the kitchen, and onto the patio.

Upon seeing the guest of honor, the group whooped and clapped, and Aiden saw Olivia join in good-naturedly.

"Happy Birthday, ya old fart!" Ellen called, walking over to kiss their dad on the cheek. "I made you some pies."

He smiled and nodded, grunting and touching Ellen's hand.

Olivia stood and smiled. Aiden took a moment to introduce her. His dad took her right hand in his left and shook it happily, giving her a squeeze before letting go.

Greetings done, Aiden wheeled his dad to the head of the table, careful not to bump his father's elbows. Once seated, his mom deftly steered the conversation away from his dad, who never wanted to be the recipient of any prolonged attention, doubly so since his stroke.

"Olivia, honey, you sit and pour yourself a glass of wine."

Olivia did so before offering to pour some for Ellen on her left.

"Ugh, thank you!" Ellen said. "I *so* appreciate you not assuming I won't have any wine because I'm pregnant. But I'm going to pass. My heartburn has been acting up today."

"Of course," Olivia said.

“Most people still think you can’t have a drop when you’re pregnant. How did you know? Are you in medicine too, in addition to the farm?”

Olivia laughed. “No, I’ve just had a lot of pregnant friends, and I’ve heard them rant a time or two on the subject.” She turned to Ellen’s husband. “Tommy, nice to see you again, and congrats on the baby.”

Aiden reached for Olivia’s hand under the table and gave it a squeeze. As he did so, he watched her face to see if he could elicit a blush. He wasn’t disappointed.

The dinner went smoothly, and Aiden’s family soaked up Olivia’s charm as easily as he had. He was happy to see Olivia was relaxed with them. She had even snuck in a few witty quips despite Ethan and Ellen’s tendencies to act as the family’s entertainment.

After pie and some loving toasts to their dad, everyone helped carry the dishes inside. Aiden was eternally grateful to his mom when she insisted they take off. He was dying to spend more time alone with Olivia.

Chapter 23 - Olivia

Olivia felt content after the delicious meal with Aiden's family. Other than the awkward moment when Sam texted to apologize because he hadn't gotten around to shipping her stuff, the night couldn't have gone any smoother.

"Thanks again for coming tonight," Aiden said.

"It was my pleasure," she said truthfully. "Your family is…entertaining. And everyone was so kind."

Sometimes being around family brought out a different side of someone, but Olivia hadn't seen that in Aiden. If anything, he seemed at ease in their company.

Though the dinner and conversation were light and positive, obviously intending to keep their dad's spirits high, at times she sensed a misstep in the flow of their conversation–as if their dad's words were missing from the dialogue.

Aiden brushed a lock of hair behind her ear with his free hand. "I think you bring out the best in my family."

She gave his hand a grateful squeeze.

"No pressure, but would you give me a tour of your farm? If nothing else, I would like to understand what a dahlia is and why Ellen is so excited about them."

She laughed. "Sure, I'd love to give you a tour, but you'll have to imagine what it's like in daylight."

They stepped out of the car. Olivia was thankful the mosquito witching hour had passed and the evening was mild. Instead of humidity, the air was thick with the sound of crickets chirping.

Olivia pointed to the bright green bugs flitting in the air. “Oh look, fireflies.”

Aiden reached out and caught one. He held up his cupped hands to let Olivia peek inside. The flickering bug lit up the insides of his palms.

“You’re so gentle. When we were kids, Grace and I would squash them and wipe the glow juice on each other. We were such little monsters.”

“It’s the Hippocratic oath. I’m sworn to do no harm,” he said with mock seriousness.

She shook her head and grinned, letting out a soft chuckle.

Letting the firefly go, Aiden reached for Olivia’s hand and deftly spun her so her body was between him and the car. He stepped toward her, backing her against the passenger door, and she wrapped her arms around his neck. Leaning against her, Aiden lowered his head to whisper in her ear.

“I really like you, Olivia.”

The hot air on her ear and his words made her shiver. She was breathless and tingly all over. *Oh god.* Once again, she was stunned by how much her attraction to him lit her from within.

"I really like you too," she whispered back, feeling the truth of her words deep in her body while also worrying about how fast her feelings were intensifying.

"Can I kiss you?" he asked.

She tilted up her face, meeting him halfway. They took their time, slowly exploring each other's lips. Olivia slid her arms from his neck to touch more of him, caressing his broad shoulders, his chest, his flat stomach, his waist.

Starting at the back of her thighs, Aiden ran his hands up her body, around and over her slight hips, along her ribs, grazing the sides of her breasts with his thumbs. He moved his lips to her neck, kissing the tender spot below her ear.

Olivia moaned with pleasure, and Aiden nipped her earlobe.

She turned her head to meet his lips with hers.

Pushing her hips forward, she rocked against him and heard his breath hitch. "Fuck, Olivia, I want you so bad."

She pulled back, grabbed his hand, and led him inside.

Ms. Darcy lifted her head off the couch when Olivia opened the door, only to curl into a ball and close her eyes as soon as she saw them.

They kicked off their shoes, and Olivia led Aiden up the stairs to her bedroom, keeping one hand intertwined with his. Her body was effervescent with anticipation.

Olivia closed the bedroom door behind them, stepped toward Aiden, and unbuttoned his shirt. As she did, he pulled the left strap of her dress down her shoulder and kissed her collarbone.

Pausing, he removed his unbuttoned shirt and lifted his white undershirt over his head. She took in his bare torso, appreciating the toned muscles and taut skin. His firm chest had a smattering of dark hair. Olivia reached out to touch his firm stomach and let her hands caress his abdomen, drifting toward his waist, grazing the hair running from his navel downward. She ran a finger along the skin beneath the waistband of his jeans where the elastic of his boxers hugged his torso.

A low rumble vibrated in his throat, and he let out a raspy breath. He stepped closer and tipped her chin up, enveloping her with his kiss. Their tongues met, exploring each other from the inside out. He pulled her hips tight against him, and his hardness pressed against her stomach. He untied the wrap of her dress, and the garment fell open and down to the floor.

He paused to look at her. Her face, her torso, her legs, her breasts.

She reached behind her back, unhooked her bra, and let it fall. Uncovered, she paused for him.

"You're so goddamn beautiful, Olivia." His words made her feel cherished.

He leaned down to take a nipple into his mouth and sucked, rolling the tip of his tongue back and forth over her bud. It was Olivia's turn to groan with pleasure when he placed his hand against her inner thigh and moved it toward her center. With his thumb, he pulled her panties aside and caressed her other bud with his fingers. As he did so, he released his pull on her nipple and caught it between his teeth, nipping.

"Ohmygod, Aiden." Olivia arched her back. "Ohmygod." It came out as a one-word prayer for him to please keep doing what he was doing.

"Jesus." His voice was gravelly and raw. "You're so wet."

He caressed and explored her opening, slipping a finger in and out, then two, while he used his palm to continually massage her.

She wrapped her arms around his neck and trembled as he worked magic on her body. The intensity of standing while the orgasm built within her was almost unbearable. Her mouth fell open, and her head tipped back as she cried out through the crest of the wave. Aiden caught her mouth with his and held her, continuing to gently stroke as she trembled through the aftershocks.

When Olivia returned to herself, she unbuttoned his jeans and pushed them down over his hips.

She backed him toward the bed until his legs hit the side, and he was forced to lie down on the white duvet. He propped himself up on his elbows, his eyes boring into her.

She crawled onto the bed next to him and connected her mouth to his. She could taste his desire.

Holding herself up with one hand, she used the other to continue the journey across the planes and curves of his body.

She tugged on the waistband of his briefs, and he lifted his hips, helping her slip them off. She took a moment to explore, gently running her fingers down his length before taking him in her mouth.

"Uhhhh." His sigh was braided with relief, pleasure, and anticipation.

Olivia sucked, nipped, and tugged, letting him in deep one moment, only to lightly kiss his tip the next. It became a game as she counted every "fuck" that escaped his lips, smiling against him with satisfaction.

After several minutes, his body stiffened. "Olivia. Stop. I can't. Wait. I want to."

Incoherent, he pushed her away, and she let him. He looked at her with drunken lust, unable to articulate comprehensible sentences.

After a few ragged breaths, he asked, "Do you want…?"

"Yes!" she interrupted. "Do you have a condom?"

His eyes darted away shyly. "Yes."

"Oh good," she said, relieved. She wanted him to know he wasn't the only one who had considered how this evening might end.

She lay back on her bed and watched him cross the room. Stroking herself slowly, legs parted for him, she admired his nakedness as he retrieved a foil packet from his jeans pocket.

Aiden returned, pausing briefly to watch her before unrolling the condom. He reached down and pulled off her panties, unwrapping her like a gift. He moved over her, his hardness warm against her sensitivity as he kissed her. He rubbed it there, gathering her wetness against him, increasing her pleasure.

He kissed Olivia across her jawline until his mouth hovered above her ear. "I've wanted to do this for so long," he whispered.

"Me too," she said, realizing it was true.

His eyes were reverent as he slowly entered her. "Is this okay?"

"Oh…god. Yes." Olivia's head fell back against the pillow, chin tilting up as her body curved in pleasure. A key deep within her turned, releasing all tension from her body.

He grinned, and a touch of ego showed on his face. She met his eyes and smiled back.

When he started to move, she raised her hips to meet him, wave after wave, thrust after thrust.

As their bodies began to know each other, Aiden rolled over so Olivia was straddling him. She moved her hips, now in complete control, and the tension returned as her body sought a second climax. He reached between them and massaged to help her get there.

She cried out once more and collapsed onto him. He continued pumping his hips from below as she shivered in ecstasy. Moments later, his pace quickened, and he drove hard into her, guttural noises escaping from deep within him as he unlocked his own release.

For a moment, neither moved from the spot. Olivia rested her body on top of his, and Aiden's hand gently stroked her back as they caught their breath, damp and panting from exertion.

After a quick, playful shower filled with kisses and caresses, they lay in bed, facing each other, silly smiles on their lips. Their heads rested on their respective pillows, but their legs were intertwined beneath the sheets. The room's darkness graciously muted the intensity vibrating between them.

"You should come down to the Cities and stay with me if you can get away from the market for a weekend."

Olivia appreciated the offer, but she didn't want him to feel obligated or to feel whatever was between them had to be something it wasn't. "Oh, it's okay, you don't have to do that."

"Do what?"

"You know," Olivia said awkwardly, trying to let him know she wasn't going to pine for him after one night of sex…she hoped.

"So, you're saying I don't have to hang out with a sweet, beautiful woman who makes me laugh? Oh man, *what a relief*," he said teasingly.

Olivia fought to control her lips, which were trying to split her face into an embarrassingly joyful smile. "This is all just very…unexpected. Like not in a million years expected. Come on, you must feel the same way."

Aiden looked at her quizzically. "I mean, I never thought you were coming back from Seattle, so yeah, I'd agree. But this attraction between us has always been there, at least from my side of things."

"Ohhh, riiight," Olivia said sarcastically. "The kindergarten kiss."

"Wait." He looked at her, his expression serious. He lifted his eyebrows skeptically, "What? You don't remember?"

"Remember what?" Olivia placed a finger on his dimple.

He looked at her expectantly. "The summer after senior year?"

Olivia thought back and remembered seeing more of him that summer. After graduation, all the different groups in their high school class started hanging out together, like all of the things keeping them apart during the previous twelve years of school had been erased by graduation.

She shook her head, not able to conjure a specific Aiden interaction. They hadn't had sex. She'd definitely still been a virgin at that point, and she was pretty sure they hadn't kissed. *Surely* she would have remembered kissing Aiden. Had they talked or something?

"We were at my family's cabin, just down the road?" He paused again, as if that would somehow make the memory click, but it didn't. "Oh wow, you really don't remember, do you?" He sounded genuinely surprised.

"I remember seeing you at a bunch of parties, and I vaguely remember a party at your family's cabin. But not much else. To be fair, though, that was the summer I discovered vodka cranberry, dare I say, cocktails? I was such a goody two shoes all through high school, and knowing I was leaving for Seattle, I think I let my inhibitions way down that summer." Olivia giggled at the memories she *had* retained.

"Now it's embarrassing how well *I* remember."

Olivia was dying to know what had transpired between them. He reached out, seeking her hand, and played with her fingers.

“So, we were at the cabin, and you were with your friend Maddy. You showed up to my party with this confidence and freedom like you didn’t care what any of us were going to do with the rest of our lives. You were there to dance and laugh and apparently drink a lot of vodka cranberries.”

“Oh funny, yeah, I mean, I actually did give zero fucks at that point. I had spent so many years trying to stay in my lane. Once I knew I was leaving, it all seemed so trivial.”

She didn’t share that she had developed a mild superiority complex because she had figured out how to get out of Minnesota when most everyone else from their graduating class hadn’t. And now here she was, sleeping with the prom king.

“It’s funny you remember that night so well. Did we dance or something?” she asked.

She prayed she hadn't been grinding on him. That was the only thing she could imagine beyond talking that would have left such an impression on him.

“Yeah, we danced.” Aiden grinned bashfully. “And…we went skinny dipping. Nothing happened, thank god. Especially now I know how sauced you were. But you kept laughing at me like I was this hilarious joke you couldn’t get over. It intrigued the hell out of me.”

Olivia tried hard once more to recall the night, wanting to have the memory for herself, but she figured she must have fully written Gresham off by then. The thought of them swimming naked together made her giddy for her eighteen-year-old self.

"So, you don't remember waiting on me like every day at Jill's for the next two weeks after that?" he asked.

"Oh, yeah, *that* I remember. That was weird. But I assumed you were perpetually hungover and really needed French Toast."

Olivia laughed, considering those brief exchanges in a whole new light.

She leaned into her pillow a little more. "I do remember you smiling at me a lot, but I figured you just wanted attention because you were such a notorious ladies' man. And I remember being sort of indignant about it and trying to ignore you."

"*Are you kidding me? That drove me insane*!" He smacked his pillow for emphasis.

Olivia burst out laughing. When she recovered, she remembered one more detail. "Wait, but weren't you with Ashley Lund?"

His eyes intensified, and his expression turned serious. "I broke up with her the morning after you and I went skinny dipping."

He gave her hand a squeeze as if to emphasize the impact their brief connection had on him.

"Shut up! You're lying!"

"No." He smiled. "I swear. I went to her house the next morning and broke it off. I think she was relieved, though. That whole high school sweetheart thing had run its course."

"Oh yeah, that whole prom royalty thing? That was tough, huh?" Olivia said sarcastically.

"Oh my god. You don't remember being naked together, but you remember that silliness?"

"Please, *everyone* remembers that."

"If you say so."

"Okay, so what happened? Why didn't you ask me out if I had you so wrapped up in knots?"

He smiled. "Well, I wanted to, but you were leaving. And the attitude you gave me every time I walked into Jill's totally threw me for a loop. I finally ran into Maddy at a party, and she gave me your number, but when I called the next day, your dad said you'd already left for Seattle."

"Yeah, that makes sense." Olivia nodded, cheek rubbing against her soft pillow. "I didn't get my first cellphone until I got to Seattle, and my mom and I left three weeks before classes began so we could stop at all the national parks on the way."

After a brief pause, Olivia said in a teasing voice, "Awww, poor Aiden, I bet you had never experienced failure before."

He unclasped her hand and playfully tugged on a lock of her hair before running it through his fingers. "You know, that summer of freedom seems to have stuck with you. You still don't care what anyone in Gresham thinks of you, do you?" His tone sounded as if he admired her for this.

"Oh, I wouldn't go that far. I'm a lot more sober these days."

"At times," he teased.

Olivia laughed, remembering her birthday party. "You know, there is something to be said for being in your thirties. I definitely feel more comfortable in my own skin. But all the same, it's hard to be fully myself here, especially if I want people to buy vegetables from me. You know how it is. The fact I don't go to church automatically puts me at a disadvantage, not to mention I'm so obviously a women's libber. If I hadn't been born and raised here, and if my dad didn't do business with half of this town, I wouldn't stand a chance."

"Hmmm…" Aiden said thoughtfully. "I think you underestimate the power of your likability."

Olivia squirmed in delight. She rolled over and tucked herself against him as a "little spoon" so he couldn't see the grin hijacking her face.

"I appreciate that," she said.

"Good." He kissed the back of her neck lightly.

After a minute, Olivia decided to make her own confession. "So, I guess I have something sort of embarrassing to admit as well."

"Yes?" Aiden sounded eager.

“I might have dreamed about you since high school.”

Aiden’s eyebrows lifted, but he didn’t say anything.

“A few times,” she added quickly.

“Did you?” he asked in a playful tone. “I think you’re going to have to tell me more–it’s only fair.”

“There’s not a lot to tell. You just showed up a few times in my dreams, and we might have done what we just did. It was random. Don’t read too much into it.”

She was starting to regret her confession, but Aiden nuzzled his nose in her hair, and she could feel him breathe in deeply. The sensation was enough to reassure her.

“You forgot to give me a tour of your garden,” he whispered.

“*Did I?*”

He chuckled.

“What time do you have to leave tomorrow morning?” she asked through a yawn.

“Five.”

“*Oofda.* That’s too early. The garden will be here next time you're in town.”

The next morning, Olivia saw Aiden off. She placed a hastily made cup of coffee in his car's cupholder while he threw his bag in the backseat.

He turned around and gave Olivia a hug goodbye. She let him in for a PG peck on the lips, hoping to spare him from her morning breath.

"Don't forget to check your schedule. I owe you a proper date." He gave her one more brief kiss before driving away.

When his car was gone from sight, Olivia returned to bed, but she was too twitterpated to fall back asleep. She relived the prior evening in her head, analyzing every word, trying once again to remember the story he had told her. After a full hour of basking, she gave up on sleep and got out of bed to start her chores.

The day was the least productive she could remember since moving home. She couldn't stop checking her phone, but she had zero regrets. She thought back to the conversation she'd had with her mom on her birthday—about harnessing joy and remembering the point of it all. She was allowed to enjoy herself, even if the future was uncertain.

Olivia was about to cave and text Aiden first when her phone vibrated.

Aiden: *Thanks again for last night and for coming to my dad's bday. Everyone loved you.*

Olivia: *That's sweet. Thank you.*

Aiden: *No, really.*

Then he sent a screenshot of a text exchange with his mom.

Mom: *Olivia is darling. Everyone loved her. Don't fuck this up.*

Aiden: *Thanks for the sage advice, mom.*

Olivia laughed out loud. Grinning widely, she typed out a reply.

Olivia: *Woah! Your mom used the F bomb! (Mouth open emoji)*

Aiden: *You should know she reserves that word for only extremely special occasions.*

Olivia: *I'm. So. honored.*

And she kind of was. She was glad she'd made a good impression on his family, but to be fair, they had made it very easy on her. Though she did worry his mom's expectations were too high. Were their moms about to start planning a wedding that was never going to happen? They still lived two hours from each other, and Aiden would be doing his fellowship in Saint Paul for at least a few more years. Those facts weren't exactly the foundation for a solid relationship.

She took a deep breath and let it out as she read Aiden's last text.

Aiden: *Let me know if you can get away for a weekend. Ms. Darcy is welcome to join us.*

Olivia smiled, grateful he had pursued the point, not once, not twice, but three times. It had removed any hint of the invite being anything less than a genuine desire to spend more time together.

Olivia: *I'm pretty sure I can. I just need to see if I can get my mom to help me out with the CSA. I'll figure something out and send you some dates.*

Aiden: *Sounds good. Let me know if you want me to ask Ethan if he can help as well. He owes me a favor.*

Olivia: *Lol...I think I'm good, but I'll let you know.*

As the days passed and they volleyed texts back and forth, Olivia grew more and more smitten. She was also more terrified. Their chemistry was fantastic, but the

longer she spent in Gresham, the more it seemed like it was exactly where she needed to be. It was becoming increasingly difficult to ignore the tug behind her belly button pulling her toward co-ownership of the farm with Philip.

Obviously, Aiden wouldn't give up his fellowship program. Even if they stuck it out with long distance for the next three years, she didn't think Gresham offered opportunities to specialize in pediatric emergency medicine.

Where did that leave them? Perpetual long distance? Olivia wasn't twenty-four anymore. If she wanted *all the things*, she couldn't have fun without an endgame. That was how she ended up in a six-year relationship with Sam, headed nowhere. At the same time, she loved being in Aiden's presence. He was kind and funny and oh-so-good in bed, not to mention the easy energy between them. She wondered how long she could keep seeing him before it would hurt too much to stop.

After an hour of obsessing, she sent out an SOS to Jessa, asking her to meet for a video chat to help Olivia sort through her buzzing emotions and half-frantic thoughts.

Jessa, a fitness guru, answered Olivia's call while riding her stationary bike. She was breathing heavily when she said, "So what's up, Olivia dear? Are you in love or what?"

"Woah, woah, woah, let's not jump the gun here. I'm just a little...overwhelmed and maybe a bit confused."

"And you can't eat, and you can't sleep, and you find yourself smiling for no reason?" Jessa teased.

"Okay, no, it's definitely not *that* bad. I mean, I'm still eating."

Jessa let out a loud bark of a laugh, momentarily pausing her bike. She recovered and got her legs moving again. "So, what's the problem, chica?"

Oliva brought Jessa up to speed.

"And so, it seems like this is a huge waste of time because he lives in Saint Paul, and I live here, and my ovaries don't have time to mess around."

"You're only thirty-one, Olivia! You've got time. Your eggs are still very much in good working order."

Unexpectedly, Olivia's eyes welled at her friend's reassuring words.

"And as for the distance thing, can't you let yourself have a little fun with a man who seems genuinely nice? Like, so much better than Sam it's not even funny?" Jessa had never pulled punches when it came to her dislike of Sam.

"I mean, I guess."

"Did you or did you not come twice last night thanks to this Aiden fellow?"

"I did."

"Case closed."

Olivia laughed, not totally sure the case had been closed, but she also knew Jessa, and in Jessa's mind, having fun without an endgame was the whole point of life.

"Also, sweetie, I know you, and I know where your head is at," Jessa continued. "There are too many unknowns and too few good guys out there to pass this up. Just…let yourself be selfish for a change. For a little while, at least."

Olivia thought about this for a moment. Though she hadn't needed to, she had been asking for permission to keep seeing Aiden and keep letting herself feel all the things for him, even though it was risking her heart.

"Okay."

"Okay?" Jessa asked excitedly.

"Okay."

"Okay! Now stop crying, and let's talk about what you're going to wear next time you see this fine man. Or perhaps what you're *not* going to wear…" Jessa laughed at her own joke.

After Olivia and Jessa ended their chat, Olivia called her mom.

"Hey, sweetie," her mom answered. "You okay?"

"Yes, I have a favor to ask…"

Chapter 24 - Olivia

Aiden: *Excited to see you. I hope you are ready to eat all the soup dumplings! (dumpling and chopstick emojis)*

Olivia: *I'm impressed by how well you speak "Olivia." How did you know soup dumplings are the things I've been missing most?*

Aiden: *Because you're human. How could you not?*

Olivia: *Good point. I'm looking forward to seeing you too.*

Olivia spent the drive to Aiden's Saint Paul apartment oscillating between thrilled and anxious. Things with Aiden had been good. Really, really scary good. And despite her conversation with Jessa, it was hard not to contemplate all the possibilities and contingency plans for her and Aiden.

Olivia looked out her window at the lush green fields interspersed with blue ponds and reedy green sloughs. As she entered the suburbs, the fields were replaced by car lots, outlet malls, and box stores, and the distance between highway exit ramps got shorter and shorter.

She had to rely on GPS since she hadn't spent much time in either Minneapolis or Saint Paul beyond the airport. Her family had made the trip once or twice a year when she was a kid, often because she or her sister had a 4-H project to show at the Minnesota State Fair. If they were lucky, their parents would also take them to a Twins baseball game and the local amusement park to ride water slides and roller coasters unceasingly until after dark.

Without a doubt, those were some of her fondest family memories, even though at the time she had been hot and sticky with a sore belly filled with sugary fried foods, not to mention totally sleep deprived from late nights watching movies in their hotel room. They'd shed a lot of overtired tears, but her mom had kept them going, usually with more sugar.

Olivia's busy brain made quick work of the drive from the city limits to downtown Saint Paul. Aiden's eight-story complex was all sleek lines and modernity. *Ah city life.* She sighed wistfully before pulling out her phone to text Aiden.

Chapter 25 - Aiden

Aiden pounded the elevator's *Door Close* button, anxious to get down to the ground floor and out the door to see Olivia. After less than two weeks, he had missed her, but he didn't want to examine that reality too closely. At that moment, he wanted her in his arms—in his bed.

The elevator finally opened, and he strode through the front door of his building. Aiden looked around until he spotted Olivia standing near her car. *Oh, thank fuck.* His body physically vibrated with energy at the sight of her. She was there, and he could kiss her.

He walked over to her and wrapped his arms around her. She looked into his eyes and tilted her head so he could press his lips to hers. The kiss sent a bolt of heat down his torso.

He wanted more. He slowly trailed his hands down her back, traveling along the delicate curve of her spine until he was cupping her ass, pulling her closer.

Olivia pulled back suddenly, and he could hear her taking air in alongside his own ragged breathing.

"Upstairs?" she asked.

He was both relieved and amped. "Yeah."

Aiden grabbed Olivia's overnight bag and guided her across the lobby's marble floors to the elevators and waited for the doors to open. He casually caressed her neck while they waited, circling his fingertips at the base of her hairline, and was rewarded with her shiver.

He strategically placed himself behind Olivia as the elevator opened to let out an elegantly dressed older couple. He wondered if they noticed the flush on Olivia's face. The thought activated a primal possessiveness in his brain. As soon as the elevator doors closed, Aiden turned and pressed his body to Olivia's, her back firm against the rear wall of the elevator. He kissed her neck and couldn't stop touching her everywhere. His hands roamed her contours, cupping her breasts, then feeling the fullness of her ass in his palms.

Her moan vibrated against his lips. Without thinking, he moved his hands behind Olivia's thighs and lifted. She wrapped her legs around his waist. Her softness pressed against his hardness, and she moved against him, tilting her pelvis up and down. He growled his frustration at the clothes keeping their bodies apart. Olivia bit her lower lip, seeming to fight back a laugh.

The elevator dinged, making both of them jump. Without thinking, he twirled around and put her back to his front, arms around her chest, holding her tight to keep her warmth against him.

When they discovered the ding had only announced their floor, Aiden guided Olivia forward out of the elevator and down the hallway to his apartment door.

In seconds, they were inside. He tossed his keys on the counter, kicked off his shoes, and pulled her by the hand to his bedroom.

"I'm hoping you want this as bad as I do," he said, "but tell me if you want to slow down."

"No, yeah, yes. I want this. Badly." Olivia's heavy-lidded eyes mirrored her words.

Aiden entered her space again as soon as they crossed the threshold to his bedroom, not bothering to close the door behind them. His hands trailed up her hips, and he grabbed her dress hem. Olivia lifted her arms so he could pull it over her head. His eyes moved from her face to the burgundy bra covering her perfect breasts.

He kissed her through the lace of her bra, remembering her pleasure. Olivia gripped his shoulders, shuddering, and he wanted to howl his satisfaction.

He trailed kisses down her chest to her stomach, to her navel, and down until he was kneeling, ready to worship at the altar of her sex, this beautiful goddess who had opened herself to him.

He moved his hand up her inner thigh, grazing her gently. The touch was fleeting as he slowly pulled her panties down over her hips until they were freed. He let them slip through his fingers as they fell to the floor. He wanted Olivia to spread open for him, so he could see all of her hidden spaces. Moving forward on his knees, hands on her hips, he gently guided her to the chair in the corner of his bedroom. Her knees splayed open for him. He paused to take in her beautiful, perfect sex.

Moving forward, he kissed her inner thighs, first one, then the other. She trembled, and he pulled back.

"Is this okay?" he asked.

"Yes, please." He could hear the pleading in her voice.

Her body jolted in response to the first lick of his tongue, and he heard her inhale a shaky "Uhn." He buried his face against her, taking in the scent of her, and she relaxed into this touch. He tasted and sucked. Placing a finger at her wet entrance, he circled the edge of her core before pressing into her. He moved his fingers to help her find her internal release as he continued to work her external pleasure with his mouth.

As the tension in her body built, she dug her hands into his hair, and her hips rocked, moving against his mouth. She moaned and begged. "Oh god, fuck, yes, please, yes, Aiden. Oh my god."

He felt like a fucking hero when her inner walls tightened around his fingers and she screamed into his bedroom.

Her body collapsed back, completely open, any lingering self-consciousness washed away by the pulsating waves of her orgasm. He pulled his head back to watch the ecstasy on her face, her head thrown back against the chair, lips parted, hair wildly strewn about over her shoulders and breasts. As he took in the stunning sight, he gently stroked her until her body was sated.

She lifted her head to meet his gaze and licked her dry lips. He was dying to have her now.

She leaned forward and motioned for him to stand. Reaching forward, she unbuttoned his pants, pulling them down his hips until he could step out of them. He was perfectly placed for her to put her lips against his sensitive tip, giving him a kiss and licking once before pulling away. The muscles in his thighs went rigid.

"Fuck, I want to be inside of you now, Olivia. Please, now."

She stood, holding him in her hand, and kissed him deeply. His tongue thrust in and out of her mouth as she stroked him. He pushed her back onto his bed, savoring the sight of her body against his blankets before pulling away to grab a condom from his nightstand.

Olivia gazed at his hands as he slipped on the condom. Responding to the desire flickering in her eyes, he stroked himself slowly as he made his way back to her.

Climbing on the bed next to her, he turned her onto her side, his front to her back, and placed himself at the rear of her entrance. She pushed back against him and reached down between her legs to guide him inside. He was overcome by the sensation of her soft, wet heat holding tightly around him as he entered her from behind.

"Uhhh." They collectively sighed at the pleasure created by connecting their bodies once again. Olivia looked back over her shoulder at Aiden and smiled devilishly.

He was finding his rhythm when Olivia began pulsing around him.

"Oh fuck, Olivia, you're going to make me come."

"Isn't that the goal?" she teased through her own quiet moans of pleasure.

"My pride says otherwise," he grunted. Trying to hold on, he set his jaw in determination.

In one fluid motion, he rolled her over so she was on top, draped over him, her back to his chest. Aiden moved inside her once again from below, but this time with more control. He slid one hand down her stomach, over her soft mound, until his fingers were against her, massaging to help her find her climax once more. She reached back and clutched the bedding, and he was pleased to be creating dissatisfaction when she had been content moments before.

"Oh, shit. Aiden. Again?"

"Yes, again, Olivia!"

She did. The thread snapped, and once again, she shook until her body went limp against his, laying atop him so he could caress every part of her. He turned her once more, this time more slowly, so he didn't interrupt her pleasure. Now she was beneath him, her face turned to the side against his smooth pillow, stomach to the bed. He found his rhythm again inside her, and she moved her hips back and forth. He came hard inside her, his body convulsing in pleasure. He groaned against her cheek, taking in deep breaths of her sweet lavender scent.

He collapsed down onto her, trying to offset some of his weight onto the mattress while also feeling her soft, warm body beneath him. After a moment, Aiden rolled to the side so they were nose to nose. He kissed her softly on the lips, and her eyelids fluttered open.

"That was…" He tried to find words to express the gratitude overwhelming his chest cavity for all of her but couldn't find any worth uttering.

"Yeah, I know…"

"We should do that again sometime."

"Yeah, it'd be a pity not to."

They lay there, close enough to feel each other's breath, and he drew circles on her back.

"As much as I don't want to leave this bed, I owe you a proper date."

"That's okay, I don't mind," she said through a yawn.

"No, no, we have to get up. I insist on showing you a good time outside this room."

Olivia smiled warmly. "If you *insist*."

"I definitely do," he said.

“Okay, but let me shower first. Also, can you make me some coffee? I don’t think I’m going to make it anywhere without some caffeine.”

“Yes.” He smiled, kissed her nose, and they bumbled their way out of bed to his ensuite bathroom.

Chapter 26 - Olivia

They drove across town and pulled into the small parking lot of an even smaller Taiwanese restaurant.

"How'd you hear about this place?" she asked, taking in the fluorescent-lit decor.

"A friend from undergrad introduced me."

"I am *so* excited." Olivia opened the menu. In the end, she asked Aiden to order for them after giving him a high-level overview of her preferences.

He ordered a couple dozen soup dumplings as well as some noodles with chicken and stir-fried Bok choy.

They barely talked while eating other than to say things like, "Oh my god, this is so good," and "Woah, yum," and "Let's never eat anywhere else ever."

It was the most flavor she'd had in months, and it satisfied cravings that had been haunting her since leaving Seattle.

Sprawling against the back of her seat, she pushed her plate away and groaned. "I am soooo full. You can put me to bed now."

"Oh no, no, no. We're just getting started. The night is young, and I have a surprise for you."

"*What?* What is it?" she demanded. Olivia had a love-hate relationship with surprises.

"Well, I remember you talking about how much you miss going to shows, so I took a chance and got us tickets to a Tune-Yards concert. They're playing at the park tonight. If you hate them or don't feel up for it, I totally understand. But I saw them in Portland with my sister, and to quote Lauren, 'they're pretty rad,' especially live."

"Oh, that sounds fun! I don't know them, but I trust your taste in music."

He quirked a grin, and his eyes sparkled with pleasure. "Why's that?"

"You won me over with The Be Good Tanyas the morning you made me brunch."

"Can I confess something?" he asked sheepishly.

"Yes," Olivia said hesitantly.

"I texted Lauren the night before to ask what music I should play to impress you."

Olivia's head fell back, and she laughed, mouth open wide. She was delighted by his confession. "Stop! That's hilarious!"

"Honestly!" He grinned proudly. "Clearly it was a good move on my part."

"Now I trust *Lauren's* taste in music. Jury is still out on yours," she teased.

"I feel like I should get second-hand credit for trusting my little sister with these decisions."

Olivia raised an eyebrow as if considering. “Okay, sure. Second-hand credit is all yours.”

Aiden reached over and chucked her under her chin like an old-timey movie. He paused to brush her lips with his thumb before pulling away. Olivia tried to hide her shiver.

“So, what's Lauren's story? How'd she end up in Portland?” she asked, hoping to distract him from noticing how much power he had over her body.

“Well, probably similar to you in her desire to get out of Gresham. And she's a lesbian, so I think she was seeking a safe space to be herself, so to speak.”

“Ah yes, that makes sense. I think Gresham has gotten more conservative since I left, if that's even possible! How'd your parents take the news?”

“It's a weird situation, to be honest. They're accepting of LGBTQ folks, but it's like they don't believe she's actually gay, like this is just a phase.”

“Huh, that’s kind of sad.” Olivia considered how that dynamic must have impacted Lauren. “It must be tough for her. Has she ever brought someone home?”

“No, but she's only twenty-three. She and Ethan are twins.” As an afterthought, he added, “So she's *obviously* way too young for something serious.” He grinned and tapped her foot under the table.

“What does Ethan think of the whole thing?”

"They've got that weird twin energy. I think he may have accepted she was gay before she did. They're still super close. They talk every day."

"Awww…that's sweet. What about Ellen?"

"Oh, she's totally fine, but she was out of the house by the time the twins were five. They've never been close. Lauren grew up surrounded by brothers, and she was always tough as nails."

"Fascinating. So what's up with your parents? Is it some sort of denial thing?"

"I hate to say this, but I think it has a lot more to do with how she looks." He paused, considering how to explain. "Frankly, she isn't *butch*. She's pretty and kinda traditionally feminine, ya know? And she dated boys in high school, so I think that confuses them. They're part of a generation clinging to an outdated idea of what a lesbian is 'supposed' to look and act like."

"Well, I guess they'll have to accept it when she eventually falls in love and it gets serious."

"I guess so."

"When were you in Portland?"

"I was there for a conference last summer and made a trip out of it. Ethan joined us, which was great. But I've never been to Seattle. Are they pretty similar?"

"Yeah, sort of. A lot of people say Portland is twenty years behind Seattle in terms of development and culture, but they mean it in a superior, less sold-out sort of way. I loved going to Portland to shop and eat since the food is amazing, and they don't have sales tax."

"That's not very progressive of you, skirting your taxes. Tsk tsk." He reached for Olivia's hand across the table and caressed his thumb back and forth across her knuckles as they waited for the check. It did things to her, but she feigned nonchalance.

Olivia flipped her hand over to interlock their fingers.

Without meaning to, she thought of Sam and how quickly the playful phase of their relationship had ended. Whatever happened between Aiden and her, she hoped this desire to touch each other, innocent or otherwise, stayed fresh.

"Meh, Seattleites are hypocrites when it comes to taxes. Washington has the most regressive tax code in the nation. Plus, I'm still from Gresham. Looking for ways to save money is in my blood."

He chuckled.

Olivia's phone buzzed, and she flipped it over to see Grace had texted her a photo.

"Speaking of sisters…" She unlocked her phone screen to see the picture Grace had sent. She assumed it would be something silly. But it was a picture of Grace and Abesh, and Grace's new engagement ring.

"Woah," she accidentally said out loud, stunned.

"Is this a good thing?" Aiden asked, sounding tentative.

"Oh yeah! Of course! Abesh is great. I was just surprised. Sorry, give me a minute to respond."

She sent her sister all of the celebration emojis she could find. By the time she was done, she was smiling with genuine joy for Grace.

"I don't mean to pry, but it seemed like your initial reaction was a little shocked. Are you worried they're not ready?" he asked.

"Oh, no, not at all." She paused to consider how she could articulate her thoughts. "I hate to admit it, but I think I was surprised." She hesitated before saying, "I kind of assumed I'd get married first." She shrugged and added, "I know it's silly. It's just…she's four years younger than me, but I'm genuinely so thrilled for her. They're a fantastic match."

"It's not silly," he reassured her. "Society puts all kinds of weird pressure on us around weddings, especially in the Midwest. If it weren't the case, I probably wouldn't be a divorcé."

"No?" Olivia asked curiously, hoping he would say more.

"No. I would have lived in sin with Rebecca until things ended naturally. Instead, we got married at twenty-three because we felt like we had to. I had a long road of medical school ahead of me, and she wanted to follow me wherever I landed. But when you think about it, it is absolute silliness to expect a modern twenty-three-year-old to be mature enough to commit to someone for the next, what, seventy years? Or at least it was for me."

"Well, I appreciate your understanding." Olivia was relieved he hadn't judged her reaction as petty.

With that, they scooted their way out of their booth, ready to head for the show.

The Tune-Yards show was "capital-F" *Fun*. Olivia loved the way the lead singer looped her voice into the music, and the band's energy had the crowd on its feet, dancing and bouncing to the rhythm.

The collective energy made her soul feel lighter than it had in weeks. She made a mental note to prioritize visits to the Cities for shows and good food. The two-hour drive from Gresham was much shorter than the drive from Seattle to Portland, and she had made that trek at least three times per year, even if Sam often instigated those trips. Sam worshiped Portland and talked about moving there, but it never appealed to Olivia in the same way. So, she resisted, using her job as an excuse not to move.

After the show, Olivia was exhausted, and they collapsed into bed. Gazing at the ceiling, she thanked Aiden for the thoughtful evening and for giving her a taste of the things she missed about living in the city.

"For tomorrow, I was thinking maybe we could meet up with some of my friends from undergrad. Would that be okay with you?" he asked quietly.

"Yes, that'd be great," Olivia whispered back.

He pulled her to him so her head rested on his chest, and her eyelids fluttered closed. She felt one last kiss on her head before drifting to sleep.

Chapter 27 - Aiden

The next morning, Aiden pulled Olivia against him, and they took advantage of their rested and rejuvenated bodies.

While the physicality of their time together was a huge plus, Aiden wanted to make sure Olivia felt their connection was deeper than purely physical. When the weekend was over, he hoped he could convince Olivia to put up with the long-distance drive between them until they could figure out something else. What that solution might be, he didn't know yet, but he wasn't ready to give up. Things between them were amazing and getting better with every hour they spent together.

Eventually, they were too hungry and in need of caffeine to lounge in bed any longer. They untangled their limbs and ventured into the mid-morning warmth.

"Let's go," he said, pulling on her hand to get her out of bed.

"Where are we going?"

"There's a coffee shop and a farmers market just around the corner."

They grabbed pour-over coffees to go, and he showed her around his neighborhood. He brought her to a farmers market a few blocks away, as promised. It was twice the size of Gresham's, and the produce was gorgeous. Olivia helped him pick some veggies to cook omelets back at his place, and they sauntered home.

The day continued at its unhurried pace as they lazed around at his apartment. It was as if a metronome was beating a lazy tempo to ensure they savored every moment. Aiden basked in their smitten feelings, knowing he had the annoying self-satisfied air of a man who had coupled up with someone a little out of his league. Their fingers and limbs naturally found each other, regardless of their location or activity.

At some point, Aiden turned on the TV to an afternoon Twins game, and Olivia fell asleep with her head in his lap as he played with her hair. In a word, the day was perfect.

Chapter 28 - Olivia

With much reluctance, they eventually got up from the couch and rejoined the outside world to meet up with Aiden's friends for dinner and drinks.

Olivia kept it casual, wearing a sundress and strappy sandals. Aiden had said the restaurant was a lowkey barbeque spot, and she was relieved to see it was as laid back as he'd promised. The interior had dark wood paneling, and the tables were mismatched—as if they'd been reclaimed from several grandparents' basements.

His friend, Ryan, had already gotten them a table for six—the three of them plus Aiden's best friend Isaac and his wife June, as well as another friend named Amber. All except June had gone through the University of Minnesota's pre-med program together, and they'd all landed jobs in the Minneapolis-Saint Paul metro.

Isaac and June arrived shortly after Aiden and Olivia. The atmosphere was relaxed as they drank and snacked on chips, hushpuppies, and chicken wings.

No one seemed fazed when a half hour passed, and they were still waiting for Amber, so Olivia assumed it was to be expected and rolled with it. When Amber finally arrived, she did so with a bang.

Instead of matching the restaurant's laid-back vibe, she looked like she was ready to party, wearing a mini skirt and a sparkly crop top that emphasized all of her ample curves. More than Amber's confidence rocking the skirt and top, Olivia was most impressed by Amber's five-inch heels—shoes Olivia would never attempt, and not just because she was five foot nine.

The table paused to say hello and tease Amber for being late. *(Again!)* But no one batted an eye at the outfit. Clearly, that path had been well trod. Olivia smiled along, mostly curious to observe the group dynamics. She was surprised when Amber sat next to her in their booth and gave her a big hug.

"Oh, hello." Olivia laughed to cover up her discomfort, which was rising as her Spidey-senses tingled a warning that all might not be right with the world now that Amber was here.

"It is so nice to meet you! Aiden cannot shut up about how great you are," Amber said a little too enthusiastically.

At that moment, Olivia's intuition grew from a tickle to an all-out warning siren that a tornado was coming and she should seek shelter immediately.

Her mother's words ran through her mind, "When you're not sure about someone's intentions, play happy and dumb, sweet pea."

Well, let the games begin.

“Awww, that's so sweet,” Olivia replied enthusiastically, leaning over and giving Aiden a kiss on the cheek. He turned his head to catch her lips with his.

“Get a room,” Isaac and Ryan said simultaneously, and they all laughed.

Out of the corner of her eye, Amber’s face took on a sour look, further increasing Olivia’s suspicions that Amber was less than enthused about her presence. But Olivia kept her dumb, happy smile glued to her face.

“So, what are some embarrassing stories about Aiden from your college days?” Olivia asked to deflect some of the attention away from her.

Isaac and Ryan grinned at the invitation to give their buddy a hard time. Aiden smiled and shook his head, and Olivia swore she could hear him thinking, “Here we go.” It was what Olivia would have been thinking if the tables were turned.

“So,” Isaac began, “did Aiden ever tell you about the time he went streaking on Halloween during our junior year?”

“Ummm, *no*. You must have been freezing.”

Ryan picked up the story, saying, “Oh yes, yes, he was quite cold. And when he ran into one of the hottest girls in our program…” Ryan abruptly paused his train of thought as Amber opened her mouth to object. “I know, I know, obviously excluding you, Amber. So anyway, he was really into her, but let’s just say she took a very good look and gave him the cold shoulder after that. She never responded to another text from him."

"It was cold!" Aiden protested. "There was shrinkage!"

The entire table was laughing, including Aiden.

"That is hilarious," Olivia said. After a moment, she added, "But I thought you started dating Rebecca when you were a freshman?"

In unison, all four of Aiden's friends said, "They were on a break!" obviously quoting Ross from Friends.

Olivia liked them all very much…well, except maybe Amber. She was still wary, but she was starting to see a pattern of personality characteristics that seemed broader than anything to do with Olivia. Maybe Amber was the attention-needing type, in which case, no harm, no foul.

The dinner continued in much the same way. Despite the Amber discomfort, it was nice to be out to dinner with people her own age.

It might be time to start making more of an effort to find like-minded folks in Gresham. Especially if this move home is more of a long-term commitment than I was originally willing to admit.

Olivia had hit a point in her life where she had great friends, even if they were in different cities. Her desire to put in the effort required to make new ones wasn't as strong as it had been in her early twenties. However, even though Olivia was very content to putter around by herself at home, her projects weren't a replacement for comradery.

After dinner, they headed to the bar side of the restaurant to play a few rounds of pool. They'd all had at least a couple of beers each, and Olivia was feeling more and more delighted to have this time to get to know Aiden through his friends. They were shocked to find out he had been a total hotshot in high school. When she told them he had been their class's prom king, they laughed so hard that people at nearby tables stopped their conversations to look over.

Olivia was pleased to know her own unique piece of Aiden's history and that their roots were inherently intertwined. She was also pleasantly surprised Aiden had chosen to humbly withhold all of that history when he'd started college, opting instead for a fresh start.

At the pool table, they played teams of three versus three. As the weakest link, Olivia was paired on a team with Ryan, the group's pool shark, and June, who was average. The game was relatively close when it came time for Olivia to embarrass herself. She fumbled her way through her turn, grateful to have steered clear of the eight ball.

When Olivia turned back around, her mouth fell open. Amber was glued to Aiden's right side, her hands hanging onto his shoulder. Olivia froze, and her heart raced as she tried to understand what was unfolding in front of her. Aiden seemed to be ignoring Amber as he spoke with Isaac, but Olivia couldn't fathom why he was letting her hang on him.

Then Amber reached over, took Aiden's beer out of his hand, and turned to look Olivia in the eye as she took a deep drink from Aiden's glass. In a flash, the beer was back in Aiden's hand, and Amber stepped up to the pool table. Amber winked as she took the pool stick from Olivia.

Olivia's stomach went sour, and she fought to steady her hands, which were beginning to tremble. She excused herself to use the restroom, a smile plastered painfully to her face, her nose prickling with the threat of tears. In the bathroom, she locked herself in a stall and took several deep breaths.

She replayed the whole thing in her mind and tried to add some logic to the picture.

What had she actually seen?

The whole thing, while super weird, had been instigated by Amber. But why did Amber feel comfortable doing that? Did they have a history? Were they friends with benefits?

Aiden and Olivia hadn't technically made their relationship exclusive, so maybe it was on her for not telling Aiden once she slept with someone, exclusivity was implied. Hell, given her track record, it meant they were about to become very serious for a long time.

Ugh, don't think like that. She didn't need to compound her worries. *God, this sucks.*

Olivia pulled her phone out of her purse and texted Grace.

Olivia: *How would you feel if another woman drank out of Abesh's beer?*

Thankfully, Grace responds within seconds.

Grace*: What? Why are you asking that? That's not a thing.*

Right? Olivia silently yelled at her phone. *Who does that?*

Olivia: *Having a debate with Jessa.*

She wanted to linger, but it was time to leave her hideout. She flushed the toilet for appearance's sake and left her bathroom stall. On the other side of the door, June was waiting for her.

"Hey." June tentatively searched Olivia's eyes.

At least she'd held it together and didn't have to worry about a blotchy red cry-face. She wasn't *that* upset, but she *was* astounded at Amber's audacity.

"Hi," Olivia said. It came out coolly, which wasn't fair to June, who had been nothing but lovely.

"Just so you know," June said, "we all saw what happened back there. You're not crazy. It was weird."

"Wow! Thank you for saying that!" Olivia said emphatically as her body deflated, releasing tension she hadn't realized she was holding.

"Of course. I remember how cold Amber was to me when I first started dating Isaac. And she wasn't even interested in Isaac. She's very possessive of these guys. And…" June hesitated. "Well, frankly, she's always had her sights set on Aiden. Isaac told me she and Aiden hooked up once in college during one of his and Rebecca's breaks, but nothing else has ever happened between them. I think it's safe to say Aiden is strictly not interested. So yeah, maybe it's weird for me to tell you all of this, but I know Aiden is crazy about you, and as his best friend's wife, let's just say I've been kept in the loop. He hasn't been serious about anyone since Rebecca, and he's totally smitten with you."

After a beat, June added, "Also, he would kill me if he knew we were having this conversation, but I don't want Amber to scare you off because it's nice to see Aiden so happy."

"Wow, that's a lot. But thank you. I did need to hear that."

"Of course. She's just…Amber." June sighed and flipped her hand dismissively.

Olivia laughed, grateful she could still trust her ability to read people. *Amber? Yikes!*

June? Lovely.

"It's all good," Olivia said. "I appreciate you looking out for me, and for what it's worth, I really like Aiden, too. Feel free to pass that back to him via Isaac."

June laughed. "Funny how the dating strategies we learned in grade school come in handy all these years later."

"You never know what's going to stick with you in life," Olivia replied.

June put an arm around Olivia's shoulder and gave her a side hug.

Fortified by June's generosity and the hand of friendship she had extended, Olivia walked back into the bar.

The evening wrapped up quickly once the pool game was over. June and Isaac had to get home to relieve their babysitter, and Ryan had an early shift. But Amber lingered awkwardly. Olivia let out several fake, exaggerated yawns, and Aiden took the hint.

On the drive home, he asked Olivia if something was wrong. Olivia knew she shouldn't ask questions to which she knew the answer, but the naughty angel won.

"Amber seems kind of into you. Do you all have a history?"

His gaze darted to Olivia's face, seeming to assess her thoughts, before training his eyes back on the road.

"No history," he said. "She…" He paused. "She has made it clear she is interested, and I have made it clear I'm not. Please, don't worry about her, Olivia. I know we haven't talked about what this is between us, but I'm very into you, and I don't plan to be with anyone else."

On the one hand, Olivia was annoyed his story didn't match June's, but on the other, perhaps she hadn't yet earned the right to expect him to tell her everyone he'd slept with.

To be fair, it was a long time ago. So, Olivia let it go.

"Okay." She placed her hand on his thigh.

"Okay?" he asked expectantly, placing his hand atop hers.

"Yeah, okay." She smiled, letting herself feel all of the goodness between them again. "And me too," she added. "This has all been such a pleasant surprise, and I don't plan to be with anyone else either."

He stopped at the next red light, leaned over, and pressed his soft, full lips to hers.

Butterflies.

In her stomach, in her feet, and a little bit in her heart.

Damn.

Chapter 29 - Olivia

Aiden sent Olivia off the next day with promises to visit her in Gresham as soon as possible. Even though the distance was not ideal, she was willing to put up with it. They were adults. They had their own lives to manage. And when they were together, they would be together.

However, the sense of calm confidence Olivia felt in Aiden's presence dissipated on the drive home. The same thoughts that plagued her drive to Saint Paul seeped into her retreat to Gresham. Though, admittedly, she felt like she had a better sense of where Aiden stood on things. He'd asked her to be exclusive, and she smiled at the sweet memory of him stopping at a red light to kiss her. It was all so romantic, and it was not something she'd experienced before with Sam. Aiden was so much more willing to put himself out there than Sam had ever been.

Still, the distance—and what they were going to do about it—hadn't changed. Two hours and two careers stood between them, not to mention the potential addition of thousands of acres of farmland.

After endless and fruitless obsessing, she arbitrarily decided she would give their budding relationship one month free of worries or decisions because no one could fall in love in one month. She emphatically ignored the voice questioning whether that road had already been crossed.

Olivia was back home in time for Sunday pot roast, so she drove straight to her parents' house. She was excited to see Ms. Darcy and hear from her mom how the CSA distribution had gone.

She'd bought a thank-you gift for her mom from the farmers market she and Aiden had visited. It was one of those cutesy "Welcome Home" signs covered in ceramic sunflowers, perfect decor for any Midwest home and particularly perfect for her mom since she adored sunflowers.

When Olivia opened the door, her mom looked up from where she sat balancing her checkbook, and Ms. Darcy nearly toppled Olivia with a running jump.

What could possibly be better than a loving dog's loyal hello?

"You poor baby," Olivia crooned, sitting on the floor to cuddle her sweet pup. "Was Jackie so mean to you? She didn't even play with you at all? And no one pet you? Aww, poor puppy."

In response to Olivia's melodramatic voice, Ms. Darcy aggressively licked her face and howled mournfully.

"Do not let her fool you. That dog is as spoiled as the day is long." Her mom sounded defensive. "I'll have you know she slept on the bed with her head on my pillow last night."

"Awww, thanks, Mom. How did Dad feel about that?"

"Oh, you'll find out for yourself soon enough, I'm sure."

On cue, Olivia's dad walked in through the door, fingers covered in mechanical grease. He turned on the sink and sprayed dish soap on his hands. "Good Lord, that dog is a spoiled brat."

"Hey!" Olivia protested, pretending to cover Ms. Darcy's ears. "She can hear you."

"Yeah, well, your mom kicked me out of bed last night so the dog could sleep next to her. I had to sleep on the damn pull-out sofa in the basement."

Olivia laughed loudly and gave Ms. Darcy more belly rubs. "Oh, good girl, Ms. Darcy. Good girl," she said in a whiny baby-talk voice, hoping to annoy her dad.

"She wouldn't stop crying," her mom said defensively. "She missed her mama."

"Oh, for heaven's sake," her dad said disgustedly. He was a firm believer that dogs had been put on earth to serve humans, specifically farmers and hunters.

Olivia was momentarily distracted by her phone vibrating. She pulled it out of her pocket.

Aiden: *Should I be embarrassed that I already miss you?*

Olivia: *(Kissy winky face emoji)*

"Look at that smile," her mom teased. "I take it things went well with Aiden?"

Olivia wasn't used to her parents being so close to her dating life. She'd kept her parents in the dark as much as possible, hoping it would minimize the pressure she already felt regarding all things Aiden, but it was hard to know what they'd gleaned from other sources. Of course, with her mom covering her CSA for her, Olivia had to fork over a few details.

"Who's Aiden?" her dad asked, characteristically clueless.

"I told you, Bill. Aiden is the Westcott boy Olivia went to school with."

Oh, how odd life is. How did I end up here in this moment?

"Dr. Wescott's son? What does Aiden do, then?"

"He's a doctor, too." Olivia silently challenged him to question the profession as not good enough.

"Hmmm…chip off the old block, eh? So, when are you bringing this young man to Sunday dinner? Why isn't he here now?"

"He lives in Saint Paul, and he had to work today," she answered with surprising patience, making an effort not to overreact to the silly things that came out of her dad's mouth.

"Well, I'd like to meet him *soon*. I don't want you dating another Sam. I knew that boy wasn't worth much the minute I saw him."

Deep breath, deep breath. How is this my father?

Likely sensing Olivia's raised hackles, her mom redirected. "Guess who I saw at the market?"

"Who?"

"Madeleine Jacobs."

"*Yeah*? How's she?" Olivia asked.

"Good! She's got a little girl, and she lives over in Naperville. I told her to give you a call."

"Oh great, it would be fun to catch up."

Olivia tried to remember the last time they'd seen each other—maybe the summer after their sophomore year of college when they both happened to be in Gresham?

Maddy had been one of Olivia's best friends growing up, and there hadn't been any particular reason they'd grown apart. The longer Olivia was in Seattle, the easier it was to simplify her visits back to Minnesota and focus solely on her time with her family. She eventually stopped reaching out to old friends to let them know when she'd be back in town. Now that she was living in Gresham, she regretted having lost touch with so many.

Her dad took advantage of Olivia's quiet to add, "She married a farmer, ya know? That Hanson fellow who raises sugar beets."

Olivia thought hard about how to respond, hoping for a reply that wouldn't lead them into murky waters.

"That's great, good for her." Short and sweet.

But she could feel it coming. They hadn't discussed the farm thing in at least a month, and the pressure cooker was bound to blow if her dad held it in much longer.

"Do you think Aiden would be interested in farming? Sounds like he'd be smart enough."

“Something tells me he's not going to give up his career in medicine.” Olivia’s words were drenched in sarcasm.

“So, what are you going to do, move to the Cities to be with him then? Going to chase another dead-end relationship? I thought we had an understanding that you're home now. You've had your fun, and it's time to grow up.”

“That's enough, Bill,” her mom said firmly.

“Well, she started it,” he said in a huff.

Childish, childish, and I'm dying to mirror him. Olivia took a few deep breaths so she wouldn’t stoop to his immature level.

“I don't know yet, Dad. I guess we'll see.”

“So, what's it going to take, then? For you to face this reality of being handed a wildly successful business that could feed you and generations to come. I didn't build this farm up for nothing. I did it to secure a future for you and your kids and their kids.”

“I know, Dad, I know. Listen, how about I give you a firm answer by October first?”

He harrumphed his acknowledgment.

“But…” Olivia paused until he was listening. “But, *if* I take over the farm, I will have conditions.”

“Of course you will,” he grumbled.

“And I'm not doing it without Philip.”

“Fine.”

She was glad he hadn't fought her on the Philip partnership. If nothing else, she hoped giving her dad a deadline for her decision would buy her some time to figure out what she actually wanted and how Aiden may or may not factor into her future.

As the tension subsided, Olivia's mom filled her in on her CSA customers' gossip. Apparently, Pam hadn't stopped to pick up her box, so Olivia's mom had dropped the box off at Pam's house. Olivia's mom insisted it was "no trouble," and she knew where Pam lived.

As it turned out, Pam had twisted her ankle at the Y that week and wasn't feeling ready to leave the house. Olivia considered whether she would be able to drop off Pam's order the following week as well. She'd have to figure out how to squeeze it in. She sent herself an email so she wouldn't forget.

Olivia's mom said several of her CSA subscribers commented on how much they loved their sweet corn, but they could use fewer zucchinis. Olivia laughed and sent herself another email to take it easy on the zukes that week. It was going to be hard given how absolutely abundant they were and how little desire she had to make more zucchini bread. Olivia had tried to get her mom to start a zucchini bread side hustle, but her mom shut the idea down immediately, having fought her own zucchini wars in years past.

“That sounds like a *you* problem,” her mom had said sassily. Smiling, Olivia asked where she had learned that phrasing. “Fiona,” her mom had replied proudly.

Oh well, Olivia sighed internally, *you can't win ‘em all.*

Hopefully, the food bank could find a use for the zucchinis along with the other veggies causing Olivia daily anxiety for fear they might go to waste. She wondered if they could send volunteers to harvest the unpicked vegetables so Olivia could focus on her customers without feeling so guilty about the produce that rotted on the vine. She sent herself a third email to call the food bank director in the morning.

The ever-constant harvest clock ticked on, and she considered how much a bountiful harvest was a double-edged sword.

Chapter 30 - Aiden

After saying goodbye to Olivia and putting in a shift at the hospital, Aiden was back at June and Isaac's house for pizza with their kids. If he wanted to see his friends on a regular basis, he was learning it was easiest to be the surrogate uncle and show up with food. His friends seemed to welcome the distraction and the presence of an extra adult in the house, especially one willing to let their kids climb all over him, which he loved. It reminded him of when he was a teenager playing with his younger twin siblings.

At bedtime, Aiden would make himself useful, doing the most obvious chores. In exchange, his friends were able to relax and hang out. Sometimes they watched bad reality TV together, which they usually made fun of or talked over. Other times, they played board games. He was slowly adjusting to this new phase of friendship.

Tonight would be more of a talking-over-the-TV kind of night. Having just met Olivia, his friends would surely want to debrief.

Isaac and June plopped onto the couch next to him, letting out long sighs. June jumped right in. "So Aiden, Olivia is fantastic. Well done."

He laughed. "Yeah, she is, isn't she?"

"Are you and Olivia locked in?" Isaac asked.

“One hundred percent.”

“Good,” they replied in unison.

After a moment's silence, June said, “I had a talk with her in the bathroom.”

“Oh?”

“Yeah, after Amber was being all Amber with you, I could tell Olivia was kind of upset.”

“She was?” Aiden asked, alarmed. Shit, why hadn’t he noticed that?

“I mean, yeah,” June chastised him. “Amber was hanging all over you. Dude, you gotta get better at self-defense around her. You let her get away with far too much, especially in front of your new girlfriend. What the hell?”

June was right, and it left him with a pit in his stomach and a tightness in his chest. At the time, he hadn’t thought twice about it because it was just Amber being Amber. She was terrible about physical boundaries in general, but Aiden knew she was the worst with him. Everyone put up with her because she had a sweet side if you got to know her. When she let down her guard, which she typically did when it was just the five of them, she was funny and smart, not that he’d be telling this to Olivia as an excuse. He would have to face the music and apologize.

“Fuck, you’re right, what’s wrong with me?”

Isaac shook his head like, *bro, what were you thinking?*

“Yeah, so I basically saved your relationship,” June said.

"Oh my god, thank you. Holy shit, what did you say?" How could he have been so stupid? What if he'd lost his chance with Olivia because of Amber of all people?

"Well, I told her you're crazy about her and not to worry about Amber."

"Okay, good." He sighed, relieved.

"And…" June was stalling. She sighed before adding, "You should know I had to explain Amber's behavior, so I told her you all slept together once in college." She cringed as she added the last part. "But I also told her you were strictly not interested in Amber, and she had nothing to worry about."

Oh god. Olivia had asked him if he and Amber had a history on the car ride home from the bar. His stomach went cold. *Fuck, fuck, fuck.* He was furious with himself. He lowered his head into his hands, trying to remember everything that was said.

"Dude, you look like you're going to barf." Isaac sounded concerned.

Rubbing his face, Aiden lifted his head to make eye contact. Taking a deep breath in and letting it out slowly, he said, "On the drive home, Olivia asked me if Amber and I had a history, and I said no."

He hung his head once more and looked down at the ground, ashamed to admit this lie to his best friends.

"Oh dear, that is not ideal." June sounded uncomfortable.

"Did she seem pissed?" Isaac asked.

"No. I guess not, but I basically made our relationship exclusive. She seemed fine." Aiden shrugged his shoulders, unsure.

"You lucky, bastard." Isaac shook his head. "Well, you better make it right. She gave you a pass, but now you're operating from behind."

"Yeah," June added, "you should tell her you know she knows and get that bad energy out of your relationship ASAP."

"I would never cheat on her. Jesus, after what I've been through, I can't even imagine doing that to someone."

Isaac let out a low whistle. "Okay, well, tell *her* that. Not *us*. We obviously know you're a good guy, and she definitely likes you, so have the conversation and enjoy the rest of your happy lives together."

"Yeah, I will. Definitely. Next time I see her, 'cause I should do it in person, right?"

June nodded. "Probably."

"Oh, god, she's only been gone eight hours, and I already miss her."

June and Isaac laughed. They knew how bad he had it for Olivia. He wondered when he could drive to Gresham, hoping it would be soon because he was tempted to get into his car and go right then. The sliver of logic he hung onto told him to slow down.

Chapter 31 - Olivia

The next morning, Olivia went to Jill's to meet Ellen and plan her wedding flowers. Olivia arrived early to have some coffee and work on her weekly farm plan. She had her computer open to the spreadsheet detailing her crop production and what she expected to produce and distribute each week, along with the actual numbers. She'd drastically underestimated her zucchini production and made a note for her future self to plant one-quarter as many the next year.

After an hour of transferring notebook scribbles and email notes into her document, the bell above the door chimed as Ellen arrived.

"Hey!" Ellen gave her a friendly wave as she walked past several booths.

Olivia stood to give Ellen a hug.

"Hello! You look great! And look, you're starting to get a bump," Olivia said excitedly.

Ellen was undoubtedly a Wescott, but her pretty features were much softer than her brothers'. She also had a handful of gray hairs weaving through her dark brown shoulder-length cut.

Ellen smiled proudly and gave her stomach a tender pat. "Thanks! We just found out yesterday we're having a little girl."

Ellen's joy brightened her eyes, and Olivia understood what people meant when they said pregnant women radiated beauty. It was a soul-deep glow as much as a physical one.

"That is fantastic! I'm so excited for you!"

Jill stopped by their table to ask Ellen what she'd like to drink. "Coffee and water, please."

"So," Ellen said, focusing their attention. "Thank you so much for meeting me here. I've been meaning to text you, but work has been crazy, and between doctor's appointments, wedding plans, and a lot of napping, I haven't gotten to it. But I'm hoping you can still do our flowers?" Ellen looked hopefully at Olivia with a hint of nervousness.

"Yes! Of course I will! So long as you're still okay with me having absolutely zero wedding flower experience."

"Yay, yay, yay!" Ellen bounced in her booth seat and clapped her hands. "That is perfect. And yes, like I said at dinner, this is going to be very laid back."

Olivia pulled open her notebook and picked up her pen.

"So what did you have in mind?"

"Ooooh, look at you! This is so official. I'm impressed. Okay, so, I'm going to need a larger bridal bouquet, obviously. I have four bridesmaids, and it would be great if they could each have a smaller bouquet that looks kind of like mine. And then…" She paused, thinking, "We're going to have fifteen tables at dinner, and I'd love to have a little centerpiece bouquet for each one of those, but nothing too fancy, just a simple arrangement of mixed dahlias."

"Okay, great! Yeah, I think I can do that. Anything else?"

"Well," Ellen said hesitantly. "Would you be willing to decorate an arch for the ceremony backdrop?"

An arch would certainly push Olivia out of her comfort zone. But that's what YouTube was for.

"I'm willing to try." She smiled cautiously. "Can you remind me of the exact wedding date and time?"

From there, they moved into the finer details of the wedding schedule, budget, and color scheme. Ellen showed Olivia several pictures of her dress and the bridesmaid dresses for reference as she planned the bouquets.

They knocked out the details, and Olivia made a final request for Ellen to create a small Pinterest board with bridal bouquet designs she liked. That way, Olivia could practice a few before the big day. For the first time, she realized it was going to be a big day for herself as well.

Olivia was about to transition their conversation into small talk before they said goodbye, but Ellen's face turned serious.

"Is everything okay?" Olivia asked, suddenly unsure if Ellen had changed her mind about hiring her.

"Sorry, yes," Ellen said. "I'm just having an argument with myself about whether I should talk to you about Aiden."

"Oh? What about Aiden? Is he secretly still married or something?" She awkwardly laughed too hard at her own joke.

Ellen chuckled and shook her head.

"Obviously not, but it *is* related to Rebecca."

Olivia's stomach clenched with low-level anxiety. "*Okay…?*"

"Screw it," Ellen said with an air of big sisterly resignation. "I'm going to say it because I don't know if Aiden will, and I think you need to know."

Olivia's body froze, and she held her breath.

"So, Rebecca really hurt Aiden."

"Of course," Olivia said breathlessly, relieved Ellen's statement wasn't anything she didn't already know, but Olivia was still wary. She quieted, waiting for more.

Ellen said, "I think we were all surprised at what she did to him. I think he was completely blindsided when she cheated on him."

Olivia nodded, having heard this from Aiden.

"He went through a rough patch. He ended up taking a month off medical school. When he went back, he went back with an intense, I'd say borderline unhealthy, perfectionism. It felt like he kind of stopped living life outside work. And now he's doing so well, but I guess I worry about him getting hurt again."

To this, Olivia could relate. Hadn't she done the same thing with her CSA farm? Other than that past weekend in the Cities and her birthday party, she had barely come up for air or made time for fun.

"Well, I can't promise anything with regard to where this thing between Aiden and me is headed. It's complicated with us living two hours apart, but I can promise you I would never cheat on Aiden."

"Thanks for saying that. For what it's worth, I hope it works out between you two."

Ellen smiled kindly, which Olivia appreciated, but she also wondered how Aiden would feel if he knew they'd had this conversation. For some reason, Olivia felt guilty, like she had crossed a line, even though Ellen had instigated the conversation. Should she have stopped Ellen from sharing?

Olivia returned Ellen's friendly smile. "I guess time will tell."

"Indeed. Anyway, I should get going. My shift at the hospital starts at noon today, and I have a few more errands I need to run before then."

They stood, hugged, and said goodbye. Olivia didn't immediately follow her out. Instead, she sat and took a moment to consider what Ellen had told her.

Aiden had been hurt badly. Would he be able to love again? Or had he been scarred too badly by Rebecca? How long had it been since their divorce was final? Was Olivia still in his rebound territory? Was he banking on the distance to keep their relationship from turning into something more serious?

On the one hand, everything Ellen said created a more comprehensive picture of Aiden and why he'd made some of the decisions he had, but it also felt like a burden. It created an onslaught of new worries and dulled some of the shine off Olivia's joy, which she'd been carrying since the previous weekend in Saint Paul. She resented Ellen a little for telling her, but she also wondered if she should be grateful to Ellen for pulling Olivia's head out of the clouds.

Her phone vibrated. Of course it was Aiden.

Aiden: *How did everything go with my sister?*

Olivia: *Good! I think we have a plan (smiley face emoji)*

Aiden: *I've been meaning to ask, I know you'll be busy with all of the flowers and stuff, but would you be my date to the wedding?*

With that one simple text, Olivia's emotional coin was flipped, and once again, her chest and stomach felt buzzy with joy.

Good lord, I feel like a hormonal teenager, riding a rollercoaster of emotions from one Aiden interaction to the next.

Olivia: *Of course! That would be fun!*

Aiden: *(two silly dancing emojis)*

Staring at her phone, Olivia didn't notice Jill next to her table.

"Who's got you grinning, girly?" Jill asked with her own knowing grin.

"Say what?" Olivia asked, all innocence.

"Mm-hmm." Jill clearly wasn't fooled. "I get it. Mind my own business. I'll go find someone else to bug."

The next day, Olivia replayed her conversation with Ellen so many times she eventually called Grace to sort through her feelings. Olivia was fixated on the piece about Aiden returning to work obsessively after his breakup. Was that what she'd done after breaking up with Sam?

But Grace reassured Olivia it took a lot of hard work to start a business. From her perspective, Grace didn't think Olivia was running from anything.

It also opened up a door to talk about Sam. Olivia hadn't yet discussed the breakup in detail. Laying on her bed, staring at the ceiling, she told Grace everything.

Grace had always been the best listener. She listened to Olivia talk for an hour about all the things that had gone wrong between Sam and her. Olivia cried hard, snotty tears. It was therapeutic, and she released some of the shame she'd had about staying with Sam for so long. She also let go of the guilt for not walking away sooner, despite knowing in her heart of hearts she hadn't wanted to end up with him.

An hour later, they'd moved on from crying to laughing as Olivia told Grace about the insane moment when Amber took a drink of Aiden's beer.

"*Who does that?*" Grace yelled.

"*I know!*" Olivia shouted back. "It was so weird!"

"Well, from what his other friend said, you don't have anything to worry about. He's super into you. So…was this a long play so you could tell me how much your boyfriend is totally obsessed with you?"

"Ha ha," Olivia said dryly.

Is he my boyfriend? Add that to the list of things to obsess over during my endless alone time in the field.

"No, but really, Olivia," Grace said reassuringly. "It sounds like you're in a good place, and everything you're doing and experiencing is normal. I wouldn't worry so much. Maybe just try to enjoy it."

"I will *try*," Olivia moaned reluctantly, then added in a whiny voice, "but it's hard when I don't know when I'm going to see him next."

"Oh my *gawd*," Grace said in a stereotypical Southern California accent, "you're *sooo* into him!"

"Yeah, yeah." Olivia laughed along with Grace.

When they hung up, Olivia realized she should just text Aiden to ask when they would see each other next. She did some calculations in her head. The next day was Friday, so she would be busy with harvest, and Saturday was the farmers market. Maybe she could drive down to the Cities on Sunday and stay for a night or two if he wasn't too busy.

Shit. Grace is right. I'm totally into him. She pulled out her phone and pulled up Aiden's contact, which was now a picture of him dancing at the Yard Tunes concert.

Olivia: *So when will I see you next?*

Chapter 32 - Olivia

Olivia was giddy, frantically picking up laundry off her bedroom floor and throwing it in her hamper. Aiden would be there any minute.

She closed her closet doors so he wouldn't see the various shoes strewn about, nowhere near their companions.

Attempting to impress Aiden and thank him for his flexibility, Olivia had stayed up late the night before making him a carrot cake using carrots she'd grown and eggs she'd traded for flowers from another vendor. When she'd inevitably snoozed her alarm twice that morning, she had only been shooting herself in the foot. Her house was a disaster, and she still had chores to do. She moved as fast as she could while taking only a moment to shower and shave her legs.

She was excited for Aiden to see her farm in the light of day, and she was curious to see how he'd handle a day in the field, especially if the drizzle didn't let up. According to Aiden, he'd wanted nothing more than to spend a day at her farm, harvesting cucumbers and green beans. Though she was dubious, she'd accepted his offer because the next two days were the only time he was free for another week, and fulfilling her CSA orders wasn't optional.

Her intuition told her the stakes for their time together were high. This would more or less be a trial run to see if they could make long distance work given their busy and erratic schedules. If these two days went poorly, she couldn't help but suspect they would be better off killing the spark before it died.

However, Aiden making a mid-week trip to spend two days with her, and his willingness to go with the flow of her life, gave her hope. With their non-traditional work schedules, this was how it would have to be for the time being. She might be able to get a day off here or there and visit him in Saint Paul, but it wouldn't necessarily mean he would have the day off. She would most likely be hanging around and waiting for him some days, which didn't sound terrible. It would alleviate her worries about consistently depleting her Trader Joe's freezer hoard. She supposed time would tell how realistic it would be for him to tag along and help her on the farm.

She peered through her bedroom window once again and spotted his car coming up her driveway. Skipping every other step, she ran down the stairs to meet him. Given the rainy weather, she'd opted for jeans and a T-shirt topped by her favorite pink and blue flannel. If she had to, she could put on her heavy-duty Seattle rain gear, which she'd purchased after several freezing wet dog walks with Ms. Darcy. She wondered how prepared Aiden would be.

She met him at his car and told him how much she'd missed him with her mouth as well as the leg she teasingly wrapped around his thigh. He pulled back and looked at her, his smile doing that cute, crinkly thing to his eyes.

"Oh, oh, ooooh, Olivia," he sang her name, and she laughed. "I have been looking forward to this all week."

"Me, too." She gave him another kiss on the lips before grabbing his hand. She pulled him toward her house so they could get out of the drizzle. "I can't decide if you picked the worst or best week to help me harvest veggies. You won't sweat to death, but you'll certainly get drenched if this continues."

"Don't worry about me. I'm tougher than I look," he said with mock seriousness.

She eyed him suspiciously.

"What? You don't believe me? I was a Cub Scout."

Olivia's head fell back as she laughed.

He feigned outrage. "Hey, I'll have you know I made it all the way to Webelos before I gave up on my Eagle Scout dreams."

"Well, in that case, I've got a lot of work for you. Really though, I'm so glad you're here and that you're willing to put up with my schedule."

"I'm just glad I get to spend time with you, and I guess we'll have to figure out this whole long-distance thing one way or another."

Aiden's acknowledgment of the bigger picture made her stomach clench. In his tone was a question, and she got the sense he was asking her if she felt the same way. She wasn't quite ready to go there with words, and they had a million things to do for her CSA.

Instead, she opted to jump right into the work. "First things first, are you hungry, thirsty, need to use the bathroom?"

"Ummm, I think I'm good. I stopped for gas."

"Great, let's get to work. Next question, did you bring any farm clothes?"

Aiden squinted at Olivia questioningly. "What would you say are farm clothes?"

"I'll take that as a no. In that case, why don't you put on something you don't mind getting covered in mud."

Aiden swept a hand to indicate his button-down shirt, jeans, and black sneakers. Then he held out his arms as if to say, *this is it.*

"Oh…all right. Well, we can wash everything tonight." She grimaced apologetically. "You *might* be able to wear those shoes again."

He gave her a bashful smile. "I believe I did ask to take a one-on-one course in farming. And to be fair, you didn't send me a school supply list."

She bit back a smile. "Right, no, totally. That's on me. I'll be sure to send you a required reading list next time."

"Thank you. I'm nothing if not a good student."

“Well, we’ll see how good of a teacher I am.”

The image may have brought some sexy thoughts to Olivia’s mind, but she mentally swatted them away. *No time for that. Must get work done so we have time for fun later.*

To his credit, Aiden was an excellent sport. So used to being alone in the field, Olivia would occasionally catch sight of Aiden out of the corner of her eye and jump, startled by his presence. Then she’d remember that it was Aiden, and then she’d see how inappropriately dressed he was, and that, of course, would lead to uncontrollable giggling.

After the third time, Aiden clued in on the joke. He walked over and pulled her to him before laying them down in the mud. They were immediately soaked and filthy. Mud squidged into her right ear, and she squealed. She howled with laughter so hard her stomach muscles ached. Aiden kissed her on her laughing mouth. She could taste dirt on his tongue, which was not as sexy as she might have otherwise thought. But her laughter made it impossible to shape her lips into anything resembling a kiss.

Aiden didn’t relent. He kissed her along her throat and down her chest. Unzipping her jacket, he had access to the top buttons of her flannel and slipped them through their holes.

She gasped when his freezing-cold fingers touched her skin. “Aiden, what are you doing?”

"Reminding myself why I drove two hours to play in the mud."

He pulled back to meet her smiling eyes before reaching into her shirt and cupping his hand around her breast. The cold sensation sobered her, and she kissed him back, pulling up his wet shirt to touch his stomach and chest.

The furnace in her core ignited as he played with the bud of her nipple, massaging it back and forth between his fingers.

Between gasps, she said, "We should…go warm up… House… Shower."

They ran through the muddy field, up and onto her porch, where they stripped off their wet clothes. Down to their underwear, they dashed up the stairs. Their bodies were streaked with mud.

In the shower, Olivia was overwhelmed by the intense response her body had to the sight of water streaming down Aiden's torso. Her heart raced when he knelt down and placed one of her legs on the side of the bathtub, opening her to him. Beyond the sensations racing across and through her sex, she felt like she could cry because she was so filled with desire for more than sex with Aiden. She wanted him here at her farm to kiss her goodnight and cuddle her awake. The terrifying realization was washed away by a thousand shooting stars rocketing behind her eyelids as her body trembled against him.

Chapter 33 - Aiden

An hour later, Aiden awoke groggily from a deep, post-sex nap. Olivia's wet hair was strewn across her pillow, and one of her arms was draped over his chest. He took a deep breath, savoring the pleasure he felt waking up next to her. He could watch her sleep all day, but she was legitimately concerned about getting her work done.

He gently caressed her cheek and gave her a kiss on the forehead before whispering, "Olivia, I think we fell asleep."

Her face scrunched up, recoiling from his words. After an hour in the field with her, he'd gotten a sense of how hard she worked to keep her CSA going. He wished he was around to help more, to take some of the pressure off. But he also knew she was independent and happy, and she was following her dreams. He'd have to figure out other ways to support her. At the moment, supporting her meant going back outside and getting everything harvested for tomorrow.

He nudged her again and spoke quietly into her shoulder, "Olivia. Vegetables. CSA customers. Lots to do."

Somehow that broke through, and her eyes snapped open. *"Fuck!"*

"It's okay, I'm here. It should go fast with two of us, right? How much work is left?"

She studied the ceiling. “Okay. We have a few hours of work, but you’re right, it’ll go faster with you here.”

They got back to work. The rain had thankfully passed. In its wake, the sun had come out, but water droplets still clung to the plants. Every vegetable sparkled like it had just been dusted with glitter in preparation for a photoshoot. The flowers were especially mesmerizing–row after row and shade after shade of reds, yellows, pinks, oranges, and purples. She’d even proudly showed him the irrigation system she’d built from scratch. Everything was a testament to her effort and creativity.

With the rain gone, Olivia turned on her Bluetooth speaker, blasting a playlist featuring mostly nineties pop music. When NSYNC's “Bye Bye Bye” came on, Olivia belted out the lyrics and danced in front of the green beans she was harvesting.

She caught him watching her and paused. “Aiden, how are you not singing right now?”

“Sorry, Olivia. I’m a loyal Backstreet Boys fan.” He waved his hands, telling her to carry on. “It’s okay,” he said patronizingly. “Some people make bad choices, and you’ve chosen NSYNC. I won’t hold it against you.”

“*What?* No way! NSYNC is clearly the superior band.”

“Well, Backstreet Boys were technically more successful,” he countered, giving her a flirty smile.

"But Justin Timberlake, am I right? He brought sexy back."

"Yeah, but Justin isn't NSYNC. He's the butterfly the NSYNC cocoon created."

"Then you should value the cocoon more," she said.

"But what about Britney?"

"Yeah, poor Britney," she said, shaking her head sadly.

Then, as if to shake it off, she turned up the volume and began dancing more wildly than before.

He loved it. He loved seeing her silly side, and he had to hold himself back from walking over and interrupting their work again. There would be time for that later.

Making love to Olivia again wasn't the only thing he was putting off. He needed to apologize for allowing Amber's inappropriate behavior *and confess his lie* about their lack of history. He kept hearing Isaac's advice to clear the air ASAP, but he wasn't ready to trade their easy energy for a serious conversation.

Chapter 34 - Olivia

Aiden surprised Olivia by cooking her dinner while she finished getting ready for the farmers market. Although her fridge was teeming with vegetables, he didn't have a lot to work with in the way of protein. He'd managed to dig out some meatballs from her freezer and make a veggie and meatball spaghetti with garlic toast. She approved, especially because she was starving after the long day in the field, not to mention the other exercise they'd gotten that afternoon.

After several large bites of delicious food, she looked up to see Aiden watching her.

"I have a question for you," he said, sounding serious.

She made eye contact, pausing mid-chew.

He cleared his throat. "Do you ever wish we'd gotten together in high school?"

She finished chewing, using the time to consider. "I'm not sure. I guess I like the idea of knowing more of you than I do today, but I also think we weren't fully cooked yet. We still had a lot of living that needed to happen on separate coasts."

He nodded.

"But," she added, feeling vulnerable, "I'm grateful we somehow found our way back here for another chance. It seems kind of crazy when you think about it—that the timing would work out for us to move back to Minnesota and for both of us to be single."

"Yeah, I've thought about that, too, and I feel lucky because being around you makes me happy. But I'm still kind of annoyed at my younger self for not making a point of knowing you sooner."

She melted at his words. She was doing a shit job of guarding her heart as well as she'd intended. His serious gaze made her feel like he wasn't saying something.

Her gaze narrowed. "What? What are you thinking?"

"Nothing. Just that you're pretty."

She shook her head smiling, totally smitten. "Such a charmer, this one. You're not bad yourself, but don't let it go to your head."

He laughed and squeezed her hand.

Chapter 35 - Olivia

The next day, they got up early for the farmers market. Aiden spent most of the day with Olivia, except for lunch, when he snuck away to spend time with his family. Olivia was amused to see some of her customers' confused expressions when they saw Aiden under her stall tent. She was a little uncomfortable when old high school classmates came over to say hello. Everyone attempted casual conversations, but their faces told Olivia they were dying to ask why Aiden Wescott was hanging around Olivia Olsen's farm stand.

Neither Aiden nor Olivia volunteered any details. They pretended it was no big deal, and it was only natural he was helping her out. She suspected Aiden enjoyed giving people something to talk about, but she was less at ease with it.

Olivia was willing to put up with the inevitable gossip to have Aiden with her. With every hour she spent being overwhelmed by his warmth and patience, not to mention his bad jokes, she became increasingly aware of her traitorous heart falling for him. He had been nothing short of amazing. He hadn't complained once that her farm had destroyed two of his outfits or that he was standing outside on black asphalt in ninety-degree heat to spend time with her. He'd also insisted there was no way she could pay him for his labor—her presence was payment enough.

Ugh, why is he so damn charming? But her attempt at exasperation was half-hearted at best.

After the market, he'd opted to spend one more night in her bed and leave early to make his shift on time, insisting he'd gotten accustomed to not needing as much sleep during his pediatrics residency.

That night, as they lay in bed, Aiden pulled out his medical licensing exam materials to study. She'd been surprised he technically wasn't a full-blown doctor after everything he'd endured. He'd told her some stories from his residency in Boston as they'd harvested vegetables the day before—the long hours, the intensity of the life-and-death situations. She was blown away by how crazy medical training was. Without any medical professionals in her family, she'd never been exposed to the commitment required by individuals to keep the human race healthy…or healthy-ish. He'd tried telling her that providing fresh veggies was a form of medicine—that a healthy diet was one of the most important aspects of preventative care, but Olivia had stared at him skeptically.

Lying under her cozy comforter, watching him flip through his tome of study materials in the light of his bedside lamp, she had to ask. "Why did you choose medicine? I suppose you knew what you were getting yourself into from your dad, or was it different for him being more rural? Did he work crazy hours when you were a kid?"

"Well, he got his start in New York, but by the time he came to Gresham, he'd made the transition to family medicine, which tends to be Monday through Friday, for the most part. That said, you're right. I did know what I was getting myself into. My dad encouraged me to pursue a different career."

She cocked her head to the side. "Why?"

"He said he wasn't sure I'd be happy doing it, but I think he was afraid I was blindly following in his footsteps. He was encouraging me to do something more artistic because he felt it had been an absence in his career."

"So, why *did* you choose medicine?"

"Well, I think our parents have a certain degree of influence on our choices, if nothing more than through the exposure to what's possible."

"Hmmm, I feel seen," she said. "Farming runs in the family."

"That's a good example," he acknowledged. "And frankly, so does medicine. Obviously, you know Ellen is a physical therapist here in town, and I ended up in pediatrics despite my dad nudging me to do something other than medicine."

"Interesting. I hadn't thought about medical professions being something you'd inherit like you would a farm or a business, but it makes sense. Why pediatrics, though? Was it the big family thing?" she added as an afterthought.

"Kind of. When my mom had Lauren and Ethan, it was a double surprise. Not only were they not expecting to have any more babies after eight years of not getting pregnant, but they were definitely not expecting to have two babies at the same time."

"I believe they call those twins," she said.

He shook his head. "No way, that term is misleading. It's two babies at the same time. Trust me." He lifted an index finger. "By the way, did you know two babies at the same time are more common for older mothers? Anyway, I was eight when they were born, and it was kind of the perfect age to be helpful without being disinterested. So, while Ellen and Nathan were very much focused on their friends, I liked helping my mom with the babies. I went from youngest child to big brother overnight, and I liked feeling important in that way, I guess."

Olivia listened thoughtfully, enjoying uncovering this new piece of Aiden. She smiled and nodded. "That's neat."

"What about you?" he countered.

"What about me?"

"Are you going to follow in your father's footsteps and take over the farm?"

"He wants me to."

"And?" Aiden prodded.

Olivia was nervous to answer. The closer October crept, the more her little inner voice told her she should partner with Philip on the farm, but she hadn't technically given her dad an answer yet. She was worried telling Aiden this would scare him off.

"Well, I told my dad I'd give him a decision by October first. But if I do commit to it, it'd be in partnership with Philip."

"Oh wow." Aiden's surprise was evident on his face. "I didn't realize it was so imminent."

"I know." Olivia cringed. "I haven't made a decision."

"But?"

"But…I have some things I need to figure out before deciding."

She'd figuratively run away from the conversation. She couldn't go there. Not when things between them were so fun and were bringing her so much light and joy.

Aiden set his study materials down on the bedside table next to him and turned to face her fully. He grabbed her hand and kissed her palm. "Whatever you decide, I hope you'll still give us a chance."

He's not going to give up on us if I take over the farm. Olivia's throat closed, and she fought back tears. She leaned her cheek against Aiden's chest and listened to his steady heartbeat. It calmed her and brought her breathing back to normal.

Once she trusted herself to speak again, she pulled back to look him in the eye. “I will. Promise.”

Chapter 36 - Olivia

A week had passed, but Olivia was still floating from her weekend with Aiden.

Her stomach was full from Sunday lunch with her family, and her heart was content. She was about to change into her farm clothes when she heard a car coming up the driveway. It was a sleek, red car, but she couldn't see the driver. Perplexed, she headed down the stairs.

Olivia emerged onto the porch, Ms. Darcy at her heels. The car door opened, and Sam's long legs swung out. He pulled himself up using the door frame, and their gazes locked. As soon as she saw him, Ms. Darcy began barking frantically and ran over to jump up and lick his face.

Olivia's heart stopped.

What. The. Hell?

"Hey, Olivia." He smiled pathetically. "I've missed you."

"Sam! What are you doing here? Why aren't you in Seattle?*"*

Olivia felt so many things at once. Shocked, pissed off, concerned, but most of all, completely baffled. They hadn't talked in months outside of a few brief text exchanges to sort out the disentanglement of their physical objects. In the years Olivia and Sam were together, he had only visited her family twice, always making excuses why it wasn't a good time for him to travel. He said he felt out of place at her parents' farm and was convinced her dad hated him.

A rare moment of insight.

"I have some of your books and old photos," Sam mumbled. "And I wanted to get them back to you."

He hadn't changed a bit. His fine blond hair still fell lazily over his forehead, his body still had the lean physique of a bike messenger, and his face was the picture of oblivious innocence. She may have spotted a new tattoo on his right forearm, but it was hard to be sure given the amount of ink decorating his body.

Seeing him there, in her driveway, at her house in Gresham, felt wrong. His Seattle bohemian vibe did not make sense on her farm, and it no longer made sense in her life. Looking at him with fresh eyes, Olivia imagined what it must have been like for her parents to meet Sam for the first time.

Her parents had been so excited to meet their daughter's first serious boyfriend. They'd built him up to be a blond Viking, the likes of which you'd find in Minnesota. Instead, they met a sullen, self-satisfied trust-fund baby.

Replaying the scene in her mind, Olivia began to laugh, a slow hiccup at first, but soon enough, tears were rolling from her eyes as she clutched her stomach through her hysteria.

Her dad had always been difficult, but the last five years between them had been worse than ever. She saw everything in a new light. Not to say he was ever correct or justified in his assumptions and prejudices; they just made a little more sense to Olivia.

Then Sam started laughing, too, which made Olivia laugh even harder.

When the wave of absurdity finally subsided, she made a *whew* noise and wiped her eyes with the back of her hands.

"So, what's so funny?" Sam asked, a clueless smile plastered on his face.

Olivia snorted, but she managed to keep from losing again.

"Ms. Darcy, come," Olivia said.

One of the worst fights they'd had at the end had been about who would keep Ms. Darcy, which was an absolute joke because Sam had done nothing to care for her. The only times he'd taken Ms. Darcy for walks were the few times when Olivia was so sick she couldn't get out of bed and had to beg Sam to take her.

"Why are you actually here, Sam? Do you think it might have been a good idea to call first? Did that even cross your mind?"

He looked like a chastised child. "I wanted to surprise you."

"Well. Mission accomplished." Olivia huffed.

"Look, Olivia." He walked toward her. "I think this is all a big mistake. I think you should come home, back to Seattle. We can start over."

Sam was standing next to her, close enough to see Olivia's look of incredulity.

"What the *fuck* are you talking about? I mean, honestly. What are you saying?"

"I'm saying I'm sorry. I made a mistake, and I can't live without you." Sam's eyes were all concern, his lips turned down in a miserable pout.

He reached into his pocket.

Oh god, oh god, oh god! Olivia's insides were screaming. All the alarm bells were ringing.

"What are you doing, Sam? Stop that! Don't do that!"

Sam got down on one knee and held up a gigantic diamond. Olivia's first impression was that the ring looked very impractical, but she barely had time to process what was happening because, at that moment, a black car turned into Olivia's driveway.

Sam and Olivia held stock-still, Sam's ring suspended between them. Halfway up the driveway, the car slowed before coming to a stop. Through the front windshield, Olivia saw Aiden, jaw open, eyebrows furrowed. Her heart ached as she watched the slew of emotions playing across his face. First, shock and confusion, followed quickly by disgusted understanding. Finally, fury and pain flashed through his eyes.

"Aiden! Wait!" Olivia yelled. She ran toward his car, praying he'd let her explain. Aiden was too fast, and his car was reversing quickly.

Olivia made a weak attempt to catch up, but his tires were kicking up too much gravel. She gave up, waving her hand in front of her face, coughing. Olivia turned back, away from the cloud of dust, to face Sam, who was stalking toward her. He had a furiously territorial expression on his pale face.

"Who the hell was that?" Sam demanded.

"None of your business!" Olivia shouted back.

Seething, Olivia whipped her pointer finger toward Sam's car. "You need to leave now. Now!"

"So, you were cheating on me? Is that what this is? Wow, all those times you claimed you wanted to marry me, but the whole time, you had someone in Minnesota that you were dying to get back to."

Olivia was flabbergasted, incredulous at his audacity. She was fighting back angry tears.

"How dare you, Sam! I thought one day you and I might be friends, but you know what? *Fuck you!"* Olivia shouted. "I'm leaving, and when I get back, you need to be gone. I never want to see you again. Ever. Go back to Seattle, and enjoy your trust fund, you shitty excuse for a human!"

Unfortunately, Sam's car was blocking hers from getting out of the driveway, and he seemed glued to his spot. Instead, Ms. Darcy followed her as she stomped toward her truck. She whipped the door open, and Ms. Darcy jumped up into the cab. Olivia hauled herself up and turned the ignition. The engine roared to life. She moved the stick shift into reverse, but in her haste to go after Aiden, the truck jolted to a dead stop.

Olivia screamed one loud "argh!" of frustration, and Ms. Darcy looked over, worry in her big brown eyes.

This is taking too long!

She took a moment to breathe and start over. This time, she let out the clutch more gradually, and the truck moved out of its parking space.

Taking more deep breaths, she prayed she'd find Aiden at the cabin.

I'm mad at Sam, not Aiden.

She just needed to explain what had happened, and everything would be fine.

It took almost no time at all to reach the pond, and the relief she felt when she saw Aiden's car parked behind the cabin was all-encompassing, like jumping into cool water on a hot day. It was going to be okay.

Olivia hopped down from the truck and jogged to the cabin, Ms. Darcy on her heels. She knocked on the door. When Aiden didn't answer, she cautiously turned the knob and opened the door.

"Aiden, hey," she said gently.

He stared at her from across the tiny room. Olivia could see hurt in his eyes, but it was masked with anger. His cheeks and neck were red, his jaw muscles were taut and sinewy, and his hands were clenched at his side.

"I know you've been texting. I saw your phone at my parents' house. I tried to give you the benefit of the doubt, and it's totally blown up in my face. Was this all a game to you?"

His words hit her like a slap across the face. "Aiden!"

"I cannot believe I fell for this. I thought…god, Olivia, I thought you were different."

"Please, Aiden. Don't say that. Whatever you saw back there, it was nothing. Why do you think I am *here*? I came after *you*, Aiden."

He was looking away from her. She wasn't sure if he'd heard anything she'd said, so she walked over to put her hand on his arm. He recoiled as if her touch was dangerous.

"So, did it work?" Aiden's voice was a growl.

"What are you talking about?" she pleaded.

"Using me to get your ex to propose? That was the goal, right? God, I feel like an idiot."

Olivia's shock left her ears ringing, and she blinked back tears.

But Aiden kept hurling painful, inane words at her. "I thought I could take a chance on you. Someone from Gresham had to be different, right? We've known each other our *whole* lives. Surely, I could trust you. Now here I am again, getting screwed over. Wow, women just can't be trusted, can they?"

It was the final straw.

"Are you kidding me right now?" Olivia's anger at Sam, which had been bubbling below the surface, surged. "You showed up without so much as a text. Maybe if you had called first, I could have told you Sam had shown up uninvited. I could have asked you to please give me some space so I could get him to leave and never come back. God, it seems you two have more in common than I thought."

Ms. Darcy was tracking Olivia's every movement, following her as she walked toward the door. Olivia paused and looked back at Aiden. "And speaking of trust, I know you slept with Amber. June told me. For the record, you're the only one of us who has been telling lies."

Furious, Olivia walked out the door and slammed it hard against the frame. It made a satisfying *whack*. Her very long fuse had run out. She was so angry at Aiden and Sam and her dad and the patriarchy. She got into her truck and gave Ms. Darcy a hug of gratitude for her presence and goodness. Tears pooled at the base of her throat as she drove away from Aiden.

Without thinking, she drove to her parents' house to find her mom. She took the backroads to give herself a few extra minutes to think and breathe.

Driving slowly, she steered the truck along a winding gravel road through a wooded area dotted with oak trees and ponds. Tears streamed in rivulets down her face. More than anything, she was hurt, but she was also a little ashamed. How could she have wasted six years on Sam? Juxtaposed to Aiden, he was such a tool. Sam's self-centered, high opinion of himself infuriated her, and she was embarrassed to have been caught up in his nonsense for so long.

Then there was Aiden. What the hell was wrong with him? How could he speak to her like that? How could she have been so wrong about him? It was *men* who couldn't be trusted.

From now on, I'm going to be as self-centered as everyone else. I am going to look out for me, myself, and I, and give zero fucks about what anyone else thinks. Unfortunately, her declaration only made her feel lonelier.

Her tears were morphing into angry sobs. She had to pull the truck over and park on the side of the road to catch her breath. Ms. Darcy whimpered helplessly. She licked Olivia's hands and laid her head on Olivia's thigh. Olivia leaned over Ms. Darcy and cried into her neck.

"Poor pup. I know you're worried about your mama. I'll be okay." Her voice caught, and she cleared her throat. "I'm just a little sad right now."

She took one shuddering breath, then another and another until she was able to drive again. Inside her childhood home, her mom was standing at the counter, chopping carrots. She turned toward the door where Olivia stood crying, Ms. Darcy licking her hand.

Her mom's face fell. "Oh honey, what is it?"

"Mom…" Heavy sobs took over her body before she could finish.

Her mom wrapped her in a hug. Ms. Darcy slunk over to lie down by Jackie, and Olivia's mom led her to her old bedroom.

Her parents had left her room as she had it in high school to make sure she would always feel comfortable coming home. The bright green and black poster from the Broadway musical "Wicked" still hung over the back of her bed. Her dresser was scattered with little knickknacks and old friendship bracelets. School pictures of her closest childhood friends were taped to the edge of the mirror.

She and her mom climbed on top of her pink floral bedspread, and her mom held her while she cried. Once Olivia calmed down, she told her mom everything. Relief filled her when her mom was equal parts angry and aghast.

"Well, this sucks," she said.

Olivia laughed bitterly, and her mom stroked her hair as they lay there quietly for a few minutes.

"I don't think I'm ready to date anytime soon…or ever."

"Oh, sweetie. You got dealt a pretty crummy hand today. You don't have to decide anything right now."

"I'm so mortified to have been with either of them. Why am I so dumb?"

"You're not dumb, honey. You're human. And so are they. We're all just bumbling around carrying all kinds of tender pain points we try to hide. But they eventually get poked, and sometimes we fall apart."

"Are you talking about Aiden?" Olivia asked into her mom's shoulder, wondering if she was defending him.

"Yes, sweetie. Aiden and all of us."

Olivia straightened to study her mom's face, "When did you get so wise?"

"After menopause," her mom said somberly but with a twinkle in her eyes.

Olivia laughed through her tears, and her mom laughed along with her. At that moment, her dad poked his head through the door to see what was going on. He looked at them, shook his head, and wandered off, which made them laugh even harder.

They hung onto each other as they rolled around on the soft bed, giggling, each of them gasping to catch their breath.

It was the reset she needed. Her well of tears had finally run dry.

"Boys are dumb," her mom said succinctly, capping off the conversation.

"Boys *are* dumb," Olivia confirmed. "Another thing you realized after menopause?"

"Indeed."

"Can I ask you something? Why have you put up with Dad all of these years?" Her mom looked at her quizzically, so Olivia elaborated. "I mean, he's a boy, and as we've established, boys are dumb. So why do you put up with him?"

"Hmmm…" Her mom thought for a moment. "Well, I suppose it's because I love him and because he has a good heart. Nobody's perfect, Olivia, and trying to force someone to be perfect is a fool's errand. At the end of the day, when you love someone, you have to decide whether you can put up with their particular faults, and your best bet is to accept them for who they are and do your best as a couple."

"I cannot accept Sam's faults."

"I know. That's why we have you back home with us."

"I'm not sure I can accept Aiden's either."

"Maybe not."

Olivia appreciated the space her mom created for her to ponder without judgment, and she was grateful for her mom's wisdom, whether or not it was actually derived from menopause.

"I don't know what I want, Mama."

Her mom smoothed her hair once more. "You don't need to know, sweet pea."

Chapter 37 - Aiden

Watching Olivia storm out of his family's cabin had left Aiden in a panic. He felt like he'd blacked out through their entire conversation, and seeing her leave was the slap across the face he needed to come back to himself. He kept replaying the previous twenty minutes in his head.

He'd remember Olivia's ex proposing, and Aiden hated him for it. A deep gut-wrenching hatred. What right did her ex have to show up like that? He'd lost that right, and Olivia was with Aiden now. Or she had been until he'd royally fucked up. She'd come here to explain, but Aiden's brain had gone primal. In his mind, he'd been back in his apartment bedroom, seeing Rebecca with another man on top of her. And the tattoos. God, Olivia's ex had been covered in them, just like the man he'd caught fucking Rebecca.

Seeing Olivia's ex proposing had felt like history was repeating itself. Another man taking a woman Aiden loved away from him.

Oh fuck. I love her. I love Olivia. And I've ruined everything.

Chapter 38 - Olivia

Olivia had fallen asleep in the small hours of the night after more crying and internal debates about how to move forward. She awoke the next day to a text from Aiden.

Aiden: *I'm so sorry, Olivia. Can we talk?*

Olivia's fingers began to type out a response, but her heart wasn't sure what to say. She locked her phone screen and got up to start working. Hours later, she still didn't know what she wanted to say to him. She had a lot of questions, but she wasn't yet sure if they were for him or for her to answer.

How could he say such awful things? How could she give him another chance? Olivia knew Aiden had been hurt by Rebecca, but she wasn't sure she had it in her to be with someone who could become so irrationally jealous and irate.

That night, Aiden called, but Olivia didn't pick up. And she didn't respond to the texts he sent every day for the next week. One benefit of a long distance was not having to see each other when things were over.

Are things over? They should be over. He'd been so unreasonable. Like he wasn't even in the room with her when she tried to explain things. Did that erase all of the other good things they'd shared? She wasn't sure.

After a week, Aiden stopped texting. The first day she didn't get a text from him, she cried herself to sleep.

The next day, Olivia video-chatted with Grace.

"Oh, Olivia," Grace said after Olivia had laid it all out for her, "I'm so sorry. That really sucks."

"Thanks," Olivia said, shrugging.

"What are you going to do? Are you going to talk to him again?"

"I don't know."

"Well, you don't have to decide yet."

"Thanks. But honestly, whatever. Let's not forget the fact that you, little sister, are getting married! Even though my life is a mess, I'm so happy for you." Olivia had to force the words out, not because she resented Grace but because she resented love in general. The idea of love burned Olivia's soul like a magnifying glass amplifying the sun's heat. "Anyway, what are you all thinking for your ceremony?"

"Well…I was going to wait for a better opportunity to ask, but I was actually wondering if we could maybe have it at your farm next summer?"

"*What?* Yes, absolutely! I would love to host your wedding. And I can grow whatever flowers you want, too!"

"Amazing! Thank you so much, Olivia!"

"Yay, my pleasure!" Olivia was genuinely honored to say yes.

After she hung up, Olivia's thoughts returned to another subject that had been plaguing her day and night…the flowers she'd agreed to provide for Ellen's wedding, which was only a month away. Olivia grabbed a pillow off her bed, shoved her face into it, and screamed.

The one thing Olivia knew for sure was she wouldn't leave Ellen without flowers on her wedding day. She would get the job done, no matter how much it sucked. Olivia promised herself that when the day came, she would hold back her tears until she drove away from the venue.

As if reading her mind, Olivia got a text from Ellen.

Ellen: *Hey, I just got off the phone with Aiden. First, let me say I'm sorry he's a fuckwit. Second, I totally understand if you don't want to do the flowers. I'm sure I can figure something else out!*

Olivia immediately typed a response.

Olivia: *Thanks, but I'm ok. I will definitely still do the flowers. Nothing for you to worry about. In fact, I've been working on a few sample bouquets for you, and I was wondering if I could drop one off for you to look at, since this is my first wedding.*

Okay, so Olivia hadn't physically worked on the bouquets, but she had been mentally working on them. She was pretty sure that counted. If nothing else, that white lie was the motivation Olivia needed to get past her fear of failure and head out to the field to cut some flowers.

That week, Olivia spent her spare moments watching YouTube videos of florists making bridal bouquets, trying to copy their every movement. She only broke down in tears of frustration four times, which felt promising. The next week, she only cried once, and by three weeks out from the wedding, she'd managed to make an objectively beautiful bridal bouquet.

That Sunday afternoon, Olivia was physically, mentally, and emotionally exhausted, so she cranked up the air conditioner and crawled under a fluffy duvet on the couch. Ms. Darcy curled up next to her as she turned on her favorite BBC period drama, North & South.

The sun was beginning to set when she heard a car pulling into her driveway.

Ms. Darcy jumped up off the couch and ran to the door, tail wagging.

Heavy footfalls sounded on the porch steps, and Ms. Darcy began to whine and scratch at the door as if she wanted to be let out. Olivia walked to the window and pulled the curtains aside just enough to peek out. It was Aiden. She jumped back.

He was handsome as ever, but stubble shadowed his cheeks, and dark circles hung below his eyes. Her heart thundered in her chest.

He knocked and called through the door, "Olivia?"

She was a statue. Olivia didn't think she was ready to see him. She examined her pride, wondering how much she cared if he thought she was a huge coward.

"Olivia, I know you're there. I just saw you looking through your window. Can you please let me in? Please? We need to talk, and the mosquitoes are eating me alive out here."

Olivia unlocked the door and opened it, stepping aside so Aiden could walk into the foyer. She crossed her arms, both in self-defense and to cover her braless chest. She looked down at her baggy clothes and imagined what he was seeing. Her hair was in a sloppy bun on top of her head, and she hadn't put on makeup in days.

Margaret Hale would never have looked so shabby in front of John Thornton. The thought was a good reminder of why it was a bad idea to watch three straight hours of British period dramas.

"Olivia," Aiden said for the third time.

She briefly met his gaze before looking at the wall behind him. It hurt to see him in her home. The last time they'd been in the same room, he'd said so many awful things. His presence brought back the knot that had formed in her stomach after she walked out of his cabin.

"I'm so sorry." Concern creased Aiden's brow. "I was a dick, and I understand if you hate me. I don't expect you to forgive me right now, but I wanted to tell you I know I was wrong. So, so wrong." He paused and took a deep breath. "I guess I'm hoping we might still be friends."

The words floored her, and she felt like she was floating above her body.

Oh, I see. He wants to be friends now. He's over it.

Her nose tingled, and her throat went tight. She coughed to clear it. "Um, I'm not sure that's going to work for me. Like I said, I don't do friendships with men who are going to be dating someone else soon, assuming they're not already."

"What? Olivia, I'm not seeing anyone else."

"Yeah, but you will eventually. So, I think I'd rather not."

Aiden's face dropped. There was disappointment and possibly even hurt in his eyes. He looked down and nodded, putting his hands in his pockets.

"Okay," he said. "Got it. I'm sorry it didn't work out."

"Me too," she said honestly.

He nodded once more and reached down to give Ms. Darcy a quick pat on the head. Then he let himself out, shutting the door quietly behind him.

As soon as his car door slammed, Olivia leaned her back against the door and slid down. Sitting with her knees folded up by her chest, she cried.

Eventually, she got up, made herself eat something, washed the dishes, and took a shower. It was time to move on.

Chapter 39 – Aiden

Aiden spent the next couple of weeks dreading his sister's wedding. Although he craved Olivia's presence, he wasn't sure he could handle another painful encounter. She'd made it clear she was done with him. She'd given him a chance, and he'd fucked it right up.

At work, he thought he was doing a good job pretending to be okay, even though he'd lost his appetite and had a perpetual stomach ache. He wasn't sleeping well, but he'd learned to live without sleep during residency.

Apparently, he wasn't hiding his misery as well as he thought because his mentor Joanna pulled him aside in the break room one morning for a chat. Initially, he assumed it was to review some of the standard emergency department procedures and discuss a unique case or two.

Instead, she asked, "You okay, Aiden? Is your dad doing alright?"

He nodded. He probably looked as terrible as he felt.

"Yeah, I'm okay. My dad's doing well, actually."

"That's good to hear. You seem a bit off is all. Your patient load okay?" she asked.

"I think so… Do I seem to be handling the patient load okay from your perspective? I respect your opinion."

It may have been overkill, but the comment he'd made to Olivia about not trusting women had been eating away at him. He was hyper-conscious of his behavior toward his female colleagues, and he wanted his advisor to know he admired and respected the hell out of her.

"You are doing well, Aiden. You know, the job and life, it can all be a lot at times, especially your first year as a fellow. I know it feels like being thrown off a cliff, but we have the mentor program to hopefully provide you with a parachute. I'm here if you ever need to talk about anything." After a beat, she added, "Or you could talk to a professional. With everything we see in this job, it's a good idea to have a therapist on speed dial. Especially working with kids. Off the record, it's a lot harder to watch kids suffer than it is a geriatric patient. For better or worse, we all want to protect their innocence."

He listened carefully and patiently. She was probably right. Even if Olivia was the core of his pain at that moment, it wouldn't hurt to create some space for all of the trauma he'd witnessed since starting his journey in medicine. During his residency program, he hadn't had time to deal with the immediate tragedies unfolding around him. He'd been forced to shove his emotions away, telling himself he'd deal with them later. However, at that moment, Aiden wanted to reassure her.

“Thank you for the advice, Joanna. I think you’re right about talking to someone, but as embarrassing as it is to admit, I’m going through a breakup, and I’m kind of a mess about it.” He all but admitted he was heartbroken, and it was a relief to offload some of the weight bearing down on him.

“Ah.” Joanna nodded knowingly. “Well, in that case, you should definitely find yourself a therapist.”

He smiled. “Yeah, you’re right. Let me know if you’ve got any recommendations.”

Chapter 40 - Olivia

Buzzing with adrenalin, Olivia got up well before sunrise on the day of Ellen's wedding. She wondered who was more nervous, she or Ellen. Olivia had lost her appetite in the days leading up to that morning, and she had been a bit of a nervous wreck. Her mom and Grace must have been concerned because they'd been sending her "You can do it!" texts all week.

In reality, she was in good shape, flowers-wise. Thankfully, her CSA subscription had wrapped up for the season. Otherwise, she was pretty sure she'd be having a stress-induced heart attack.

Ellen's bridal bouquet and her bridesmaids' bouquets had been in Olivia's air-conditioned house since the night before. She'd finished Ellen's on the first try—or was it the thirtieth if she counted all of her practice attempts?

For the last push of work that morning, Olivia was tasked with making somewhat identical table centerpieces. Fortunately, Ellen had approved a relatively casual aesthetic featuring large dahlias, so she hoped it would only take her a couple of hours until it was time to go to the venue and set up the final arrangement—a flower arch that would be the backdrop for the ceremony. Now, it was only a matter of execution.

Like clockwork, Olivia's mom pulled up two hours later in the white minivan she'd been driving since Grace and Olivia were in middle school, and Olivia sent a thank you to the Patron Saint of Midwest Frugality.

Once inside, her mom looked around. She oohed and awed, which Olivia really needed at that point. So much was riding on the day ahead. Olivia wanted Ellen and Aiden's whole family to feel like she had fulfilled her end of the agreement. That way, she could close the chapter that was her brief affair with Aiden and move on. It was also an opportunity for her floral business to take off. Not only might it lead to more weddings, but Olivia could potentially parlay it into an opportunity to sell wholesale flowers to professional florists. Ellen had even generously offered to have her photographer snap photos of all of the arrangements and provide Olivia with copies.

When Olivia and her mom arrived at the venue, Olivia's anxiety was hovering around a five out of ten, so that felt promising. She was praying they would be in and out before the wedding party, or more specifically, Aiden, arrived. If everything went according to plan, Olivia would have everything set up well before pre-wedding pictures started. She needed to focus on getting the job done.

Her mom distributed the table centerpieces while Olivia got to work on the arch. After setting the bouquets out, her mom walked over to help.

Olivia had the greenery in place, and her mom was holding various dahlias, sunflowers, and zinnias for her to arrange in the arch's structural armature. Thankfully, it was going much faster than she'd expected. Taking a step back, she stretched her arms and shoulders while looking at the arch in full detail.

Someone said her name.

Aiden.

Olivia didn't need to turn around to know it was him. She and her mom pivoted their heads in unison and saw him standing there in a tux.

Fuuuuuuck.

Olivia's stomach did a somersault.

His presence alone was enough to cloud her brain, but there he was, looking amazing in black and white. The tux fit him perfectly and made his broad shoulders look somehow even broader.

"Sweetie, I need to use the potty," her mom whispered.

Her words were a record scratch.

"Hi, Aiden," her mom added cheerily over her shoulder, already halfway out of the room.

Olivia didn't even have a chance to cling to her arm and cower behind her. Aiden waved halfheartedly toward her mom's back.

"Hi, Olivia," he said again.

“Hey.” She forced a smile and met his eyes briefly before he took in all of her hard work.

“Wow, this looks beautiful. You’re incredibly talented.”

Damnit. It would be so much easier if he was being a dick right now.

“Thank you. I’ve learned a lot, thanks to Ellen.”

Aiden didn't say anything. He looked into Olivia's eyes with a piercing stare, full of questions she didn’t know the answers to, but she couldn't look away. Her heart was beating fast, and sweat prickled at the nap of her neck. *Ugh, when is this intensity going to fade?*

“Sorry, was there something…?” Olivia didn’t know what question to ask.

“Oh, sorry.” He shook his head, and his shoulders drooped. “My mom texted me to ask if I could grab Ellen’s bouquet for her first-look photos. I guess it was a last-minute decision?” He sounded uncertain.

“Hmmm…interesting.” Olivia suspected their mothers had a hand in her current predicament–standing face-to-face with Aiden.

“Yeah, I’m starting to think so, too.” He’d read her mind.

They grinned knowingly, and Olivia had to admit it was a relief to see his smile and his dimples again.

He reached toward her as if to take her hand, but she instinctively pulled away before quickly asking, “How’s your dad doing?”

His eyes widened slightly, but his smile remained, if a little tight. “He’s doing well. Thanks.”

Aiden dropped his hand to his side.

“I’m glad to hear that. I’m sure this is all a lot for your whole family, but I know it’ll be a lovely day.”

“Sure. We’re all really happy for them.”

“Anyway, Ellen’s bouquet is over there.” Olivia pointed toward the honorary bride and groom chairs and crossed to the arch to put more distance between them. “You should take the vase so Ellen can keep her bouquet hydrated between photos.”

“Right, thanks.” He nodded once. “Again, this is all perfect. I hope you’re ready to be flooded with wedding requests. My parents’ friends will definitely be talking about this.” His words were friendly, but his tone was reserved.

Olivia nodded and gave Aiden a closed-lip smile. “Thanks. And congrats again to your family.”

He grabbed the bouquet and, with a final wave, walked out the door.

As soon as he left, Olivia’s mom reappeared.

Olivia raised a dubious eyebrow. “Really, Mom?”

Her mom’s whole body cringed, and she shrank several inches.

She covered her red face with her hands, the picture of guilt. “Eeek. Don’t be mad. Aiden’s mom made me do it.”

Olivia shook her head. "Was the weed hers too, Mom? Were you just holding it for her?"

They burst into laughter, and it cleared any remaining tension from the air. After wiping away a few tears, both from laughter and sadness, Olivia wrapped up the final touches on the arch. She spritzed all of the bouquets one last time and triple-checked to make sure she hadn't left a single leaf or flower petal out of place. Olivia hoped Ellen and Mrs. Wescott would feel as though flower fairies had come and gone.

Then they were off. Back to home. Back to safety.

It was Olivia's first market-free Saturday, so she had intentionally made plans to distract herself from all things Aiden Wescott. She was finally meeting up with her old friend Maddy for dinner at Los Guapos, the slightly better of the two local Mexican restaurants, and she was looking forward to it.

Chapter 41 - Aiden

With Ellen's wedding ceremony over, the bridal party was enjoying a brief respite in a private suite before joining the rest of the guests at the reception. Aiden, Ethan, and Nathan were all groomsmen, along with Tommy's best friend, Will.

Tommy and Ellen had gone off to have some alone time, and Will was flirting with one of Ellen's bridesmaids. That left the three brothers standing around a high-top table, talking about the Major League Baseball playoffs.

Their sister, Lauren, joined them, two bottles of beer in each hand. Her dark Wescott hair was swept up behind her head, and she was wearing a burgundy bridesmaid gown.

Handing out the beers, she asked, "So, Aiden, what's the story with Olivia? What happened? Ethan has been very stingy with the details."

"Yeah, Ethan hasn't told me anything either," Nathan confirmed.

"That's because I don't know anything." Ethan sounded defensive. "And…I respect Aiden's privacy," he added less convincingly.

The four clinked their bottles, and Aiden groaned. "Ugh, I was an idiot."

"Well, yeah," Aiden's three siblings said in unison.

"But how exactly were you an idiot?" Lauren asked.

Begrudgingly, Aiden told them the whole thing. He wanted to omit the more incriminating details, like what he'd said about not being able to trust women, but in the end, his shame led him to confess it all as penance.

"You said what?" Nathan laughed. "How are you so smart and so dumb at the same time?"

"Dude, she is never going to forgive you," Ethan said.

Aiden slumped over the table and put his head in his hands.

"Hold on, hold on," Lauren said. "Let's not give up hope just yet."

She gave their brothers the stink eye, which Aiden appreciated but also felt was pointless.

"What we need here," she added, "is a grand gesture. Aiden, you need to apologize for being an ass, and you need to humiliate yourself while doing it."

"I don't know…" he said skeptically, not sure Olivia was the grand gesture type. She seemed too low-key for something like that.

"No, no," Nathan said. "Lauren's right. Women love that shit."

"Really, Nathan? Have we learned nothing from Aiden's dumb-assery about generalizing women?" Ethan asked, laughing.

Lauren saluted him with her beer.

“Okay, fine, but what am I supposed to do? She stopped replying to my texts after I fucked up.”

“I bet I can find her,” Ethan said matter-of-factly. “If she’s out tonight, and if I can locate her, do you agree to a grand gesture, brother?”

In elder brother fashion, Nathan jumped in. “Aiden, do you or do you not accept the terms of Ethan’s bet? If Ethan can find Olivia by the end of the night, assuming she’s not at home, do you agree to make an ass of yourself?”

“Fine,” Aiden acquiesced. “Whatever.”

He rested his chin on the lip of his beer bottle in defeat.

Chapter 42 - Olivia

After a nap and a jog with Ms. Darcy, Olivia showered and got ready for dinner.

When she arrived at the restaurant, Maddy was sitting in a booth toward the back. It was shockingly good to see her. Her hair was as curly as ever, framing her big round face and even rounder blue eyes. Maddy had always been naturally curvy, the same way Olivia was naturally thin.

As Olivia made her way to Maddy, she passed the generic Mexican-family-restaurant-décor of gold sombreros and hand-painted green cacti, which stood out against the bright orange and red walls. Olivia was pleased to see tortilla chips and salsa already sitting on the brightly tiled table in front of Maddy.

"Mad-Eye Moody!" Olivia exclaimed excitedly.

"Ollivander!" Maddy stood for a hug.

Olivia had the comforting sensation they were picking up exactly where they'd left off a decade or so ago—two giant book-loving theater dorks.

They looked at each other and smiled.

"It's so good to see you!" they said in unison.

They sat down, smiling so big that Olivia's face hurt in the best way.

"So, there's something you should know before we hang tonight," Maddy said. She pulled open her phone and slid it in front of Olivia. "Your mom sent me this text about thirty minutes ago."

Olivia's Mom: *Please show Olivia a good time tonight. She needs it. I will be your DD. Just call me when you're ready to be picked up or when the bars close down.*

Olivia read the text and burst out laughing.

"I almost died when I saw this text," Maddy said. "So…it sounds like we're drinking margaritas tonight?"

Olivia smacked her palm against her forehead. "Oh, boy."

"I know we have approximately fifteen years to catch up on, *but what is going on*? And please make it juicy! I could *really* use a juicy story in my life right about now."

Olivia took a deep breath and let out a resigned "woe is me" sigh. "Do you remember Aiden Wescott?"

Maddy snorted. "Yuh."

"Well…"

Olivia caught her up between bites of a burrito. Two margaritas later, she was pounding the table for emphasis as she told Maddy about the Sam-Aiden fiasco.

"Holy smokes," Maddy said in awe. "You're back for less than a year, and your life is more interesting than the last five of mine combined. Didn't you get the memo? Gresham is boring."

“Ha, must have missed it. Also, I call B.S. You've gotten married and given birth to an adorable human. That's not boring.”

“Well, not boring, but it's definitely monotonous at times.”

“Please,” Olivia said with a sweeping gesture. “Help yourself to my drama anytime.”

“Don't mind if I do. You know, Aiden had a thing for you that summer after we graduated. He asked me for your number.”

“Hmm,” Olivia said thoughtfully. Maddy had just inadvertently corroborated Aiden’s story.

“So, what are you going to do?” Maddy asked excitedly.

“What do you mean?”

“About Aiden.”

“Ummm…what is there to do?”

“Well, it sounds like he was a jackass, and he apologized. Are you going to give him another chance?”

Olivia sighed before launching into the final piece of the story. “So, basically, he said he wants to be friends, and I'm not into that.”

Maddy looked skeptical. “That sounds like he was just trying to get you to reopen the metaphorical door to being with you since he screwed up big time, and he knows it.”

Olivia bit her lower lip, considering that perspective. “I don't know.”

"I'll admit I wasn't there, but it sounds like he's still into you. It also sounds like he has some baggage, which doesn't mean he's less into you, just that he was being a jealous idiot."

"Do you think I should forgive him?"

"Woah, woah, woah. That's a '*you'* decision for sure."

"Well, I appreciate your perspective, but now I'm sick of talking about me. Tell me all about your life! I want every detail I've missed since we left for college. Start there!"

Maddy laughed and said, "It was a cool autumn morning. I was eighteen years old. The world was my oyster, and I walked into my first day of freshman orientation."

Olivia giggled and reached across the table to poke Maddy in the arm.

"In all seriousness, I would love to catch you up, but I don't think I can have a third margarita. Let's go somewhere we can get a beer and give them back this table."

"Okay, good thinking."

They settled the bill and walked toward the restaurant's heavy wooden front door. Olivia used her whole body to push it open, emerging into the humid evening.

Olivia looked over at Maddy for direction. "So where should we go? I haven't cracked the Gresham nightlife scene. In fact, I'm usually asleep by nine every night. Apparently, I'm turning into my father."

“You and me both,” Maddy said, trailing behind her. “But people our age usually end up at The Whiskey Warden. They make decent mixed drinks and have a solid beer selection. And bonus, it's walkable.”

They ambled the short five-minute distance along Gresham’s quiet Main Street to The Whiskey Warden.

Olivia looked around, rubbing her arms for warmth. “Oh my god, this place is freezing.”

“Don't worry,” Maddy reassured her. “In an hour or so, there will be a hundred bodies in here, and it'll warm up. Then you'll appreciate the AC.”

“Okay, I trust you.”

Olivia took in the ambiance. The bar was darkly lit, which allowed the backlit shelving to show off the various liquors and liqueurs lined up like soldiers behind the bar. Black wainscotting edged the parameter along with a handful of vintage leather sofas, giving the bar a speakeasy vibe.

Olivia and Maddy found an empty booth in the corner and took turns buying rounds for the next several hours. Despite her immediate decision to switch to Coors Light and water out of self-preservation, Olivia’s intoxication level matched the energy of the bar as more and more folks streamed in.

Eventually, they transitioned from catching each other up on their life stories to Maddy pointing out various people and telling Olivia everything a Greshamite should know. Who owned which business. Who had slept with whom. Who was married or divorced to or from whom. Throughout their conversation, former classmates had stopped by their booth to say hello to Maddy and reconnect with Olivia.

"How do you keep track of all this and remember everyone's name?" Olivia asked, astonished.

"Well, I used to bartend here in the summers during college and for a few months while I was looking for a job. People don't realize it, but bartenders see *everything*. And I think when people drink, they forget bartenders are sober. They treat the bar like drunk therapy."

Olivia laughed hard at this, thinking back to one of her first conversations with Aiden about drowning sorrows in beer.

"What?" Maddy asked.

"Nothing, it just reminded me of a conversation I had with Aiden."

Olivia's face fell because she wanted to tell Aiden about how this confirmed their theory.

Maddie tucked her chin in. "Girl, I hate to say it, but you're still into him."

Olivia groaned. Maddy was right.

Needing a moment, Olivia excused herself to pee. She checked her phone. It was almost midnight. She couldn't remember the last time she had been out this late. In the bathroom mirror, she saw droopy, drunk eyes, which made her laugh. Straightening her shoulders, she resolved not to let thoughts of Aiden ruin the lovely time she was having with Maddy.

Back at their table, Maddy was typing something on her phone. Two new beer bottles sat on their table. Maddy looked up and smiled.

"Oh boy," Olivia said. "This has to be my last beer."

"I just want to make Mama Olsen proud. We'll call her to come pick us up after this."

The words had barely left Maddy's mouth when a particularly loud and over-dressed group of attractive individuals breezed through the door.

Olivia immediately spotted Aiden. He must have felt her gaze because his eyes locked on hers. His smile faltered momentarily, but he pulled it back onto his face. He gave Olivia a brief wave and turned back to his group.

Ethan was next to make eye contact with Olivia. Grinning, Ethan elbowed the man and woman next to him and pointed in Olivia's direction. There was no question the people standing next to Ethan were his siblings, Nathan and Lauren. The family resemblance was uncanny. Olivia continued to watch the group, trying to read their thoughts. Ethan shouted something into Nathan's ear, then he turned, smiled broadly, and waved. Olivia nodded in acknowledgment before swiveling back to Maddy, groaning with self-pity.

Olivia giggled despite herself. "Fuck my life, I'm moving back to Seattle." Laughing harder, she said, "Just drink fast so we can leave."

"Okay, okay." Maddy complied. They were now chugging their beers between giggles, which was somehow the most hilarious thing of all.

Then she heard it—the opening vocals of NSYNC's "I Want You Back."

Out of the corner of her eye, Olivia watched a mob of white shirts, black dress pants, and one burgundy dress coming their way. Ethan and Lauren were frog-marching Aiden forward until he was standing next to her…and the group was singing…to Olivia. Her brain felt like it wasn't processing the action in real-time.

Aiden, who had been pushed to the front, succumbed to the pressure. He knelt in front of Olivia, his hands outstretched, and belted out the lyrics, *"So tell me what to do now, cause I, I, I, I want you back."*

Olivia covered her face in horror. She peeked out between her fingers, wanting to see but unable to experience the full intensity of the moment.

All of Aiden's siblings began dancing and singing along with him.

Olivia's mouth fell open in shock. She was simultaneously delighted and mortified. It wasn't long until the entire bar had turned to watch. Many of the patrons sang along or whooped encouragement.

Out of the corner of her eye, she saw Maddy pull out her phone and point it in their direction. *How dare she!* Olivia shook her head desperately at Maddy, who reluctantly put down her phone. Tears of mirth streamed down Maddy's round cheeks. *What a traitor*.

Olivia laid her head down on the table against her forearms and succumbed to her own hysterical laughter.

When the song finally ended, Aiden gave Olivia a bashful grin and said, "Sorry, Olivia, I lost a bet. I promise we won't bug you again."

Behind him, his finely dressed backup singers high-fived each other, looking proud of their performance. Aiden glanced over his shoulder and shook his head. He stood up and pushed his siblings toward the other side of the bar.

"Well, I think two things are clear," Maddy said between fits of giggling. "Ellen's wedding was a good time, and that man is not interested in being *just* friends."

"I'm way too drunk for this." Olivia was stunned. "Let's go call my mom."

They made their way through the crowded, noisy bar. People clapped for Olivia and yelled, "Give him another chance!" Others offered less encouraging things like, "Marry me instead!"

Olivia was a good sport, but she was thankful when the doors closed behind her, muffling the din.

The quiet of the night immediately sobered her. “Oh god, I think I'm gonna be sick.”

She ran to a garbage can next to the bar’s entrance. The smell of cigarette butts was the last straw, and any remaining shreds of dignity escaped with every heave. When she came up for air, Maddy pulled a bottle of water from her purse, handed it to Olivia, and placed a steadying hand on her back.

“Thank you.”

Olivia sipped the water as they waited in silence. Ten minutes later, Olivia’s mom pulled up as promised and rolled down her car window.

“Your *You-Ber* is here,” her mom called through the open window.”

Maddy and Olivia giggled as they literally crawled into the back seat.

“Sorry, Mom, I'm so drunk, and Aiden sang to me, and I think I have to take over the farm.” Words. So many words were coming out of Olivia’s mouth.

“Okay, sweetie, we'll talk about it in the morning. Why don't you just close your eyes for a minute.”

Chapter 43 - Olivia

Olivia woke up in her bed next to Ms. Darcy and an empty bowl. Her mom must have somehow gotten her into her jammies. A glass of water and two ibuprofen were on the nightstand.

The memories of the night before started to crystallize in her mind. Had Aiden and his siblings sung NSYNC in front of the entire bar? It made her cringe all over, which made her head ache and her nausea more acute. When she peeled back the layer of embarrassment blanketing the entire scene, she remembered Aiden on his knees, asking her to take him back.

Could she? Even if they started over, nothing else had changed. He still had a career in Saint Paul, and Olivia was all but committed to taking on her dad's 'legacy.'

What was the point of getting back together just to get hurt all over again when distance and logistics would inevitably kill their relationship anyway?

Hangovers impacted Olivia on an emotional level. She had a theory that drinking used up twice her allotted happiness budget, so her misery the next day was like paying off a debt.

Olivia got up, took care of Ms. Darcy, made some coffee, and crawled back into bed. She opened her phone and turned on a movie, too deep in self-pity to bother opening her laptop. Some people had hangover meals, but Olivia had hangover movies, and her favorite was a relatively old French movie called Amélie. Something about being forced to read the subtitles helped her drift in and out of sleep.

Olivia eventually felt normal enough to shower and get dressed. She made a halfhearted attempt to tidy her house and wash the dishes, but she was moving at a snail's pace. An hour later, she was once again in a prone position when she got a call from Aiden.

She swiped her thumb across her phone to accept it, and her voice came out rusty. "Hi."

"Hi," Aiden said, sounding tentative. "I'm hoping I can come over so we can talk, but I wanted to call first."

"Okay, yeah. I'm home."

"Oh, good, 'cause I'm at the end of your driveway," he admitted. "Change is incremental, right?"

Olivia let herself chuckle at his admission and walked out to the porch to greet him.

Chapter 44 - Aiden

Aiden was grateful to see Olivia's big white farmhouse and the fields of flowers and veggies behind it. He was even more grateful to see Olivia standing there with her dark red hair pulled up in a messy bun, wearing a baggy ripped T-shirt and basketball shorts.

She invited him to sit on the porch swing, but he was careful to leave plenty of room between them so he didn't overstep his welcome.

"Hi, Olivia."

"Hi, Aiden."

"Oh man, I've really missed you."

Olivia just nodded. She wasn't giving him any sign of hope, and he started to feel more nervous than he had been as he'd laid awake all night wondering whether his siblings had been right or dead wrong about the grand gesture.

"I know," he continued. "I know I messed up. Bad. But I think we have something special between us, and what you saw of me at the cabin that day…what I said…that's not who I am. I promise you. And I'm actively working to root out and examine how I could have lost my head like that."

Olivia finally met Aiden's eyes.

"I'm honestly so ashamed of how I acted," he continued. "I took a colleague's advice, and I found a therapist. We had a few video sessions, and I think I owe you the full story. If you'll let me share it."

She nodded. "Okay."

"I know what I'm about to say doesn't excuse my behavior, but hopefully, it'll provide some context." Aiden raked his hand through his hair and let out a deep breath.

"Things ended badly with Rebecca. The move to Boston, medical school, and having to work all the time…it was all very hard on our relationship. She was lonely, and I was so perpetually exhausted that I stopped making an effort. It took her a long time to find a job, and the one she found was only part-time. So I encouraged her to find a hobby, and she took up yoga."

Aiden looked down at his hands as he continued. "It seemed to be helping. I thought she was happier, ya know? Anyway, things between us were still kind of stale, but I stopped worrying about her. Honestly, I was just relieved not to feel so guilty.

"Then…I came home early from a shift one evening. I was supposed to be on an evening rotation, but I had the flu and couldn't stop vomiting, so they actually let me go home. I was barely holding it together on the train ride. When I got back to our place, it looked like Rebecca had just hosted a friend for dinner. There was leftover food on the table and an empty wine bottle and two half-full glasses. Wow, I can still see it perfectly."

At this, he laughed caustically. He still couldn't believe it had happened.

"I found her having sex with another man in our bed." Aiden paused, cleared his throat, and rubbed his jaw. After taking a deep breath, he continued, "It's taken me a long time to trust people again. So…when I came here, albeit uninvited, and I saw you with your ex, and he was obviously proposing…well, I fell apart. And yeah, it's not an excuse, but hopefully it provides an explanation."

He stopped, letting the story settle heavily between them.

"I'm sorry Rebecca cheated on you." Olivia's voice was replete with sympathy. "But what you said to me was terrible because I never asked Sam to come, and I certainly didn't expect him to propose. And as you can see…" she made a sweeping gesture, "all of that is very over. I'm not going to pretend it was easy or that I'm not still sad at times, but I'm also one hundred percent confident it's in the past. I've moved on in a very different direction. He wasn't good for me, and it took me far too long to figure that out."

Hearing this, Aiden prayed she would give him another chance. "I get it, and I should have trusted you. I do trust you," he corrected himself, sounding desperate to his own ears. "And if you couldn't tell from my willingness to make a complete ass out of myself last night, I'm pretty crazy about you, Olivia. I love spending time with you, and I hope you'll give me another chance."

Olivia's hands went to her face, and her shoulders began to shake, quiet sobs escaping through the cracks in her hands. Aiden's heart dropped into his stomach.

He felt helpless. He scooted across the bench toward Olivia and wrapped his left arm around her shoulders, pulling her hands away from her face and cupping her cheek with his right hand, turning her face toward his.

He forced Olivia to look him in the eye. "I'm so sorry I made you cry." He wiped away Olivia's tears and kissed her forehead before wrapping his arms around her and holding her tight against him. "I'm *so* sorry," he said again, aching with the sincerity of his regret.

Olivia let him hold her, and they stayed in a quiet embrace for several minutes. Occasionally, he kissed her forehead and rubbed her back.

Olivia pulled away and wiped her face and nose on the edge of her T-shirt.

"You look so sad," he said, a lead weight in his stomach.

Olivia took a deep, shaky breath. "Aiden." Her voice quaked, more tears falling.

The way she said his name tore something inside of his chest. His stomach ached as if it knew what she was about to say.

"Aiden," she repeated. "I can't."

Tears formed in his own eyes. He tried to fight them, looking up and blinking, hoping to keep them in, to keep her from seeing him in such a vulnerable state.

Olivia swallowed once and spoke through shaky breaths, "I've decided to stay here and take over my parents' farm. The whole thing is so much bigger than me. I want Philip and Cassie to be able to create a stable future for Fiona. She lives in a world built for others. Philip and Cassie have to work five times harder to make sure she gets what she needs, so if this is a choice I can make to guarantee them long-term stability, financially and otherwise, I have to make it. And I want to make it. I'm content in Gresham. There's so much space to just *be* here."

He nodded and swallowed back the pain clawing at his throat.

Olivia continued. "But I want you to know I have forgiven you, and I'm sorry too, for getting so mad and comparing you to Sam. He's got absolutely nothing on you. You've so thoroughly put him to shame by showing me what a relationship should look like that it's comical. I just don't think either of us should give up on our dreams, and I can't do long distance indefinitely."

Olivia's vulnerability pushed him over the edge, and his tears fell. He brushed them away and reached to hold Olivia against him once more. They sat there quietly for a very long time, their arms wrapped around each other.

Eventually, a sense of calm sadness settled between them, and Aiden knew it was time for him to go. He pulled away, and the cool autumn air rushed in to fill the space between them.

“I’m sorry, Aiden.” Olivia’s voice was a hoarse squeak.

“Me too.” The corners of his mouth turned up in a forced, shaky smile.

They stood, and Olivia walked Aiden to his car. He gave her one final hug before driving away. He didn’t stop driving until he pulled up to his apartment in Saint Paul, unable to face his family or anyone. He needed to be alone.

Chapter 45 - Olivia

As the weeks passed, Olivia busied herself with putting her farm to bed for the winter. Dahlia tubers and tulip bulbs had to be dug up and stored in her basement. Tools needed to be cleaned, oiled, and stored in sheds. The irrigation system that started the whole mess in the first place had to be wound up and put away.

Although those chores and Ms. Darcy got her out of bed, the heavy sadness wouldn't let go, and the return of her optimism still hadn't come.

Olivia continued having dinner with her parents on Sundays, and every Sunday, her dad casually mentioned another young, single, or recently divorced farmer. Olivia assumed these comments were for her benefit, but she was also pretty sure her mom had made it clear he was not allowed to explicitly mention dating.

On October first, true to her word, Olivia gave her dad an answer. "I'm going to take over the farm in partnership with Philip."

He was thrilled, but his excitement was dampened by Olivia's next words.

"We know this is going to be a big change for you, and we're not trying to shut you out by any means, but we have some conditions."

She handed her father a contract she and Philip had created that detailed a list of conditions her dad would have to agree to for them to take over joint ownership. She forced him to read and initial each bullet point and sign off his total agreement at the bottom.

As he did so, he grumbled under his breath—words like "Unbelievable," "Oh for god's sake," and her personal favorite, "Good grief, already."

When he was done, Olivia took a photo of the document and emailed it to her dad, copying Philip as a witness.

When it was all said and done, Olivia was relieved a decision had been made. She no longer felt like she was living in ambiguity. She had a plan. She was making project lists, and she and Philip were having weekly farm meetings to discuss where things stood and where they wanted to take the farm. Olivia had some ideas regarding more sustainable farming practices she'd been reading about, and she wanted to start testing a few in their fields.

Throughout this time, she was grateful to have the calmer winter months ahead of her to give her some time to absorb the farm's current business state and immerse herself in the plan for the year ahead. The deeper she got, the more it became glaringly obvious she wasn't going to be able to keep running her CSA without help. Maddy immediately came to mind.

The morning the first snow fell in Gresham, Olivia was reviewing some financial plans when she got a call from her mom.

"Olivia?" Her mom's cautious tone told her something was wrong, and her stomach dropped. Olivia's first thought was her dad had been injured in a farming accident. She held her breath as her mom continued, "I'm on my way to pick you up. Fiona had a seizure this morning. She was stabilized, but they're sending her down to the Cities with Cassie in an ambulance. I'll be there in ten. Pack a bag, honey. We don't know how long she's going to be in the hospital."

This wasn't Fiona's first seizure. Epilepsy was a more common occurrence in individuals with Down syndrome, but her doctors had never rushed her in an ambulance to the Cities before.

"Oh my god, Mom, is she going to be okay? Why are they taking her in an ambulance?"

"Honey, we don't know yet. They're taking her to the Gillette Children's Hospital. She's been unconscious since her seizure."

"Fuck! No!"

The walls that had been threatening to collapse since she and Aiden broke up were caving in. She didn't have the strength to hold it all up anymore. Despite her belief she couldn't keep going, her adrenaline got her moving. She grabbed random clothes and shoved them into a duffle. Olivia didn't know what to do with Ms. Darcy since she didn't know how long she was going to be gone, so she packed a bag for her, too.

Her mom pulled up exactly ten minutes later, and Olivia and Ms. Darcy piled into the car. Olivia gave her mom a hug, and her mom took a deep breath as she squeezed Olivia's arm.

"I know you have your own beliefs, but honey, I just want you to know I've alerted the prayer circle, and we are going to get the powers that be intervening. She is going to be okay. I'm sure of it," her mom said confidently.

The car ride was tense. Her mom silently moved from one rosary bead to the next, and Olivia made to-do lists on her phone. *We do what we must to cope.*

Twenty minutes later, Olivia's phone buzzed. It was Aiden. She held her breath as she clicked on the message.

Olivia wasn't sure she had any more willpower left to resist him.

Aiden: *I'm sorry if this is inappropriate, but my mom just called and told me Fiona is on her way to Gillette Children's. I'm here if you need anything.*

"Mom." Olivia looked up. "Is Mrs. Wescott in your prayer circle by chance?"

She squinted at Olivia questioningly. "Of course, honey, why?"

"No reason."

"Oh-kay." Then she caught on. "Did Aiden just text you?"

"Yeah."

"That was sweet of him," her mom said hesitantly. "I know you might not be ready to hear this, but it would probably be a good idea for you all to make amends because your paths are going to keep crossing."

"I know, Mom. I know you're right. It's just hard."

Her mom nodded and let a beat of silence hang between them.

Olivia's stomach clenched as she thought about how her breakup with Aiden had likely caused her mom a fair bit of stress as well. She'd been so wrapped up in her own feelings and her own wants and needs that she'd never even considered if it had put a strain on her mom's friendship with Aiden's mom. She felt like a selfish teenager instead of a grown woman.

“I’m sorry, Mom. I’m sorry if my mess has made your life harder or hurt your friendship with Mrs. Wescott.”

Her mom patted her knee. “Oh you know I’ll be fine, sweetie girl. But…one thing that might be helpful is if Aiden could keep Ms. Darcy at his place while we’re in town.”

Oh crap.

Her mom was right. Hotels didn’t allow dogs, and who knew if they were going to be able to find a vacation home that allowed dogs without having to pay a significant last-minute premium.

Her heart raced at the prospect of asking Aiden for help. Of seeing him.

Then her phone vibrated again.

***Aiden**: Sorry…again…I was just thinking, do you need me to watch Ms. Darcy?*

The text gave Olivia goosebumps. She shook her hands to calm the nervous energy vibrating under her skin.

Olivia’s mom looked over at her questioningly.

“He texted me again and asked if he could watch Ms. Darcy.”

Her mom let out a tiny snort. Olivia looked over, but her mom’s face was unreadable, and her eyes stayed focused on the road.

Olivia was only a little annoyed. “Yeah, yeah.”

Twenty minutes later, her stomach was in knots at the idea of seeing Aiden, or not seeing him, and she caved. Aiden had been brave enough to offer help after all of the rejection she'd put him through. The least she could do was summon a modicum of bravery in herself.

***Olivia**: Hey, thanks for your texts. I'd really appreciate that. Just for a few days. I can swing by to take care of her. I don't think a hotel is going to allow us to bring her in.*

His response was immediate.

***Aiden:** Yes! Of course! I'll be home from work around 5. Does that work?*

***Olivia:** Yes, thank you so much.*

Her mother gave her a knowing look. "So, should I just drop you off at Aiden's then?"

"Very funny, Mom. Really. When did you become a stand-up comic?"

"Hmmm…" her mom said as if she were considering the possibility. "When my kids gave me a lot of material?"

Olivia shook her head. She closed her eyes, trying not to let the joy she felt about seeing Aiden reach her face, but the corners of her mouth had a mind of their own.

She had been trying so hard to move on from him. She'd thrown herself back into work. She'd even downloaded a few dating apps, but she hadn't been able to stop thinking about Aiden.

Her brain kept trying to come up with ways they might still make it work. Through it all, she hadn't been able to kill the last little flicker of hope they might somehow have another chance at being together. All of these thoughts ran through Olivia's mind for the zillionth time. Then she'd remember Fiona and feel horrible.

What is wrong with me? Our little girl is in a coma, and I'm sitting here thinking about Aiden.

She was so disgusted with herself that she actually stopped thinking about all things Aiden and instead turned to internet medical advice, which was arguably also a bad idea.

After a bit of research, she asked, "Mom, do you know if Fiona's coma was induced?"

"No, sweetie, I don't know. Why do you ask?"

"It looks like, in some cases, they induce a coma after a seizure, so I was just curious if you knew."

"Well, hopefully, we'll get some answers once they've had a chance to take a look. You said Aiden is a pediatrician, right? Does he work at Gillette?"

"No, he works at Saint Paul Children's."

"Okay, well, it'll be good to have a doctor around to help Cassie and Philip translate all of the medical-speak."

"I don't think he's going to be around, Mom. He's just watching Ms. Darcy."

"Right, yes, that's what I meant."

Olivia side-eyed her mom and scrunched her face.

Her mom waved her off with a flap of her hand, and Olivia let it lie.

The next ninety minutes of their drive felt like ten hours. Olivia finally dropped her mom off at the hospital and took Ms. Darcy to a dog park to kill time until Aiden was home from work. The air was chilly, and she was grateful she'd grabbed her puffiest coat and mittens while she watched Ms. Darcy run around happily, chasing the other dogs through the light dusting of snow covering the park.

Eventually, they had to hop back in the car to warm up, and her phone pinged.

Unknown: *Hey Olivia. This is Aiden's friend Isaac. He asked me to meet you at his apartment so you don't have to wait for him to get off work. I've got a key I can give you.*

Olivia: *That would be amazing. Thanks! I can be there in about twenty. Does that work?*

Isaac: *Yup. See you there*

Olivia and Ms. Darcy drove over to Aiden's apartment, and Isaac was waiting for them outside.

"Hey, thank you so much for meeting me here," she said.

He greeted her with a hug, and she returned it warmly. He reached down to let Ms. Darcy sniff his hands before giving her a quick pet.

"No problem. I'm so sorry to hear about your niece. I'm sure this feels awful, but you should know the doctors at Gillette are excellent. She'll be well cared for."

Olivia smiled gratefully. "Thanks, that's nice to hear right now."

Isaac nodded. "Anyway, here's the key. Aiden told me to tell you to make yourself at home but also not to judge him for the state of his apartment because he didn't know he was going to have company."

She laughed. "Oh, I'm just lucky he offered to host Missy here."

"Well, I know he was happy to help. And, for what it's worth, it's nice to see you again. June and I were bummed it didn't work out for you two."

"Thanks," Olivia said, letting out a deep breath. She attempted a "tough luck" smile. "Yeah…it's been hard."

He nodded. "Sorry, I didn't mean to pry. I'll let you go. I'm sure you're anxious to get to the hospital. Let June and I know if there is anything we can do. We have a guest bedroom if your cousin and his wife ever need a place to stay."

"Wow, thanks. That's so generous. I'll be sure to pass that along."

When she and Ms. Darcy got inside, a few dirty dishes sat in the sink, and Aiden's shoes were strewn about, but it was in no way the mess Olivia thought it might be based on Isaac's warning.

More than anything, the place smelled like Aiden. She let herself breathe in deeply once before forcing herself to snap out of it. Her inner weirdo was tempted to crawl into Aiden's bed and take a nap under his covers. Instead, she focused her anxious energy on setting Ms. Darcy up with some water and her bed, making sure she couldn't get into anything dangerous or delicate. Once she felt safe leaving Ms. Darcy alone, she headed to the hospital.

Chapter 46 - Olivia

When Olivia walked into the hospital room, Fiona was asleep, surrounded by family. Philip and Cassie, Olivia's mom, Cassie's parents, and Philip's mom were all there, filling up the tiny space. Olivia made her way around the room, giving hugs to each of the people who loved Fiona best.

"Any news?" she asked tentatively.

The group looked at each other. Cassie's face was white with worry and exhaustion, and her eyes were red-rimmed.

She cleared her throat and said, "She's in stable condition, but she's still in a coma. They have a few theories about what happened, but they won't know for sure until the blood test results come back. For now, they're monitoring her. They've got her on an IV drip, and they've intubated her." Cassie's voice cracked, and Philip put his arm around his wife's shoulders.

They held each other, crying. Olivia hated everything about that moment, watching them suffer. But she also admired and envied the love and support they had for each other—they weren't facing this alone.

Olivia sat on the bed next to Fiona and rubbed her hands. She told Fiona that once she got better, Olivia couldn't wait to have another slumber party at her house. She told her they could braid their hair and practice tricks with Ms. Darcy, and they could watch Frozen one hundred times in a row if Fiona wanted. Olivia kissed her on the forehead before walking over to perch on the arm of her mom's chair.

An hour later, a knock sounded on the door before it slowly opened. Fiona's family looked up hopefully, waiting for a doctor with news. Instead, Olivia was stunned to see Aiden. He looked like he'd come straight from work in his button-down and slacks. He stood hesitantly in the doorway.

"Hi," he said tentatively.

Cassie took the lead as Olivia stood, mouth agape. "Aiden, hi. Come on in."

He was so goddamn beautiful, and she had missed him so much. In true Midwest fashion, he hadn't come empty-handed. He was holding two bags full of Jimmy John's sandwiches, and tucked under his left arm was a small stuffed rabbit he must have bought at the hospital gift shop.

"I thought you all might be hungry, so I just got a bunch of sandwiches. I hope that's okay. If not, I'm happy to run out for whatever sounds good."

Philip spoke this time. "Thank you so much, Aiden. We appreciate it." Philip took a bag from Aiden and shook his hand in welcome gratitude.

Aiden was there. With food and a cute stuffed animal. At that moment, Olivia realized she didn't have to go through this alone either if she didn't want to. She had someone who would stand with her in hard times. All she had to do was figure out a way to make it work, and she could see by his presence that Aiden was willing to work for it, too.

The little flicker of hope in her chest grew to a warm flame, and she beamed at him, so proud to be associated with this man who was so kind and thoughtful in a crisis. When he made his way to Olivia, she gave him a big hug, and she felt the tension release from his body, as though he had been waiting to hear the verdict of whether or not she wanted him there. She did. She was so fantastically happy to see him, and she desperately wanted him by her side.

Olivia didn't want to let go of him. She wanted to stand there all day hugging him, but her basking was interrupted by a gentle pinch on her butt—her mom's not-so-subtle way of telling her to simmer down because they were in a room full of family. She'd have to get her mom back for that one.

They pulled apart, but in the transition, their hands intertwined. The room fell back into silence, and despite the gratitude for Aiden's thoughtful gesture, the bags of sandwiches sat untouched on the table.

After an eternity and several nurse check-ins, a doctor came in to give them an update. She was tall with brown hair worn in a pixie cut. Her dark-rimmed glasses and pants suit beneath her white lab coat, along with her no-nonsense attitude, exuded competence.

"Hi there, I'm Dr. Richardson. Thank you for your patience, Mom and Dad." She addressed Philip and Cassie. "First of all, let me say your Fiona is a very strong little girl, and we think we have some answers for you.

"Fiona's blood work results show she is Type 1 Diabetic. We believe her blood sugar became dangerously high, which may have led to status epilepticus, also known as a prolonged seizure. Sometimes, when a body experiences status epilepticus, the brain goes into a coma in an effort to protect itself.

"While we won't know for sure until it happens, I believe once we get her glucose levels stabilized along with a good bit of rest, she should regain consciousness and be back to herself soon after that."

Huge sighs of relief and "Oh, thank god" echoed through the room. Aiden squeezed Olivia's hand and smiled down at her. Her mom rubbed her back.

"In the meantime," the doctor continued, "we'll have a nurse and a dietitian teach you how to help Fiona manage her diabetes. I'm not saying diabetes is an easy road, but it's definitely something you can learn to manage. And it's good to see you have a strong support system." The doctor gestured toward Fiona's family. "She's a lucky little girl to be so loved and well cared for."

The doctor's final statement sent half of the group over the edge, and they cried happy tears. Cassie and Philip gently hugged and kissed Fiona around her tubes and cords, patting her head and telling her how much they loved her.

As the doctor took her exit, Olivia pulled Aiden into the hallway.

She waited for the door to close before asking Aiden, "Is this good?"

"Yeah. It sounds like her doctor is taking good care of her, and she thinks Fiona is going to make a full recovery."

"And the diabetes? How bad is that?"

"Unfortunately, diabetes is more prevalent in children with Down syndrome. It's never ideal, but her doctor's right—it's manageable, especially when parents have the resources and time to be attentive. I think Fiona's going to be okay."

"Thank you." Olivia wiped away the last of her tears. "Thank you for being here for my family…and for me."

He hugged her again and said softly, "Of course, I'll always be here for you."

Pulling back, she met his gaze.

Without thinking, the words slipped from her mouth, "Aiden, I'm in love with you."

His face transformed from dim to brilliant, radiating hope and joy. He pressed his lips to hers and overwhelmed her with his kisses, in the best way possible.

"Excuse me?"

They jumped apart, looking toward the nurse standing next to them with a cart. Laughing, they apologized and found a corner waiting area that was mercifully empty.

"Olivia, I love you so much." He kissed her briefly once more before pulling back and becoming serious. "There's something I need to tell you." He sounded nervous.

Olivia held up a hand to shush him. "Wait, I have something I need to tell you first. I'm sorry for everything. I was mad at Sam and myself and the whole stupid situation. I gave up on us too quickly, and I promise I won't do that again. I will make more of an effort, and I'll try my hardest not to shut you out again."

She gasped a breath. "The drive up with my mom, seeing Fiona, your text…I've been selfish. I don't know how we'll do it, but if you need to be in St. Paul, if that's where your work is, if that's where your heart is… I'll get someone to run the CSA so I don't have to be there day to day. I'll work remotely to help Phillip with the business side of the farm. I love you, and I'll—"

"Olivia." Aiden pressed his lips against hers, quieting her. He pulled back and said, "I'm moving back to Gresham."

"What?" Olivia exclaimed. "How? Why?" Unable to help herself, she added, "Who, when, where?"

He laughed, shaking his head at her, and said, "What am I going to do with you?"

"You tell me! Seriously, are you really moving to Gresham? What about your fellowship? I have so many questions."

"You're right." He nodded. "The biggest challenge I was having when trying to figure out whether we could make this work was the distance and my fellowship. I technically still have to take my medical board exam in a few weeks before it makes sense for me to transfer, and I'll have to wait a month or two to get my results. But I thought a lot about what you said…about being there and showing up for Fiona and how she's not afforded the same opportunities as other kids. It made me realize my impact in Gresham could be much larger than if I were to stay in Saint Paul, where there are hundreds of great specialists to choose from. I also want to be there for my dad and my family. And most importantly, I want to be with you, Olivia. I'm so in awe of you and your drive and your talent. I'm happiest when I'm with you. I think I might be a little bit addicted to you."

"I think I might be a little bit addicted to you, too. Seeing you today. I guess it really hit me…I grow vegetables. You help people like Fiona and Cassie and Phillip every day. You save lives!"

He flashed a sheepish smile. "Well…vegetables help make my job easier."

Olivia laughed loudly, tears once again pouring from her eyes. She reached up, put her arms around his neck and kissed him, vaguely wondering where the nearest supply closet might be.

He pulled away first. “As much as I want to take you home right now, you should be with your family. I’ll take care of Ms. Darcy until you get back. When things settle down here, we can figure out what the next few months will look like. We’ve got time.”

She threw back her head and laughed from the overwhelming joy bursting inside of her chest. She was so intoxicatingly happy. With one last kiss, she pushed away from him, and they returned to Fiona’s room. Aiden waited a beat before popping his head in to say goodbye. He received a chorus of “thank you again” before making his exit.

Philip looked at Olivia with a knowing grin on his face. “So, did Aiden decide he wants to be a farmer after all? Am I gonna need to look for a new job?”

“Ha ha.” Olivia tried to keep a straight face but failed miserably. “He’s moving back to Gresham.” Her joy was contagious. Everyone was smiling.

“Yay!” her mom whispered happily, clasping her hands together against her chest.

“Oh, thank God,” Cassie said. “We could really use a doctor in the family.”

They all laughed, and Philip reached for a sandwich. Olivia and the rest followed his lead. With each bite of food, Olivia’s pride in Aiden grew. She had to admit it felt good to be taken care of every now and then, and she looked forward to returning the favor.

After an hour of hashing out a round-the-clock schedule to be with Fiona, Olivia drove her mom to her hotel a few minutes away.

Before stepping out of the car, her mom asked, “Honey, are you or are you not engaged to Aiden?”

“Not.”

“Well, are you at least boyfriend and girlfriend?”

“Yes!” Olivia let out a quiet "Eeek," unable to contain her joy.

Her mom kissed her on the cheek.

“Mom," Olivia said.

"Yeah?"

"Thanks for always taking good care of me.”

“Oh, well now. Of course, I’m your mom.”

“I know,” Olivia said. “Just thank you.”

“Oh, okay, you’re welcome, sweetie.”

Olivia got out of the car to help unload her mom’s luggage and gave her one last hug, “I’ll see you in the morning.”

“Sounds good.”

Olivia’s mom squeezed her hand before heading through the automatic sliding doors into the carpeted lobby.

Olivia got back in the car and drove to Aiden’s. The only thing keeping her from speeding to his apartment as fast as she could was the stop-and-go traffic. But the traffic didn’t bother her because she knew where she was going and how she was getting there.

Olivia stood in front of Aiden's apartment door, bouncing on her toes and fidgeting with the edge of her phone case. When he finally opened it, his hair was wet, and he had a bath towel around his waist. His bare arms and chest did Olivia in.

“Hmmm, this should be fun.” She reached out for the hem of his towel and unhooked the knot, letting it fall to the floor.

Aiden laughed and pulled her into his apartment, closing the door behind them.

“Such an exhibitionist,” he muttered as he pulled Olivia toward his bedroom.

They made up for lost time, and fortunately, there was a lot of time to be made up for. Afterward, Olivia lay next to him, naked and happy and curious.

“So, what happens now?” she asked.

“We live happily ever after?”

“I’m not sure that’s how it works.”

“We *try* to live happily ever after?”

“That sounds more realistic.”

With a laugh, he pulled her tight against him and kissed the tender spot on her neck, just below her earlobe.

Epilogue - Attempting Happily Ever After

(Six months later)

"So, do you want to go skinny dipping?" Aiden asked Olivia.

She'd met him in their front yard when he got home from work.

Olivia was covered in mud. She had been in the field helping Maddy get another set of vegetable seedlings transplanted and trying to get all of their dahlia tubers into the soil in time for them to bloom before the growing season ended.

"It's sixty degrees outside," Olivia said dubiously.

"Hmmm, you're right. We should probably just hose you down."

She walked toward him casually. When she was within a foot of him, she dove, wrapping him up in her muddy arms. She smeared her dirty face on his button-up shirt, and he hollered in protest.

"What are you doing, you wild woman?" he said, laughing. His clothes were shot, so he pulled her down to the ground, tickled her side, and covered her giggling mouth with his.

He pulled back and asked, "So, did you get all of your dahlias planted?"

"Pretty much."

"That's good. I heard they're critical for wedding bouquets."

Olivia laughed. "Oh, we'll make a farmer out of you yet, Dr. Wescott."

His smile broadened. "Well, I was wondering…if we were to get married, who would make your bouquet?"

Olivia pulled back, her eyes wide as she searched his face.

Aiden pulled Olivia up so they were on their knees facing each other. He reached into his pocket and pulled out a small black box. When he opened it, a light shone onto a beautiful, old-fashioned diamond ring. It sparkled under the tiny light.

Olivia immediately recognized the engagement ring as her great-grandmother Olivia's. It had been added to her mom's jewelry collection when her grandma passed away, and Olivia had loved playing with it as a little girl.

She looked up from the ring into Aiden's eyes, breathless with anticipation.

"Olivia Olsen, will you marry me?" Aiden asked.

"Yes." She laughed. "Yes, Aiden Wescott, I will marry you."

She let him slip the beautiful ring onto her left hand, over the dirt and the calluses, before pushing him back onto the cool earth and covering his body with hers.

Thank you for reading!

Wishing you could spend more time with Aiden and Olivia? Scan the QR code below to access the extended prologue.

Acknowledgements

Thank you so much to all of my wonderful family and friends who helped make this book possible from reading the early, very ugly drafts, to telling me you liked it. It gave me the courage and hope I needed to keep going.

Dan, thanks for teaching me that writing requires community. Noella, thank you for being my first reader and the best-door neighbor a girl could ask for. To my other early readers and supporters, Ilyssa, Logan, Ka Bao, and Courtney, seriously, your encouragement was everything to me when I needed it most. For every other friend who read some or all of the book, embarrassingly, there are too many of you to list, but please know that I'm still so grateful.

Lara, you were a fantastic mentor. I don't think these words would have made it into book format without your keen eye.

Leau Macy. Holy smokes. Who knew life would send me a fairy godmother just in time to guide me to the finish line. You are the most badass sponge I've ever met. I can't wait to read yours!

About the Author

Annie Marcus lives in Seattle with her handsome husband, energetic son, and the best dog girl ever.

She grew up in rural Minnesota and has spent her adult life in the Pacific Northwest. Like Olivia, she owns a small farm-to-table flower business.

Annie looks forward to publishing a novel for each of the five Wescott siblings.

Follow along via Annie's Newsletter:

www.AnnieMarcusBooks.com/Newsletter

Made in the USA
Columbia, SC
02 July 2024

37994799R00214